SENTIMENTAL JOURNEY
THE MONARCH

By D.M. Cipres

Special Editor |K. Fulton|

Cover designed and illustrated by |Mekenna Cipres|

1

DEDICATION

This is dedicated to my family who probably started to wonder if I even lived here anymore. Thank you for giving me hundreds of hours to journey back to the Tempus Vector, and return with the Monarch.

FOREWARD

The first time I met Mrs. Cipres, I was in the same kindergarten class as her son; back then, I just knew her as one of the moms. Fast-forward nearly two decades, and now I get to call her a dear friend.

When Dena asked me to write the foreword to her second book, I, no joke, almost cried. What an honor it is to be a part of her story! Before her first novel Sentimental Journey: Tempus Vector was published, she let me read early drafts of her writing, and I was quickly captivated by the depth of her talent and creativity. She is the most imaginative person I know and has the rare ability to turn words into worlds and pages into people. She has written a truly beautiful narrative celebrating life, adventure, love, sacrifice, and courage, and I am so excited that the story continues in book two, The Monarch.

She not only pours her heart into her books, but also into those around her. I see so much of her in the character Adina. She is the compassionate caretaker of her family, always ready to sacrifice herself for those she loves. She is the family matriarch, beloved by her children. To read the Sentimental Journey series is to get a glimpse of DM Cipres—the vibrant, hilarious, kind, intelligent, hard-working, imaginative authoress. I have enjoyed reading this book almost as much as I have enjoyed being her friend.

I can think of no one better than Dena who has the ability write about the lives of strong, complex women who have difficult circumstances thrust upon them. As Dena penned Beni and Adina's stories of duty and heartbreak, she herself traveled a similar journey. She, too, grappled with a burdensome calling. The inspiring stories of these fictitious women came straight from the author's heart. In her time of grief and uncertainty, Dena walked alongside the brave women in her novels and infused them with her own courage, grace, humor, and faith.

Now enough about the author, back to The Monarch! Book two in the Sentimental Journey series follows Beni into her new life and explores the cost of sacrifice. She must make difficult decisions as the keeper of the Tempus Vector, and now that she is married to her love Carig, she is nearly pulled apart by conflicting responsibilities. In my experience, you will not be able to put down The Monarch, and when it's over, you will want to hear more!

Reader, I hope you enjoy this novel. I hope Beni's adventure inspires you to be courageous and full of faith, even when dark times make you want to give up. And I hope that when you read *The Monarch*, you remember the dedicated, passionate, relatable authoress who crafted it for you.

-Melissa Chesney

P.S.- Dena did not ask me to write all those nice things about her. I was not bribed by money or food (among her many literary talents, she is also a great cook). I promise, she did not write this herself and create a fake name. I'm real.

TABLE OF CONTENTS

Our journeys are commonly marked in one of two ways: either by the light gold dusting from angels' wings, or the dark-blistering brand of the devil's tail upon our backs.

|M A L A C H I   C O F F E E|

Chapter 1

THE REGRET

*"Regrets are like an empty frame positioned on a wall; a painful souvenir of a flaw once permitted, that forever torments the soul." ~**Malachi Coffee**~*

Time seemed to stand still as I stood eye to eye with Adina. The incomprehensible had become reality. She wore an expression that I had never seen before, one of fear and uncertainty at my ill-timed presence. It was evident through her fidgety body language, along with the disapproval on the faces of the other citizens of Friedlich, that I was not welcome. Their discriminating expressions confirmed their eagerness for me to finish my business, and get out.

No words seemed to come as I opened my mouth to speak, leaving my audience even more attentive to my motives and forthcoming declaration. I wondered if Adina could tell how frightfully nervous I was, or if I succeeded in masquerading my apprehension through my shroud of

7

navy blue tulle. Carig often commented on the fact that I had the gift of camouflaging my true feelings. In this instance though, it would be a blessing rather than a curse to hide my uneasiness.

Taking a deep breath and trying to focus, I pointed to the door and in the general direction of Schuh Coffee. She must have thought I was a borderline lunatic as I blurted out the words that would forever change her life, and mine for that matter, "Schuh Coffee."

There! I said it! It's done! Before the final "e" abandoned my lips, and although hindered by a fitted skirt and high heels, I turned around and exited the store as swiftly as I had entered. I longed for the comfort of my faithful jeans and tennis shoes that would have come in handy right about now - my longstanding allies, that would abet my escape and see me home.

But be that as it may, there was nothing comfortable about this place, or how I felt at this moment in time. I was lost, overcome by the confusion of where to go next. Paths moving in every direction appeared infinite and dark, no inkling of light, no point of compass. I was in the middle of a strange place, and couldn't help but feel that the hands of time had thrown down a gauntlet of contest, heralding an omen, a warning that I was not welcome on this cobblestone page of history. The rusted timepiece would now faithfully stand watch on every corner, ready to defend its fossilized record. With its objection to my presence, it was puzzling why it wouldn't open a clearing for my departure. But like a final clang of caution from this gloomy pendulum of yesteryear, I sensed a frightening revelation that refused to be silenced. It threw me into a spiral of fear, suggesting that the door to this place only opened one way, and it would forever hold me captive.

Trying to shake off what felt like a cruel joke, I quickly escaped into the narrow recesses of a nearby alleyway. My already frantic feeling was compounded by an overpowering fear that someone or something was chasing after me. With eyes fixed on the passersby, I felt like a trapped animal soon to be discovered within the shadows. But after a few tense, but undiscovered moments, I breathed a sigh of relief while practically melting into the side of an old dirty building. With everything within me, I hoped that speaking those few words to Adina was my purpose here and would fulfill the requirements of this journey. I waited, even longed for the discomfort to come - the inner affliction that would, in effect, be my green light to return home, but I felt nothing.

"Get it together, Beni. You can do this!" I squeezed my eyes shut, somehow believing that the strained process would generate a solution. "Think, think! What now? What now?"

As suddenly as the question escaped my lips, I knew! I knew exactly where I needed to go. If meeting Adina was not the purpose of this journey, surely Malachi *was*. I had to see him. The same affirmation that prompted me to tell Adina to go to Schuh Coffee, reaffirmed that Malachi was my next stop. The agonizing but similar intensity that alerted me to come here in the first place, was now compounded by an inner stirring of anxiousness, one that reminded me of the effects of too much caffeine. *He* was my purpose for being here.... I was here to correct Adina's greatest regret. I was certain of it.

Mindfully observing my surroundings, I took a quick glance from around the corner, making sure that the way was clear. Assured, that no one was watching me, I made a swift right turn heading straight for Malachi's shoe store. As I was nearing his shop, I sensed an atmosphere of oppression among the people. Their obvious anxiety created a backdrop of disregard for anyone or anything

11

outside of their own personal ventures. Unfriendly gestures, and quick cold-hearted glances, became evident symbols of a clear division of alliances. As hundreds of people bustled around me in all directions, focused on their daily tasks, they were completely unaware that they had a visitor in their midst from another time and place. One who sadly knew what was soon to enter their lives. Distracted faces and blind eyes all around me, having no idea that they, and their country, would be marked forever in history as a people who conformed to the decrees of a mad man.

Finally reaching Malachi's storefront, I found myself standing before a beautifully carved green door that I couldn't help but pause and admire. A chime rang out as I passed over the threshold, alerting the shopkeeper that a customer had entered. Hanging my valise on a coat rack sitting by the front door relieved my burning hand that had grasped the worn handle so tightly. Then as I entered the chamber filled with boots and shoes, a unique aroma of both peppermint and shoe polish greeted me The room was quiet and peaceful apart from a faint tapping noise that was resounding from the back room. Like clockwork, when the chime pealed, he yelled out for me to sit down.

"Bitte hinsetzen!"

Resting my purse against the leather waiting chair, I sat down feeling both nervous and excited to meet this mysterious shoemaker for the first time. Well, I guess this would be the second time for me, if truth be told. The tables had certainly turned. When we met at the airport, he knew exactly who I was, but to me he was a curious stranger. This time it would be me catching him off guard. While reflecting on my unforgettable encounter with his ancient blues and crown of splendor, Malachi, Adina's Malachi, walked up behind me carrying a measuring tool to begin the process of sizing my feet for a new pair of shoes as he did with all of his customers.

Comparable to an artist making ready his masterpiece, each tool sat unhindered within the pockets of his weathered apron. His routine was flawless, and like a well-oiled machine, his unvarying method of creation had begun. After a quick crack of the knuckles and wringing of hands, he opted to wipe away any polish residue, even though every line and crevice was shadowed with tones of a charcoal and brunette glaze .

Without even looking at me, he rattled through a conversation, assuming that I understood his German tongue. Casually looking up and seeing me for the first time, he pushed his spectacles from the tip of his nose.

"Hallo, fraulein, wie kann ich ihnen heute helfen?"

After the hello part, I was kind of lost and wasn't exactly sure what he had said to me. Thankfully, I knew from Adina's letters that he knew how to speak English, but I was at a loss as to where to begin. This was the moment that could revolutionize his future, simply by voicing words of discernment and truth. Yet at the same time, I couldn't just blurt out a warning and walk out of his store. This plight of deliverance would require artful wisdom, with a hefty side of skillful finesse. As he bent down before me on the floor that bore sanded scars matching the shape and size of his tired knees, he prepared to measure my foot, unaware that my mission was not the pursuit of shoes, but of his ultimate salvation. Just as I remembered from our brief airport encounter, his eyes spoke warmth and kindness. At first glance, I felt a connection as if he remembered me. I peered deep within his eyes, hoping that my purposeful stare would somehow jog his memory. I'm not certain what I expected to happen. After all, we hadn't officially met. That is not for another seventy-five years or so.

"Malachi?"

"Ahh, you are American?"

15

"Yes, yes I am!" I continued looking at him, and he at me. I somehow believed that my prolonged gaze might stir a prompting of recollection. "Malachi, do you know me?"

He paused for a moment, taking a deeper look.

"No my dear, should I? Have we met?"

"No, I guess not."

"Well, you have come a very long way for a pair of shoes. What can I make for you today?"

Before I could say another word, he slipped off the shoe from my right foot. Upon noticing "Coffee" stamped on the insole of my navy blue pump, he gasped, taking a deep breath as if he were about to choke, and then quickly jerked away from me. Completely forgetting that I was wearing his shoes with his stamp, it unnerved the both of us. Honestly, in all of the preparations that I considered, I didn't give my shoes a second thought. How was I to know

16

that I would be coming here of all places? There was nothing that I could do now. I only wished that I would have considered every possibility, and had been more careful.

"What is this? Where did you get these shoes? These have my name, but I didn't make them! I have never made shoes like this before...who are you? What do you want?"

Malachi looked at me as though I was his enemy. He was sorely frightened, and this unintended shoe fiasco had quickly put him on the defense. He would never listen to me now.

"I don't know you! What do want here?"

The fact that I had frightened him bothered me greatly. Exactly what I *did not* want to do. Somehow, I needed to fix this quickly as I had no idea how much time I would have here with him.

"Malachi, wait, it's ok!"

"And how do you know my name? Why do you know me? I have never met you!"

"My name is Benidette Crawford, I mean ... Hammell ... Benidette Hammell." I nervously started babbling about how I was recently married, and that this was the first time saying my new name.

Malachi looked at the ring on my finger, but was not moved nor amused by my newlywed story.

"I've come here to tell you something very important. You see I'm...well, something is going to happen."

Oh my gosh, what was wrong with me? I kept stumbling over my words, and like the people back in the market, Malachi was practically bleeding fear.

I was thinking that somehow, I needed to calm the situation and put his fears to rest, when unexpectedly I was drawn away from my thoughts by a welcomed distraction -

his enormous wall of frames. At the mercy of only one

shoe, I slowly limped over to where they hung. It was hard

to tell how many hundreds of frames had been placed on

his wall, but just like Adina's sewing room, there were far

too many to count. Lightly brushing my fingers over the

adorned photos, I could feel Malachi curiously watching

my every move. Still touching the frames, I glanced back at

him.

"Malachi, these are your journeys?"

Until this very moment, I had never actually

witnessed someone's color changing from fleshy tones to

chalky white, but before my very eyes I watched as poor

Malachi turned as pale as a sheet, accompanied by an

altered disposition. Still looking completely shocked over

my profound comment, he walked over to where I stood

and placed his hand on my shoulder.

"Come, my dear. Come sit down. Tell me what you know."

Returning me to my seat, he once again kneeled on the floor before me, and gently reached up and held my face.

"You, Benidette Hammell, are chosen, yes? When are you from?"

His warm hands and soft voice calmed my soul and set the stage for the long awaited, life altering conversation. I was so relieved that he knew who I was. No longer did I feel alone, so without further delay I resolved to tell him everything.

Regrettably, my peace was short-lived, and my disclosure ill-fated. Before I had the chance to reveal even one word of warning, we were both startled into silence as the front door slammed open followed by a fast-paced charge of thunderous footsteps stampeding through the shop. Like a downpour bursting forth from dark shadowy clouds, a trio of Nazi soldiers rushed over to where we sat, blocking the light of day with their towering brawn. The commander was dressed in a fine green uniform, lined with buttons and buckles of shimmering silver. Not a hair was out of place beneath his perfectly matching cap that was grotesquely branded with the infamous and contorted Nazi skull. That, along with the notorious eagle and iron cross displayed beneath his collar, reminded me of a most gaudy and overdone Christmas tree, practically begging for a toss of sterling tinsel to complete the crude ensemble. His intimidating stature was amplified by his showy floor-length leather overcoat. Not only was it adorned with braided silver shoulder boards, but the bulky collar stood stiff and at attention, not unlike his lower ranking minions who never varied from their principled stance. Although his attire was brazen and showy, I couldn't help but be distracted by his face. Initially, he appeared quite decent looking. Along with near perfectly proportioned features, his electric blue eyes were framed by a crown of white-blonde hair.

His true nature both inside and out, quickly reared its ugly head when he brutishly grabbed my arm and yanked me from my chair. Now forced to stand toe to toe with him, he loudly barked out German threats only inches from my face while the other two had their weapons aimed and ready to fire. I didn't yet know the name of this commanding and most annoying officer of the group, but as for me, I would refer to him as the bete noire, as every inch of his marrow was pure evil. This was the first time in my life that I had ever encountered display of military intimidation, not to mention burning hatred that would find pleasure in my demise. Without a doubt, I was in terrible danger and in way over my head.

"Wie lautet dein name?" I said nothing to him. I knew that he was pressing to know my name, but I just wasn't sure how to answer him. "Wie lautet dein Name?!!"

he demanded again in a more elevated tone. Still reeling

from their abrupt appearance, and wondering why I was

being targeted, all at once it occurred to me that the two

women at the counter in the market must have called the

Gestapo, or whatever authority this was, and reported me as

a threat.

Even at his second request, I still remained silent,

feeling a strong conviction to by no means reveal my actual

name. The journal entries that I had read thus far said

nothing about what name to give if confronted, but for

some strange reason I felt compelled to give them a false

one, something other than my own. But what that identity

was, I didn't yet know.

His anger at my silence elevated, causing him to

push his swagger stick to my chest and then grunt out the

same command, "Wie lautet dein name, Fräulein?!!"

Like a streak of lightning, flashing photographs rushed through my mind and I was given wisdom of how to respond to his inquisition. Within these mental images, I repeatedly saw the face of my roommate at Yardley Academy replay through my mind. But it wouldn't be her name or her story that would become my own, but her grandmother's, Valentine Brannigan.

Apart from being my roommate, Rae Brannigan had become heiress of Brannigan Steel at the age of nine. Rae and I had come to Yardley at about the same time. She was desperately shy and withdrawn, and no one else wanted to be her roommate, nor mine for that matter. Her immense wealth was kept very hush-hush amid the school population as her guardians realized that she needed some normalcy in her life. From the moment we met, she and I hit it off and our lifelong friendship began. Her shyness and my quirkiness just worked. Rae's Philadelphia-born family became billionaires in the manufacturing of steel at the end of the 19th century. As time passed, and we opened our flawed lives to one another, we spent many a late hour discussing her illustrious, but peculiar family and their incredible history.

Her grandmother, Valentine Brannigan, lost her father on the RMS Titanic on April 15, 1912. Because Valentine had just been born that February, her mother chose to stay behind and not accompany her beloved husband, Magnus Brannigan, on the long ocean journey from Southampton to New York. His presence on the maiden voyage was greatly solicited by White Star Line, as Brannigan's hefty contribution of steel plates had allowed for the completion of the great ship. Similar to my relationship with Adina, Rae was practically raised by her grandmother, Valentine. Valentine's life stories, combined with the extraordinary role that she played in furthering Brannigan Steel during the turmoil of World War II, was highly impressive, although quite unusual for a woman in

25

that day and age. She had an amazing head for business and kept the family company strong and thriving while others were failing around her. Because she was an extremely wealthy woman in a man's world, she was quite well known in the United States, and the world, for that matter.

Call me crazy, but during those few seconds that seemed like an eternity, I made the decision to assume her identity in hopes that her name and status would be acknowledged and respected, even by the Nazis. This would be a risky move to be sure, but one thing I did know, these fascists and power-hungry people group, were always looking for avenues that would benefit and further their cause. In this case, I would have to make my presence all about raw steel, as it would aid their quest for more weapons and tanks. I only hoped my charade wouldn't backfire.

"Mein Name ist Valentine Brannigan."

Malachi looked at me in a most confused manner, then lowered his head as if he were ashamed and disappointed in my decision to be deceitful. Oh no! Had I chosen unwisely? Perhaps what I believed to be wisdom, was actually stupidity in the highest degree. By his disheartened response, I felt that I had failed miserably. There was probably some unwritten rule about giving a false name that I didn't yet know. But it was too late! My deceptive alias had been unveiled, and there was no going back. Making the choice to give them an assumed name was the wisdom given to me at the moment, and I went for it. I may forever regret this avenue of dishonesty, this lie that flowed so easily out of my mouth, but like it or not, I had just become Valentine Brannigan.

The highest ranking officer turned around and looked at the others, and laughed out loud. Together they jeered as if they knew something that I didn't.

"Sie ist Amerikanerin!"

27

Obviously pleased with his keen evaluation of my allegiance, he removed a small silver case engraved with the initials "HS" from his leather overcoat pocket. With the push of a button, a long skinny cigar surged from the pack. Suavely placing it between his lips, he stood still waiting for a light, bearing the resemblance of a spoiled child. Without skipping a beat, one of the lower ranking officers stepped forward, struck a match, and ignited the tip. It was apparent that his two insignificant comrades feared "HS" and knew that there was no room for error, even in the lighting of a cigar. Inhaling deeply, he moved closer to me, blowing smoke in my direction. Insanity marked his stare. It was apparent that this man's gifts were twisted, exclusively in the art of intimidation, mind games, perverse diversions, and administering the third degree and heinous torture, all in the name of the Third Reich.

"Show me your papers!"

It was difficult not exposing my insurmountable fear to this individual who would have found great pleasure in watching me cower before him. Not only was his tone harsh, but he spoke down at me, as if I were no better than a bug to be smashed. I could tell that he was just waiting for the opportunity to destroy me, and his decision to do so would only take one wrong move on my part. I knew at that moment that I must resort to stupidity and ignorance, two things I hated, but the duo of brainlessness could very well save my life.

"Honestly, I would really love to show you my papers. I really would, but silly me, somewhere between the train station and here, I lost my purse. I wish I could tell you that was the first time this has happened to me, but it seems to happen all the time. If my head weren't screwed on, I would probably lose that too! All I have is my suitcase, right over there!"

I pointed over at the door where I had placed it

upon entering the store. Causing my heart to skip a beat,

the demented beast bellowed out an order for one of the

soldiers to look through my bag. Their obedience to him

was like a dog's to its master. I watched as my suitcase was

thrown upon the counter and opened, where they rigorously

searched through all of my belongings. Thankfully,

everything that was important and that would give me

away, including the Tempus Vector, was in my purse.

As the probing continued, Malachi attentively took

notice of the bag itself. It must have been a very strange

reality to observe his personal leather suitcase, exposing his

initials "MC," on the counter of his very own store. All that

he could do was stand there and watch, unable to claim it as

his own as time had made it the property of a perfect

stranger. Obviously troubled, he looked at me plagued by

concern. I shared his anxiety, knowing that he and I were

thinking the same thing. To us the letters "MC" stood out

30

like a sore thumb. We only hoped that they wouldn't take notice of the initials on the bag, the revealing evidence that it was not mine. My particular presence here had put Malachi in a very dangerous and quite impossible situation.

We both stared watchfully at the head officer, trying not to appear nervous, and hoping that the suitcase and the contents of it raised no red flags. My heart sank as I watched him walk over to the open carryall, taking heed of my personal items lying on the counter, thoroughly examining each piece carefully. Malachi and I looked at one another fearfully as the officer's interrogation commenced.

"Well, what do we have here?"

With his back turned to me, I could only hear his deplorable and hiss-like tone, unsure of what he had happened upon. What did I have mingled among my garments that would raise concern? As I looked once again at Malachi, he in turn asked me the same question with his eyes while impressively remaining calm and collected. He swiftly pivoted on one heel, and in a single determined move, lunged towards me holding a pink lacey bra that I had packed, then proceeded to dangle it in front of my face.

"What is this? This is the underclothing of a whore and a spy. No respectable heiress such as yourself would wear something so offensive."

He then efficiently examined the front and back of my fancy and most disagreeable brassiere.

"These metal wires placed under each side - very clever - possibly some kind of transmitter, Fräulein? And what do we have here?" He spread out the tag so that he could read it more easily. "A secret so it says! So, I am correct, fräulein, this is some kind of camouflaged weapon, created in the name of the queen perhaps? Perchance you are British? No, only an American would be so stupid as to label their weapon."

If I wouldn't have been so frightened by the situation, I would have laughed out loud at his accusations about my pink foundation.

"This will stay with me, and it will be thoroughly examined. I'm sure you now realize how foolish you are to think you can hide something so obvious in women's undergarments. You see, Fräulein, we are always a step ahead of the rest of the world. Your technology is scheisse compared to the boundless intelligence of German science."

I was both relieved and dumbfounded as I watched him tuck my bra in the side pocket of his overcoat. If that was the extent of what he would take from me, I was more than alright with it. But even so, I had to take a step back.

Although I had only been here a short amount of time, it was already clear to me that I was in the middle of a very dangerous situation, surrounded by vile men. But regardless of the peril that stood before me, it was comical to watch this grave-looking officer standing there holding my highly secretive "Brassiere of the Queen," actually believing the wires were some kind of spy device. While I found humor in the whole episode, Malachi did not. As a matter of fact, he didn't think it was a bit funny. Reminded by the photos hanging on his wall that this current experience, while difficult, was most probably not the first time that he had dealt with an alarming situation, I was, however, certain he had never experienced anything quite like this before.

The officer looked at me in a most irritated manner.

"You will come with us now. There is someone who wants to see you ... Fraulein Brannigan."

34

Everything about him, from his towheaded crown to his lustrous boots, was disturbing, including his full-toothed grin of crooked, tobacco-stained teeth. The most beastly part of his sneering, leering expression, however, were the menacing, arctic, blue-toned windows that reflected his soul; they were unnatural at best. He oozed a depravity and evil that was fermenting and spilling over with every word he spoke. Even the tone with which he spoke my name was like fingernails on a chalkboard that set my teeth on edge. Although everything about him was bizarre, and I detested being in his presence, he was smart and certainly one to be feared. When it came to this devil man, I would have to be careful. It may have just been my guilty conscience, but I sensed that somehow, he knew that I was lying about everything.

"We first spotted you a week ago, and have been looking for you ever since. Lucky for us, someone reported seeing you earlier today. You see, Fräulein, we have faithful patriots everywhere."

"Wait, that wasn't m ..."

Without thinking, I nearly revealed proof of innocence. I almost told this man who was waiting for me to trip up, that I had just arrived today. But thankfully, I didn't. It suddenly occurred to me that they had been searching for someone of my likeness - most certainly my Aunt Adina. She's who they saw a week ago, and our close resemblance made them believe that I was her.

"You were saying, Fräulein?"

There was no way that I would tell them about her as it would most definitely complicate things, endangering her life as well as Carson's. I would just have to play along with their game and figure this out on my own. Still overcome with guilt, haunted by the lie that I was living left me feeling like a common criminal rather than the reality, that I was completing a divine mission. In this case, was lying right or wrong? I had always been taught that there is never a place for lying, never! But not only was I trying to complete a task brought about by the power of the Tempus Vector, but I was also in the middle of a soon-to-be war-torn Germany. The old adage that "the first casualty of war is truth," now made more sense to me than it ever had. I now understood what it meant - I was living it. I had not just sacrificed the truth of my identity, but in the last hour of time I had ravaged everything that was true in my life, and it grieved me.

In a desperate effort to help and prevent the Nazi trio from taking me, Malachi stood up and proclaimed that I, along with the rest of the Brannigan family, were regular customers.

"You see, Fraulein Brannigan comes all the way from America to buy the finest shoes in the world. Come now gentlemen, let us reason together. As you can surely see by what she has in her baggage, she is only here for a short amount of time. She means no harm. Please, please, she has been here many times before."

Then he pointed down towards my feet.

"Look for yourself. She wears my shoes!"

Not only had I perjured myself at the highest level, but I also made it necessary for Malachi to lie for me. If they did discover that I was truly not Valentine Brannigan, they would come after him with a vengeance.

"SHUT UP, you stupid old man! It is best you say nothing!"

Malachi, knowing that there was nothing that he could say to change their minds about taking me, grabbed my left hand as if to hold it, and pulled my wedding ring from my finger. As he removed it from my hand, he continued looking straight ahead so as not to draw attention to his action. At first, I resisted, and pulled my hand away, but then I realized that he had the foresight to know that a wedding ring would only complicate whatever situation I would be walking into.

"Am I allowed to put my other shoe on?"

As I bent down, I spotted my purse still sitting by the chair which I had discreetly nudged deep beneath the seat, attempting to hide it from the Gestapo. If he was in fact going to take me, I couldn't risk him searching my bag and finding the Tempus Vector, which he most certainly would. I knew that Malachi was a man of wisdom, and once he spotted it, would know exactly what to do. The head officer nodded at the soldiers, signaling them over to where I stood, and each of them proceeded to grab an arm and pull me towards the door.

"Wait, you have no right to take me. I'm an American citizen. I've done nothing wrong! What do you want with me anyway?"

"You are sadly mistaken, Fräulein, if you believe that you have any rights here! You've done nothing wrong? You stand guilty *because* you are American! Your beloved democracy means nothing here! Make no mistake, I will put a bullet through that pretty head of yours if you so much as look at me the wrong way."

"I think you misunderstand, sir! I am here at my family's request. Our company, Brannigan Steel, has been selling our finest gird to Russia, and I am here only as an ambassador to see....well, to see if all of this talk of Germany rising up and becoming a great nation is true or not."

I was fairly sure that most of what I was saying was bogus, but hopefully he was ignorant to such political matters and to this level of information. It was difficult to tell by his nonchalant reaction to my proposal of good will. He, along with the others, completely ignored me, responding as if I had said nothing of importance. Escorting me out of Schuh Coffee, it was obvious that they had their own agenda, and couldn't care less about mine or anything I had to say. Somehow I knew that their intention from the moment they walked into Malachi's store was to abduct the brown-haired, blue-eyed American who had been pursued and finally tracked down.

I turned my head, taking one last look at Malachi while struggling to release myself from my captors, and yelled out a number that would make sense to only him.

"Malachi! Malachi!.... two thousand sixteen! Two thousand sixteen!"

Quickly placing me in the backseat of a very large black sedan that proudly displayed Nazi flags on each side of the car, I found myself sandwiched between the pompous HS on one side and a simple-minded private on the other, leaving no possibility of escape. I was at a loss as to why this officer hated me, and why he continually glared at me with such hostility in his eyes.

"By the way, Fräulein, my name is Halag Sauer, assistant to Field Marshal Richter. I hope for your sake that your story checks out. If it does, well, we can all be friends, yes?"

His attitude and arrogance infuriated me, and while I should have stayed quiet, I returned with my own snotty retort.

"No, that will certainly not happen. When my family finds out how I've been treated, Brannigan Industries will refuse to supply Germany with steel for your weapons and tanks, all because of you! When that happens, and I promise it will, you will no longer be the assistant to the Field Marshal. Perhaps they'll shove you straight to the front lines and let you be the first one to get shot!"

While my reply was not wise for the moment, I found great satisfaction in observing Halag's annoying smirk vanish from his face with every syllable I spoke. But with his fading grin came a fury that could barely be contained. I could feel the heat of his anger radiating from the pores of his leather coat. What was I thinking? Only a fool would pour gas on a fire. For my own safety, I needed to remember where and when I was, not to mention what I was here to accomplish. Most importantly, I had to bear in mind that I was not in the presence of a reasonable man, but rather one whose deep-seated anger towards me was provoking him to violently grit his teeth - which was freakishly generating gross clusters of bulging veins in his forehead. I could tell that it took every bit of restraint for him to even be the least bit civil in his reply.

"We will see about that! DRIVE!"

It was apparent that whoever it was that wanted to see me had instructed Halag to deliver me unharmed.

Malachi stood in his doorway, helplessly watching me drive away. There was nothing that he could do except digest the unfathomable. I had begun my journey by breaking the first and most important rule, "Keep the Tempus Vector close to you at all times, and protect it at all costs." This was the first day of my calling, and I was already parted from the frame, but all for the sake of keeping it safe. I couldn't see another option, and I knew that it would be protected and in good hands with Malachi. I could only imagine what he must be thinking - that I'm a stupid girl who should have never been given the responsibility of carrying the frame. My fear now was that I would be called to return home while separated from the Tempus Vector. That horrifying scenario of being trapped here forever unnerved me. I only hoped that the mystery person I was meeting would release me quickly. Otherwise, there was a high probability that I would remain in 1940 forever, never to return to Carig.

My poor Carig! What must he be thinking? Already
I had been gone far longer than either one of us expected. If
I were to be completely honest, finding my way back to
him was all I cared about at this moment. I had to
escape! But there would be no escaping if I didn't pay
close attention to the route that we were taking out of the
city. It wouldn't be easy, but somehow I had to find my
way back to Malachi and the Tempus Vector.

Chapter 2

THE PERFECT STORM:
Carig's Chronicle

"Remember lad, the finest steel used to build the greatest ships and highest buildings, must first be refined by fires as hot as Hades. So too, within this life will the flames of hell rise up with a sword made of blue fire that will ei' destroy ye, or rarefy yer soul.... strengthen and empower ye for the battles that wait on the or' side of the bridge." **~Killen Hammell~**

"Thus far, my life has paralleled that of a mariner, dwellin' within a vessel forever at the mercies of the lawless sea, days and years of stormy waters ragin' all about me. Aye, there have been many blessed ones as well, filled with sunshine and gainful winds. But it wasn't till Beni came back nearly six weeks ago, that the tides changed. She transformed my world from craggy rocks, to smooth sands. I was nearly convinced that I would be forever parted from her, and the truth was, if I couldn't have her, I would have chosen to be alone. I nearly accepted that lot; she was just too far gone in every way.

Not just in breadth, livin' beneath the bright lights of the southwest, but her mind never varied from 'er goals, and her heart had hardened over time, leavin' no place for love.

"Adina had different ideas about the whole thing though, makin' somethin' beautiful out of somethin' so bitter. Her prophesy that Beni and I would someday be one, came to pass. Her death created a beginning for us, revealin' a legacy that she left behind for her most precious niece. It truly is a miracle, the whole thing. Beni comin' here the way she did, and turnin' in a completely new direction. Although my stubborn lass dug in her heels, kickin' and screamin' along the way, both her heart and her mind transformed before my very eyes. Beni not only yielded to her new calling as the Carrier of the Tempus Vector but also made Bar Rousse, Maine her new home, not to mention that she married me, her best friend and love of her life. Somehow, in a most mysterious way, all of

it together has led to this very moment of both sufferin' and obedience."

Watching her disappear through the balcony door left Carig as cold as the wind that followed her parting. The concern that he felt for Beni reminded him once again of the cry of Edmond Dantes, "All human wisdom is contained in these two words - Wait and Hope." For some strange reason, waiting and hoping, especially when it came to Beni, seemed to be his endless plight. He had waited his entire life for her, but even now he felt as though she was like the wind, and that he would never truly be able to hold on to her. He knew he couldn't allow himself to think like that, to fall into a pit of despair, things were different now. Beni was not just a fair-weather friend who may or may not return, but she was his wife and he had no doubt that she loved him. Carig was reminded that he too played a crucial role in this mysterious calling of the Tempus Vector, and had to stay focused on the task at hand. He promised Beni that he would be there waiting for her when she returned. So until she did, he would wait and hope.

Like his Grandfather Killen before him, Carig made himself comfortable in the same armchair that was tucked in the far corner of the room. It was more than a seat of vigilance, rather the Hammel pioneered symbol of faithfulness, which of course faced the balcony door. This most comfortable plaid velvet chair filled with down pillows covered in green and white ticking, was surrounded by mahogany shelves that kept all of Killen's favorite reads. Directly behind the chair was a standing brass lamp that embodied a radiant beacon that would illuminate the space. Still sitting by the chair was a small side table that held an antique smoking box filled with Killen's tin of tobacco and three wooden pipes. Carig grew up sheathed in the fragrance of a vanilla and bourbon mist, which still reminded him of his grandfather. He simply could not bring himself to discard Killen's pipes even though the years of smoking was the cause of his demise. Many a night when Carig was missing his parents, he would sit on his Gran's lap and listen to stories about his father's childhood and how Carig was the spittin' image of his "dadaidh," all the way down to the red birthmarks on the palms of his hands. But being a romantic at heart, he most loved the tale of the day his mother and father first met. He found great comfort in this place filled with happy reminders of time spent with his mentor and teacher. He even enjoyed the lingering fragrance of tobacco that had deeply permeated the cushions. Somehow just being in the mix of his Gran's favorites filled Carig with warm memories.

Directly behind the light was a cuckoo clock that Adina retrieved from her belongings, the remainder of which were left behind in Germany. Somehow the cadence of the ticking clock calmed Carig's nerves as he remembered that Beni's journey, no matter how long for her, would only be minutes for him. So, in reality, he fully

expected her to walk through the door at any time. He had

some experience watching Adina leave and return. She had

done it so well, it almost seemed effortless and predictable.

Somehow though, he felt more confident about Adina than

he did with Beni. Adina had journeyed for many years, and

this was Beni's first time. He only hoped it would be swift

and successful, and that she would come back to him

quickly. He already ached for her.

As minutes ticked by, Carig attempted to lose

himself in a book so as to take his mind off of Beni, but it

seemed impossible to focus. All he could do was watch the

door, waiting for the moment she would come home. With

eyes glued in the general direction of the balcony, he

noticed one single snowflake fall, marking the beginning of

this season's first snow in Bar Rousse. It ironically

reminded him of their first season of life together. Every

thought of her face and her body consumed him with

pleasure. His love for her was abounding within him, and he couldn't wait for her return. But like the frigid beauty of the snow, the continual thought of his bride, and the misery of her absence, was both delightful and cutting at the same time.

Accompanying the snow came plummeting temperatures with a bone-chilling bite that crept like fog across the room. This unexpected frost prompted Carig to light a fire, ensuring warmth for Beni when she would return through the door. In lieu of a fireplace, a black pot belly stove sat atop a matching pedestal just steps from his Gran's chair. The stove was small but mighty in efficiency, and once set ablaze would radiate like the sun, not only providing toasty warmth to the third story but also boiling water for a hot cup of tea. With the strike of a match, flames ignited the dried kindling, setting the iron belly aglow, consuming the chill in the air.

Watching the flames rise up sparked reflections of
their honeymoon night in the bothy. With a dismal smile,
he recalled Beni's playfulness as she lured him onto the
fluffy pillows that lay on the floor around the roaring fire,
prompting him to join her. It was hard to believe that this
time last night they were together - somehow it seemed like
an eternity ago, a far off but beautiful memory. Flame-
tipped shadows dancing on the walls reminded him of their
glorious and impassioned night of discovering one another
for the first time. The vivid recollections of Beni's face and
the essence of her soft skin against his, made him
desperately want her back, not in a minute or an hour, but
right now! He would never get enough of her, always
wanting more. His heart ached as the haunting reverie
intensified the already confirmed awareness that, until she
returned, his heart would lay dormant.

Suddenly, Carig's already uncomfortable
predicament was interrupted by something even more

intense and entirely unexplainable. As if struck and carried away, he was hit by the feeling of being swallowed and bound by a crushing wave. He had encountered this sixth sense once before. It was the same exact swell that consumed him only moments before the car accident that killed both of his parents. He knew that this oppressive awareness meant only one thing. Something had gone terribly wrong - not with himself, but with Beni. Even though he was a man, no longer a child, this familiar feeling of calamity left him feeling not only helpless but instantly enraged. The idea of knowing that Beni might be in some kind of danger, and being unable to help her, was already wearing on him. Generally, his temperament was as cool as the sea, but as of late, particularly since Beni arrived, he found himself battling against the demon of anger. The excruciating reality of his limitations, and trying to make sense of any of it, was making him feel completely psychotic. Not helping the matter any, he then heard

Beni's voice calling him from out of the dark waters that held him captive. All of this combined convinced him that he was losing his mind while feeling at the same time that he was in a paralyzed state and unable to move. He had the sensation of being trapped, and it was a struggle even to call out Beni's name, trying to let her know that he was there. Straining to break the spell or whatever this conjuring of dreaded insight was, he had to break free, get out of this room and pull back from the moment, or these feelings and thoughts would drive him crazy.

As if he were running for his life, he barreled down the stairs, barging through the front door of the house, paying no heed to leaving the entry wide open. He was oblivious to the frigid elements that were bombarding him, focused only on one thing, getting to the lighthouse. This was the place he could go where everything seemed to make sense, his refuge … just him and the sea. No matter the storm, no matter height nor depth of the restless waters, they were always faithful to bring about peace.

There were two things that stirred fire within the hearts of the Hammell men: women, and being in a situation that they couldn't control. But mixing the two, especially when undying love was involved, was like throwing gas on a fire. These two elements merging not only made their Scottish blood boil, but it brought about the spirit of the "Gaisgeach." Killen raised his grandson to stand strong as a gaisgeach, or a Scottish warrior of virtue, in all situations. Along with his instruction to always take the higher road, his Gran referenced every painful and difficult lesson with the well-known words of old, "Remember lad, the finest steel used to build the greatest ships and highest buildings, must first be refined by fires as hot as Hades. So too, within this life will the flames of hell rise up with a sword made of blue fire that will ei' destroy ye, or rarefy yer soul … strengthen and empower ye for the battles that wait on the or' side of the bridge."

Not knowing exactly what his grandfather meant, Carig heeded his words as best he could, but there was, and had always been, something about Beni that made his inner strength of steel melt like wax. Perhaps it was because of the inferno that burned within him when it came to her, but whatever it was, it, along with the deep roots of his Scottish heritage, made his level of frustration rise. There had always been an element of lovesick frustration when it came to Beni, but what he was feeling at this very moment, the uncontrollable anger and paralyzing intensity of helplessness, was something new and altogether unwelcome. He was struggling to understand what was going on within him.

"Gran, *I dunno if I can do this! I thought I could, but now I dunno! I know ye did it for Adina many odd years, but Gran, Beni's my wife. I miss her every moment*

I'm apart from her, and I can't stand the thought of losin' her. Is it too much to ask just to be with her and live a normal life? I love her so much, I always have, ye know that as well! Her bein' in a place alone, and me havin' no way of gettin' to her or knowin' if she's ok, is killin' me! I feel as though I'm dyin' inside! Most of all Gran, I'm feelin' wildly furious, like I'm somehow a different person than who I was, and don't know why. I'm plagued with uncontrollable rage within my spirit, and nothin' makes it better. I hate to say it out loud, but the very moment Beni walked up behind me, a stirring of heat rose up like I'd never felt before. She ignited an inferno of ill temper in my soul. Yet she, and she alone, is the one that can satisfy the affliction. Her rapturous passion is like rain falling from the heavens that drenches the raging fire. I cannot stand it, I can't! I just don't understand how this all works."

Carig was not only unaware of the time that had passed but also indifferent to the freezing temperature and blanket of snow that had all but covered him. But he didn't care. He would rather be on a peaceful ledge of snowy ice than in a heated room full of torment. His peace, however, was short-lived as the unsympathetic winds howled all about him. Within them, he heard Beni screaming his name. "Carig! Carig! Help me!"

Unaware of his feet even touching the winding steps as he raced down from the tower, he sprinted to the house and up to the third story, hoping to see Beni standing there. As he flew into the room, he was fiercely disappointed ... the space was exactly as he had left it. The door leading out to the balcony was still closed, and there was no sign of her. He collapsed into the chair, fighting back tears that were burning in his throat. Even his skin burned as the heat from the wood stove began to thaw his frozen flesh.

Carig had to do something to keep his mind occupied or else he would go completely crazy; he was never one for sitting still or being idle. Taking out his knife and a small piece of wood, he began sculpting. Scraping back and forth with his knife, he caught sight of his grandfather's books. He coveted peace. The kind of peace that Killen demonstrated as he sat for hours reading so tranquilly. He never seemed a wreck like Carig felt. Maybe reading was his secret to staying calm in the storm of Adina's travels. The problem was that Carig never really loved reading, always being distracted by the slightest movement in the room and unable to focus on words on a page. But hearing Beni read was an entirely different thing. He could sit for hours listening to her voice and her stories. She had a gift of bringing any tale to life with her great enthusiasm for the written word.

Eventually, with thoughts of Beni swirling in his mind, the sounds of the crackling fire, and the ticking of the clock, he was lulled into a deep and much-needed sleep.

Startled awake by the sound of a high-pitched scream, Carig found himself in a lather of sweat, at first not knowing where he was. Like waking out of a drunken stupor, his head was filled with fog, and ears still recovering from the peal of the cuckoo. He stood up and turned around trying to concentrate on the clock face. But no matter how hard he tried, everything was out of focus, even fuzzy, as he strained to make out the time. When his eyes cleared, his spirit sank within him as he discovered that it was one-thirty in the morning and Beni still had not come back. What would normally be only minutes of waiting, had turned into hours. In all of Adina's instructions and warnings to him, she never mentioned a reason for not returning, or that such a thing would ever occur. He remembered Beni telling him about the time when Adina fell in love, and almost chose not to return, but he knew Beni, and he knew that was not the situation in this case. She would never choose to stay. It was something else, but he had no idea what it could be. Was there another unspoken govern of the Bearer that he was unaware

61

of? Something had gone wrong, he could feel it. His mind went crazy thinking of all the possibilities of what could have happened to her, and how helpless he felt. He came to the conclusion that she was either hurt, somehow separated from the frame, or even dead. He sat on the edge of the chair, holding his head in his hand. "What do I do, God … what do I do?"

Resigning himself to the fact that there was absolutely nothing he could do except wait, he turned his head in the direction of the case of books and began reading the titles one by one from left to right: The Grapes of Wrath, Jane Eyre, an entire row of Sherlock Holmes, To Kill a Mockingbird … As his eyes arrived at the bottom of the shelf, he noticed Beni's ceramic mug filled with bookmarks that was separating the novels from two small journals that were tied together with a leather strap. He grabbed both of them and saw that beneath the strap was a piece of paper folded with a dried flower on top. He pulled out the note, and started reading.

Carig,

Until now, I didn't know what it meant to have a love like ours. Words can truly never tell you how much I love you. I know that it's not fair to leave you alone so soon after our marriage - I miss you already!

There's something I want you to know, something that I have never told you about my past. Like everyone I guess, I have regrets that I wish I could put away and never think about again. Two times I tried to give my heart away, surrendering what I knew was wrong. I was convinced it was meant to be. At the time, they seemed right in so many ways, but as it turned out, they each took their turn at trampling my heart,

leaving it spread about in many pieces. You

remember me growing up. I always seemed

to be the friend, never the girlfriend. I finally

came to the conclusion that I was not meant

for love. I couldn't quite figure out what was

wrong with me. All through school, the cute

flirty girls were the endgame for the

handsome boys, but never me. It seems silly

now, but I used to cry for hours thinking I

was too ugly, too fat, too skinny, had too

many pimples. The boys didn't care that I

was a nice girl. As a matter of fact, they

didn't want a nice girl, nor did they want

me, but I didn't know why.

One night when I was so upset,

spilling my fractured stories of heartbreak to

Adina, she told me why. My affliction was

both a blessing and a curse, she said. She

then explained it in a way that I will never

forget, and from that point on, it changed my

life.

God is everywhere, sees all things

and works everything out for good! Through

their blindness, He was protecting me. He

was guarding me from the wrong people,

and from making decisions that could

ultimately ruin my life. She promised me that

the One who made me had the perfect

person picked out, and when he came into

my life I would know. Until that time, I

needed to stay focused on my goals and

work hard, which was what I chose to do

from that point on.

I remember the day you told me that

you loved me - I was a silly teenager who

was in love with Omar Sharif. I think I

laughed and said that you were simply

infatuated. I hurt you, I'm sorry! Somehow

you knew, and for some reason, you still

loved me even when I didn't deserve it.

When I came here, several weeks ago and

saw you standing there, my love, God

opened my eyes and heart, and I knew. I

didn't admit it at the time, but at that

moment, at that second, my heart became

yours. Through my years of wondering and

tears, God brought me you, and I am forever

thankful. I could never ask for a better man.

Even as I sit here writing this, getting ready

to leave, I'm thinking about you, every part

of you, and I can't wait to be with you

again.

We both knew that this would be

hard, and I hope with all of my heart that

you're not regretting marrying me. I'm

sorry that you're the one left behind, I'm so

very sorry! I just want to reassure you of

how totally crazy in love I am with you, and

that, will never change. You are, and you

always have been, the one for me. I am

blessed! While you wait for me to come

back, I've left Adina's and Malachi's

journals for you to read through. I have

read only a fraction of them, and I feel like

all of their experiences should be yours as

well. I couldn't do this without you, and I

wouldn't be doing any of it if not for you.

Please don't ever be afraid; I will always

come back to you. I'm not frightened of what

my journey holds for me because I feel you

with me, Carig, I always have. You're in my

heart and my soul everywhere that I go.

I will see you soon, my love!

Forever Yours!

Beni

Carig leaned back in the chair and inhaled deeply, overwhelmed with relief by Beni's reminder of love for him. Little did she realize that he always thought she was beautiful, even through the teenage years of pimples and braces. He had heard her tears of brokenheartedness as Adina held her, and cursed those who caused such pain. He wanted to be the one to comfort her, but she wasn't ready to see him in that way.

Even though they had known one another for years, this uncharted step of marriage was new and untested. He was thankful for her insight into knowing how much he

68

needed to hear from her at that very moment. The idea of reading these two diaries took on a whole different level of interest for Carig, far more interesting than Killen's well-loved novels. He was definitely more familiar with Adina's travels, but everything about Malachi was a complete mystery to him, and that's where he would begin.

Page by tattered page, he read all about Malachi's beginnings after his father died, and how frightened he had been. It seemed that every Bearer of the Tempus Vector had that in common; they all began at the same place, on the corner of unsure and afraid. But also having in common a spirit of fortitude, none of them allowed their fear to stop them from moving forward. Minutes turned into hours of reading and studying Malachi's journal, which was nothing less than fascinating. Nearing the end of Malachi's diary, believing that his story had come to a conclusion, Carig was caught off guard as he zeroed in on one particular name that nearly jumped off of the page; Benidette Hammell.

He sat there frozen, only able to stare down at the name that belonged to him, not to a ghost of the past. His eyes were glued to the page, unable to read anything before or after it, not knowing if he even wanted to. For a split second, he thought perhaps that Beni wrote her name in the diary, but could tell that the penmanship belonged to Malachi, and the paper was old and weathered. He even considered the fact that Malachi could be referring to when he saw Beni at the airport, but her last name was still Crawford at the time and he had been dead and gone for years. None of it made sense. All at once, the truth of the matter occurred to him. Beni's first journey had taken her to Germany, and she had found Malachi.

Chapter 3

THE SAGACITY

"The cryptic timepiece was strategically assembled and driven by divine authority, like a finely made watch with an impeccable movement. Hence, the journey is driven by the hour hand, with the minute hand of precision marking the task, and the mortal pendulum keeping the device grounded and moving forward."
~Malachi Coffee~

Finding it difficult to continue, Carig decided to read on despite what he may find. The incredible events that he discovered within the pages of Malachi's journal, had occurred three-quarters of a century ago, and were simultaneously including Beni at this very moment.

October 3, 1940

I am an old man now. I have seen many things, I have many regrets, but also many accomplishments, many blessings, and many things to be thankful for. I know my days as the Carrier are coming to an end.

Father told me that some, not all, ever have

the privilege of meeting the one who will

follow them. He told me that there was no

doubt that he knew from the moment my real

father traded Estee and me for shoes that I

would be the next Bearer of the frame.

    Sadly, now I see my home on the

verge of war. When Hitler's men come to

pick up their boots, I am afraid. I feel they

somehow know that it's here. I don't know

how long I can keep it safe. I pray every day

for the wisdom to keep it protected and to do

what's right. Oh God, please send me a

sign...something showing me what to do.

    The next entry in Malachi's journal was dated the

following day, October 4, 1940. The fated parallel that was

soon to reveal itself would catch Carig completely off

guard. He had no thoughts that Malachi's antique chronicle would in a million years involve Beni at such a deep level. His passage into Malachi's past would set him on a vessel made of webs, spun together by the unthinkable events that were commanding her journey. She had become unreachable in a place and time that seemed to have swallowed her up.

Praise the God of heaven and earth, I have seen a miracle. How can it be? No one would believe me if I told them, I hardly believe it myself. I heard the chime ring out at the door like I have a million times; a customer, so I thought. So very busy making boots that I did not wish to see any patrons, not today. But, "Never leave a customer waiting," that's what Papa said. When I walked out to see who it was, I was taken aback by a beautiful young woman, a stranger, who was dressed like someone

important. She looked at me and smiled as if

she knew me, but I did not know her. She

even asked me if I knew her, but of course, I

did not. How could I? At first, I was afraid

... I know every person in this town like the

back of my hand, but not her. Because I feel

the eyes of Nazi spies watching me, I

thought perhaps she was one of them. All I

could do was remain calm, and treat her like

any customer who would walk through my

door.

A shroud of darkness fell upon me as

I removed her shoe and saw my stamp. I

hadn't been that frightened since the day I

unknowingly arrived in the middle of a

hailing firestorm on the streets of the

Golden Gate City. The insole bore my name,

74

but never had I made such frivolous shoes.

The people in this town are simple and

would never have need of such things. At

first I thought her a demon of sorts, like a

dream laced with darkness had entered my

presence and become real. But then

something happened that changed

everything; she was drawn to my wall of

frames, closely examining each one. She

knew what they were! She knew, because she

is a Carrier of the Tempus Vector. Benidette

Hammell was her name.

Oh my dear, forgive me, I can't

believe I stood here and watched as you

were taken away by the Gestapo. This is a

very bad turn of events that could ruin

everything. They don't know what they've

taken, what chain of events they set into

play. Their act set in motion the flow of unaltered time. Only the world of those serving the call of the Tempus Vector would know the consequences of such an action. When a Carrier is taken or held against their will, time will no longer stand still for those who wait for them.

Let my words bear witness to you, the one who bears the great burden of waiting in the realm of the unknown. She has been taken, and there was nothing I could do to stop it. Everything that could go wrong, has gone wrong. The matter of time and how it moves, sometimes slowly, sometimes quickly, is an unknown truth that I discovered when my father traveled. I thought he had died after a month of waiting had passed.

Benidette mentioned another name

by accident, "Crawford." It appears to be

her maiden name. Poor girl, she said she is

just recently married. This calling is not

meant to go hand in hand with marriage. If

somehow this finds you, the one waiting, you

surely feel a great weight upon you. Being

bound to the Bearer of the Tempus Vector

will never be easy, and will always be

attached to great worry, this I promise. For

that, I am sorry! But this I will say, love will

cast out even the darkest of nights. I do not

know where she is, or if she is safe. Estee is

trying to find out. I have no idea how long

she has been here, my Benidette. The

Gestapo said they have been watching her

for many days. After seeing her drive away,

I came back inside, unsure of what I should

do, except this...I had to make this known to
you.

Only one thing can be done to help
her... to lay prostrate on the floor begging
God for help, only God can help ... I pray
that He helps you too!

The Lord has opened my eyes. For while
before the Lord, I spotted her handbag
beneath the chair. It was pushed so far
under that I almost did not see it. I know
why you did it, Benidette. You were wise to
leave the bag here that contained the frame,
but my dear, it is not good that you are
parted from it. I fear that something
unforeseen will happen and you will be
forced to remain here forever.

Carig couldn't believe what he had just

encountered, and sat lifelessly back in the chair. Just like

Malachi had said, this was the worst situation possible,

other than her dying. He closed his eyes tightly, hoping that

this was all a bad dream, but it was real, and staring him

straight in the face. "Oh God, no, please no! This cannot

be real! Aw Beni, you've been captured in the most horrid

place, by some of the most vile people in history, and now

you have no way of gettin' back and there's nothin' I can

do to help! God! Did you spare her from the Devil's

Knuckles only to be lost forever? Have I done somethin'

wrong that you would take her from me?" Carig was

sickened by this new information. He just couldn't believe

what he was reading. He found some comfort in at least

knowing what was going on, and why she hadn't returned.

"She can't return, and all I can do is wait." Once again, he

became enraged at the fact that she needed his help, but he

was here, and she was there, it seemed like a complete

waste. He found himself more and more angered over this nonsensical arrangement.

Malachi's journaling didn't end there though. There was yet another entry on the same day. He was leery of what he might find out, but at the same time, intrigued, and so continued to read.

My hands are still shaking! As if this day has not already been filled with such peculiar and curious affairs, I thought for a moment that I had been visited by a ghost! This time, however, when the chime rang out, I was at first irritated at the disruption. I was busy and couldn't be bothered as I was preoccupied with my search through Benidette's bag. I stood in awe as I discovered the frame cleverly hidden within the lining. In my mind, now was not the time to wait on a customer, I had to put all my efforts into finding Benidette and helping

her to escape. But then it occurred to me

that maybe the Nazis had returned. What did

they want now? Frantically, I hid her bag in

my box of tools. She had sacrificed

everything for the safety of this frame, and I

would not risk it being discovered.

When finally I had gathered my wits,

and calmed my tremorous hands, I went out

front to see who had come into my shop. It

was then that Benidette's ghost appeared, or

so I thought. Walking through my store, as if

she had never been here before, was a

young woman who bore an almost identical

resemblance to Benidette. There she stood,

looking a little bit lost, clinging to a box that

was clearly important to her. It was as if my

new friend had never left, well, a version of

her remained anyway. Initially, I was filled with great relief, that is until I took a closer look at her face. This girl, although young, somehow seemed older than her years. A soul that had already weathered a life of disappointment. It was obvious that she did not know me - most definitely not Benidette!

I could tell by her demeanor that she was also American. What a strange coincidence! No, providence! She must have believed me rude, but my words were adrift, without even so much as one breath to speak them. My normal flowing tongue does not generally allow such a halt in words, nonetheless, this was the second time today that I felt that my heart had stopped beating.

She told me that her name was

Adina, not Benidette, and that she came to

buy boots for Leta. We talked very little, but

I did discover that she too was married. I

inquired as to her surname, but she was

hesitant to say. I then did something that I

have never done before, I offered her a

position in my store. Somehow I knew that

this was divine providence, she was meant to

be here. Lucky for me, she can sew clothes

quite well, so... she will sew shoes. She

begins tomorrow, and seemed so happy at

the prospect. Like the fragrance that

accompanies rain, these two souls go

together, I feel it! The only difference is that

Adina belongs here, and Benidette is but a

sojourner. My poor Benidette, there is very

little that I know about you except your

name, and a short but profound message
that you revealed to me as you were being
dragged away. I know now that you are
from the next century to come, two thousand
and sixteen, so you said. You are so far from
home, but more tragically, parted from the
frame.

I believed that nothing could divert
my attentions from Benidette, but now there
is Adina. There is no doubt in my mind that
she is my successor, like a miracle dropped
from the heavens, and undoubtedly,
Benidette is hers. I knew from my many
years of being the Carrier and keeper of the
Tempus Vector, that nothing is by chance,
no accidents, but only divine intervention.
Benidette was here for an even greater

purpose than I could know, and I needed to

help my new dear friend.

It has now become my highest goal

to find out what has happened to her, and

where she's been taken.

Fear not, Benidette. I have hidden

the frame for now, keeping it safe until your

return. What a smart girl, leaving your bag

here with me! You had the wisdom to know

that the Nazis surely would have discovered

it, and then all would have been lost. I will

help you, my dear! So very strange to see the

photo of Ira's bakery as the centerpiece of

your frame, and not me or my shop. You

were meant to come here, but why, I do not

know. Yet, you came to Schuh Coffee, and

here I stand holding the frame. I am certain

that you have spoken with Ira, now I must go

and speak with him. For now, the photo in the frame remains as is.

Ira, my dearest and closest friend, couldn't remember a name if his life depended on it, but remembers his customers by what they order. Benidette though, he remembered.

"She was like a cherry on a brulée!"

He said that she ordered his famous kasekuchen, and spoke of it as if she had tasted it before. He told me that she was a curious one because she asked him what town she was in, and then acted surprised at his answer. She remained in his bakery until she saw a woman walking on the other side of the street going into the market, then she hurriedly ran after her, leaving far too much money for her tea and dessert. That was all

he knew, all he could recall. I still do not

know why she's here, but there's a reason -

there's always a reason.

Estee just returned from seeing Etta.

Etta's daughter works in the household of

Alrik Richter, Field Marshal of Germany.

Benidette has been taken to his residence for

questioning. This is all that I know right

now.

"Wait! No! That can't be it!" Carig flipped to the

next page and then the next. Malachi said nothing more

about Beni. It ended there. She had been taken to the

household of Field Marshal Alrik Richter. "The end?

Damnit!!" Carig stood up and threw the journal to the other

side of the room with such force that it left an indentation

in the wall.

In a bout of fury, he ran downstairs to the sewing

room, and sat at the computer to research this Alrik Richter

to find out what his story was. Hopefully, history would

reveal insight into what was going on, or what was about to

happen with Beni. As he searched, he was surprised to find

page after page of information on Beni's captor.

This is what he uncovered: "Alrik Kuno Richter

born in Friedlich, Germany, August 22, 1910, born to one

of the wealthiest families in Germany. His father, Count

Stephen Richter, made his fortune in automobile

manufacturing and ball bearings. By the turn of the century

he was one of the richest men in all of Europe, with a net

worth of what would equal $17 billion today. Count Richter

was one of the greatest sole financial contributors to the

rise of Hitler's cause and movement. Alrik's mother died

when he was young, leaving him devastated and to be

raised at the hand of a harsh and unloving father. Alrik

experienced a *complete* Nazi education, being trained and

educated in the "Way of the German" at the School of Goring, beginning at the age of five. In 1929, at the age of nineteen, and against his father's wishes, Alrik married Caprice Moreau, daughter of the Richter Estate's groundskeeper. Family objections, mainly from the Count, were severe due to her low status and French heritage. It was the Count's desire to maintain a *pure* German bloodline. Caprice died during childbirth on Christmas Day, 1935, leaving the young Alrik embittered and alone. His father, the Count had only one goal for his son - a high ranking position within the Third Reich. In order to assure his position, Count Richter donated excessive financial contributions to Hitler's movement. Alrik Richter was commissioned as Field Marshal to Hitler in 1939. Upon his father's untimely and mysterious death during the commission ceremony, the massive Richter fortune was left solely to his son.

"He is most highly known for the enormous 50-acre indoor farm located on his historic 200-acre estate. Using the most brilliant botanist minds of the 20th century, Alrik Richter created a forward-thinking greenhouse system of farming and solar science that revolutionized the food production of that time, and is still used and studied today.

"In 1942, the highly regarded Field Marshal and his daughter, Annaliese, disappeared from Germany, never to be seen again. Abandoning his post as Field Marshal to the Fuhrer, he was marked a traitor and criminal of war by the German Republic. He died February 1, 1999 in Portland, Maine, survived by his daughter, Annaliese Richter."

"Bloody Hell! Portland, Maine? He lived here by us, all these years?" Scrolling to the bottom of the page, there was a picture of Alrik Richter, and directly next to him was a photo of a painting. Beneath the painting was the name "Caprice Richter, Beloved Wife." It went on to say that this masterpiece could still be found in the Kristall

Himmell Art Gallery, in Portland, Maine. Carig became

frantic and then tormented, as he meticulously inspected

the image of Caprice. Positioning himself closer to the

computer screen, he noticed that not only was this a picture

of Beni, a perfect likeness to be exact, but it said that she

had been dead since 1930!

Chapter 4

DR. CARSON

"I will surely die ten years earlier than what the good Lord intended. The moment I saw her standing there wearing the brooch, in the arms of another, my heart went portside, and died a decade's worth." **~Carson York~**

Keeping track of the route as we sped out of town to wherever we were headed, was becoming more challenging as the roads were tedious and a thick fog had set in. After several miles, and without warning, the already bumpy road turned into a rickety and unsteady byway as we began crossing a wooden bridge that had been constructed over a raging river. Upon arriving at the other side of the one-lane crossing, the heavy mist broke into sunshine, as we approached an unquestionably more elite section of town. Friedlich, like many other cities in the world, contained neighborhoods of both higher and lower status, and we had obviously arrived in the so-called upper east side section.

I could feel the eyes of my brutal abductor glaring at me.

"You seem a bit nervous, Fräulein."

"No, not at all! I'm just not accustomed to being taken prisoner!"

Nervously gritting his teeth, he attempted to make small talk. Even this slight but pathetic gesture of goodwill was done in the most scheming manner.

"I am afraid I have neglected to introduce myself. I am Halag Sauer. I have indeed heard of your family. When I was a boy, my family visited America. While we were there, we stayed in your hotel in New York City. Do you know the one?"

Was he kidding me? How could he already have me figured out? Somehow, in the short amount of time that we had spent together, he discovered that I was lying about belonging to one of the most affluent families in the world.

93

He was evil, but certainly not stupid. This Halag Sauer somehow knew from the first that I was not Valentine Brannigan. Surprisingly, he refused to accuse me out loud - not yet anyway. Perhaps he wasn't completely convinced of his own ideals, or maybe he was waiting to reveal my secret upon a stage of his own making, before a crowd of his choosing. It was obvious that he was skilled in the art of intimidating threats and bogus accusations, and I couldn't help but feel that his twisted game of cat and mouse had just begun. I loathed his inflated ego and sense of superiority. His obvious goal was to frighten me, but little did he know, that his underhanded method empowered me, turning my fear to malice. My position was swiftly revitalized, and I was determined that *my deceitfulness* would have to be bigger, broader, and more convincing than the inklings of this fascist pig.

"Ah yes, Mr. Sauer, The Ritz Brannigan, it's merely one of my many homes. I stay there often! As a matter of fact, the penthouse on the top floor is for my own personal use."

Little did he know that I would often stay in the penthouse, but it was with my best friend, Rae Brannigan, who actually did have her very own place at the top of the hotel, and I was fortunate enough to have lodged with her many times. He had no idea that my knowledge of the hotel came from the great granddaughter of Magnus Brannigan. Hopefully, I would be able to continue this charade effectively, and most importantly, *believably*. Mr. Sauer, or whatever his title was, was conniving and anxiously waiting for me to slip up. He looked at me with such hatred, and words that flowed from his mouth were filled with venom and malice.

"Just as I remember, beauty queens, millionaires, ridiculous records, and Hollywood."

I looked over at him with an expression of disgust.

Even though I had only encountered a few dreadful interactions with Halag, I quickly came to the realization that he was foul and deranged. He was one of those psychopaths that would smile at you as he slit your throat.

"Excuse me?"

"That's all you Americans care about, and *you* are the worst of them all!"

After the extremely bizarre exchange between us, I decided that I was done with him. He obviously hated Americans, and hated me from the moment he laid eyes on me. For the duration of the drive I looked straight ahead through the front window, trying my best to ignore him. Unfortunately, his scrutinizing glare continued, which made me terribly uncomfortable.

Finally, we arrived at the intended location which was not at all what I expected. I had anticipated a small concrete torture room with one single interrogation light shining in my face, and of course the torment being

conducted by a group of brutal Germans similar to Halag

Sauer, but to my surprise, we turned down a long pebble

driveway that was bordered with perfectly groomed shrubs

and white statues. Apparently, we were not headed for a

torture chamber at all, but someone's home. At the end of

the driveway was a roundabout with an enormous dark gray

fountain decorated with gold cherubim crowning the center.

The house that appeared at the end of the private road was

extraordinary. So much so, that I was confused as to

precisely what to call this magnificent residence - my guess

would be a manor of some sort. There were three main

sections, which all together formed a U-shaped, three-story

structure. The middle section was the main entry where,

standing outside at attention, were all of the housemaids

and butlers in their finest uniforms, ready to receive us. The

sections on either side appeared to be filled with many

chambers, and were the size of a grand hotel. It was a

stunning array of pale yellow and white hues canopied by a charcoal gray roof. This was by far the most beautiful and inviting home I had ever seen.

Sitting in the car awaiting instructions of what I would be forced do next, left me feeling even more unsettled. I was able to stay calm and collected on the outside, but on the inside I was nervous and afraid for what was coming. When the Gestapo officer finally got out of the car and away from me, I was relieved. Sitting next to him made my skin crawl. Even the two officers who remained with me were far better alternatives than being with him. At this point, I wasn't sure if I would even be getting out at all, or if this was simply a pause before a longer journey.

However, after a few moments, I watched as Sauer came back to the car and opened my door. He motioned with his hand for me to get out. Slowly, I slid across the black leather seat and set my feet on the ground. Before I even stood up, both of my transports were each grabbing an arm and guiding me through the assembly of servants towards the front door. I refused to be kept on a leash, and continued in my struggle to break free from their grips, but my attempts at freedom only resulted in a tighter grasp. Interestingly, as we walked past each of the workers, none would make eye contact with me. None, that is, except one. An older heavyset woman who stood closest to the door, looked straight into my eyes with an unusual expression of both joy and sadness.

Finally making our way through the opulent and quite exquisite front doorway, I was overcome by an even grander entry area entirely enveloped in white and gray marble. The gray veined marble continued up the spiral staircase, that was, of course, embellished with gold scrolled balusters. In the center of the room was a large round glass table with an arrangement of fresh flowers that was massive in size, stretching towards the baroque ceiling.

The demeanor of the Head Gestapo officer completely changed as he stood at attention, as if someone of great importance was about to walk into the room. I fully expected to see Hitler himself arrive at any moment, or someone who was highly regarded by all. Whoever lived here was extremely important and immensely wealthy.

My impatience got the best of me, as I glared at Officer Sauer demanding he give me some answers.

"Enough of these games - why am I here? Where am I? I demand to know!"

For the first time, he chose not to engage with me, but only glared. The two officers still clung tightly to each of my arms, as if I might run away.

"Take your hands off of me immediately!"

After my outburst, they held on even tighter, and my battle for liberation continued. From the top of the stairway, I heard a command ring out in a deep militant tone.

"Let go of her!"

Instantly, their arms dropped to their sides, and I was free. I looked up to see where the voice came from, and standing there was a young man, probably early thirties with blonde hair, a strong chiseled chin, and intense blue eyes staring down at me. Our eye contact with one another was powerful. I felt an incredible sense of deja vu come over me; this was not the first time I had seen this man. I had seen him before, but where, I wasn't sure. This unfamiliar environment was throwing me off, but him ... his face ... somehow I knew it.

Everything happening at once was causing an explosion of panic within me. It was overwhelming and upsetting, but I had to hold myself together. Halag would enjoy nothing more than to watch me fall apart.

This familiar face was wearing an all-black uniform decorated with several gold insignia, and trims of red. He slowly walked down the flight of stairs looking at me in a most curious manner. Once he arrived at the bottom and stood right before me, he grabbed my hand and kissed it. Strangely, he didn't smile or even seem very friendly, but maintained a stern expression.

"Fraulein Brannigan, welcome! I hope your coming here has not inconvenienced you!"

"Inconvenienced me? Are you kidding? I have been extremely inconvenienced and I am highly offended! I came here as a visitor, a friend of Germany, and I have been treated like a criminal. I demand you return me to town so that I can finish my business there and return home. My family will be terribly worried."

He stood there just watching me rant, not saying a word. I felt as though I was an actress on stage, and he was my audience. He watched me as if he were looking right through me.

"You know, I also came here to possibly offer the services of my family's company to supply steel to Germany. But now, after the way I've been treated, I just want to leave - so can you please return me to town?"

His continued silence thoroughly annoyed me. Then from out of nowhere, his harsh looking, but perfectly sculpted face broke into a partial smile.

"I am so very sorry, Fräulein, that was never my intention."

"What is your intention? Are you the one who wants to talk with me? The one who's been watching me for a week now? Well, here I am, what do you want?"

The look on his face as he glared at Sauer spoke a thousand words, all laced with raw hatred. He was obviously irritated at him for leaking this particular bit of information that should have remained confidential. Right, wrong, or indifferent, I found extreme gratification in the visual scolding.

"I would like to make amends. First of all, I am Alrik Richter, and all he meant to say was that we keep abreast of the goings-on of all foreigners who come here without notice. Please forgive me! Obviously, he misunderstood my instructions. How can I make this up to you?"

Alrik casually moved into my personal space, coming far too close. My mind was racing. Oh my gosh, I've seen this look before! He's giving me *that* look. It's the kind that a married woman shouldn't encourage, but rather run away from as quickly as possible! Trying not to make a scene, even though I was at the center of everyone's attention, I turned around and walked over to the door.

"Well, it's simple. Take me back to town, that's all I want - that's how you can make it up to me."

Pursing his lips and nodding his head, he reluctantly walked out the door with me, proceeding slowly, as if he didn't want me to go. He stopped, and stood silent with an empty stare; his body was present, but his mind was somewhere else. I could tell that my mysterious captor was busy chasing abstract thoughts of something that was consuming him - something deeply rooted in the recesses of his mind, perhaps some alternate agenda?

I stood as an invisible monument at the top of the stairs, unable to move. Her face was like a love song. I found myself consumed and inspirited by her delicate features, mastering every line and curve. Would she really be there when I finally reached the ground that she graced? I scarcely had faith in the evidence before my own eyes. The moment she looked up at me, it was so familiar, so comfortable, so right that she was here. She belonged in this house. Once in possession of her delicate hand, I couldn't resist brushing her ivory velvet to my lips, all the while growing more enraptured by her presence, her scent, feeling as if my soul was leaving my body and enveloping her. Even though her words were filled with fury, I didn't mind her scolding. Nothing she could have said would have offended or changed my thoughts towards her. I felt that this was my second chance at happiness. My life filled with pain, and the bitter pill of loneliness, had gone on for far too long. But what could I do - what could I say to stop her from leaving? I couldn't just allow her to go. It had only been moments since her arrival, and yet I was consumed by her ... how could such a thing be? I didn't understand it - this fixation was not like me at all. It had been days now since I first saw her, and it seemed like an eternity waiting for the car to finally arrive, for her to finally enter my life. She didn't understand, and would never know, that her presence here had been finely orchestrated by my hand.

106

This obsession that even I didn't understand, began in town

a few days back, and since that time, I could think of

nothing else. Although the initial encounter was barely a

glimpse in the side mirror of my car, I was bewitched. The

spell had been cast. She stirred a longing inside of me that

I believed died many years ago, one that could only be

satisfied by her nearness.

Despite a distant glimpse that only lasted mere

seconds, I ordered the driver to quickly turn around and

return to town, but like a vapor, she was gone. I thought

perhaps I'd seen a ghost; it wouldn't have been the first

time. I ordered Halag to find her, and not to think of

returning without her. He thought it a foolish task,

believing that war should be at the forefront of our

intentions, leaving him more embittered than ever.

"Of course, Fräulein, I will take you wherever you wish to go."

Halag looked at me, confused at my offering of freedom after he had attempted in vain to retrieve her. Halag and the two others followed us, but I assured them that their assistance was no longer necessary.

"I will take her!" *I opened the passenger door holding her hand as she stepped into the car. It was my goal, my hope, that she never leave. I would somehow create a way to make her stay, to make her love me.*

As if all of this was not already an entirely strange experience, I was now being ushered with kid gloves into the most cutting-edge automobile of the day, one I had only seen in pictures until now. This Mercedes transport was the golden carriage of the highest ranking officers who arrogantly paraded down the streets of Germany as if they were gods. But to me, it was simply a historic museum relic - a symbol of beastly atrocities.

I watched as Alrik walked back over to where the three dumbfounded men stood. From a distance, I observed angry gestures and overheard hushed grumbles from what appeared to be a heated conversation between Alrik and Halag. As they continually looked back in my direction, it was obvious by shifting glares that they were discussing me. Halag strode away in a huff, clearly irritated at the outcome of the conversation. He motioned for his two stooges to follow him, and together they quickly walked away in the opposite direction, as if they'd been sent on a mission.

As the car spun out onto the main road, I spotted an unusually large cement building surrounded by trees, far behind the estate grounds. It was a massive structure with no windows, and one large door in the front. I wouldn't have thought too much about this somewhat-of-an eyesore, except the entire roof of the building was an incredible glass dome which shone brightly in the sunlight, as though the ceiling was made of crystal. The ugliness of the structure was redeemed by the beauty of the dome. I couldn't help but stare, and my curiosity was piqued.

"What is that building over there?"

"*That* is the greatest achievement of my life!"

I looked over at this high ranking German aristocrat who bore the air of a typical cookie cutter Nazi, but then noticed a gentleness about him, something in his eyes. After incessant gushings of undying love over his "greatest achievement," he became exceedingly more amiable and soft-hearted. This seemingly stoic man slowly revealed details with a childlike enthusiasm that was quite charming, to say the least. It was extraordinary! My preconceived ideas that his extensive education in Nazism had devoured his mind since youth, were clearly misguided. His goals were not at all motivated by a lust for power, but by something pure and far more worthwhile.

"So, this is the passion of your life?"

He hesitated answering, almost as if he wasn't sure how to respond. But then he looked at me, a perfect stranger, with a longing in his eyes. It seemed that he was going to reveal something more profound than his concrete and glass achievement. There was something he wanted to say, I could practically see it on the tip of his tongue. But he quickly tucked away the notion to speak freely, and changed gears to a most unlikely subject, farming.

"So, my dear Fräulein, before I take you back to town, let me show you what's in that domed building. I think it may interest you, and your family."

Then he gave me some background for the motivation behind the construction.

"Because of the cold weather that so often consumes this part of the world, farming, and producing bountiful crops is not always an easy task. Germany is trying to be more efficient at taking care of and feeding its

people and its soldiers. Producing healthy and mass

quantities of food is critical for our survival and success.

So, may I show you, Fräulein?"

Not only did I feel compelled to say yes, but my

curiosity to see the inside of this massive greenhouse that

was hidden from the rest of the world stirred my blood.

"Well, if it won't take too long, and also, you can

call me Valentine."

"As you wish!"

He turned the car around, and started towards the

windowless conservatory.

From a distance, the gray building appeared merely

quite large, but the closer we got, the more massive it

became. There was one single metal door in the front which

was secured by two guards. When we stepped out of the car

and walked up to the door, the two stood at rigid attention, raising their arms to salute and acknowledge their

allegiance to the Fuhrer. At Alrik's nod, one of the men

removed the key from his belt and unlocked and opened the

heavy door. As it slammed behind us, I could hear the locks

simultaneously re-engage.

The initial room leading inside was dark and

claustrophobic, and the dense humidity created a shortage

of oxygen. Aware of my uneasiness at the lack of

breathable air, Alrik grabbed my hand and escorted me

down a rather long hallway filled with a progression of

windows on either side. With each step, the humidity

intensified and was enhanced by the aroma of dirt and an

even stronger stench of fertilizer. Strategically placed

opposite one another, were labs filled with shelves and

rows of many different species of plants labeled with exotic

names and various dates. Cooking over high-tech lab

burners were beakers filled with colorful concoctions

blowing toxic steam into the atmosphere. There in the

midst of it all, were dozens of men dressed in lab coats, goggles, and protective masks. As a whole, they were completely engrossed in their experimentations, not varying one inch from their tasks at hand.

"These scientists are the finest in all of Germany. They have been working for months, researching new and better ways to feed plants and enhance soil and growing conditions so that crops will develop quicker, and double, even triple, the size of normal plants."

As he continued boasting about this revolutionary structure and the great things they were accomplishing, the more giddy and excited he became, like a child with a toy.

"They have done amazing work, and their research keeps evolving and escalating. It's truly incredible!"

Well, he was right, I could tell that this was indeed his passion.

"Now through here is something so unimaginable, you will not believe your eyes!"

At the end of the hall was another door. As we entered, it was as if we were walking outside, only the climate was ideal, still a bit humid, but quite pleasant. The room was filled with an immense amount of light, but perfect, with sun filtering through the panels of staggered clear and white glass that made up the domed roof. The room went on for acres in both directions, an incredible indoor farm that appeared to be complete with every vegetable and fruit tree as far as the eye could see. As we walked down each aisle of plants and trees, I noticed that every stalk was unflawed with no blemish, no pests, no disease, just perfection. He was right, I was thoroughly impressed by what he was doing here. The nucleus of the entire structure was a mass body of water resembling a pond. In the center of the pond, a flame rose up beneath a large tent of plastic, sending dripping water into irrigation watercourses that spread throughout the entire indoor farm. It was magnificently designed and built to keep the soil moist and the plants perfectly watered. It felt as though I had entered the garden where all life began; it was flawless and complete.

"So, what do you think?"

"I'm blown away!"

He looked at me strangely … "Blown away?"

"What I meant to say is that it is truly amazing. It's like a miracle!"

Alrik was so pleased by my reaction. It seemed that I was the first outsider who had entered his Eden. In all truth, it was difficult *not* to be impressed by the vast creation that he had masterminded.

"So what you see here is not even the best part. Look up at the glass ceiling."

As I looked up, I noticed that spaced every ten feet or so, directly below the ceiling line, were large brackets, each one holding what looked like a motorized pulley system. Cables extended from each pulley, attaching through an entire row of glass panels. Apparently, throughout the day, and based on the position and strength of the sun, the panels were constantly repositioned to capture and direct the luminary energy.

"As you have probably noticed, the window panes are staggered with both clear and white panels. These multi opaque panels allow for proper amounts of light to come into the room as the sun moves throughout the day. But if you notice, there are also black panels that have been strategically placed in particular sections to be raised when the sun is strongest, protecting the plants from too much heat, while also absorbing and storing energy. Through the incredible work of our mechanical engineers and scientists who were brought in from around the world, we have harnessed the sun and then stored it within large battery units that can be used on cold sunless days."

What I was looking at was solar energy in a most magnificent greenhouse. They had taken an underused and unpopular concept of the time, and created something new and revolutionary. Even though I had come from a period when this science was being commonly used as a popular source of energy, I had never seen or heard of anything like this before.

"I am most fortunate to have acquired a brilliant master engineer who has made this all possible. You must meet him. He too is from America. Through abounding automation, he has set a standard of food growth and development that will change the world. In exchange for his help, I have given my permission for him to take this science back with him to America when he returns."

We continued walking to the far side of the building, where I noticed an entire work area and machine shop that contained, what appeared to be, every piece of machinery and tool known to man. It was unique to say the least. Like an auto shop/laboratory all in one, that was pristinely clean, well kept, and organized. I wouldn't have been surprised by the look of it if a caretaker was employed just for the primary task of purging dust and grease from these notably prized instruments of 20th-century technology.

The men were all dressed in black coveralls and hard hats. Some had been hoisted up high to the ceiling, working on and repairing panels, while others were adjusting the black panels and working on tubes and wires that were attached. It was obvious that each individual had a specific task at which they were extremely proficient. The men in the workroom were wearing welding helmets for protection as they fused large pieces of machinery. The

119

diligence and commitment of each worker was impressive. Not one of them stood around in idle conversation, but they were all focused on their particular skill. I could tell that Alrik's passion for the success of this project was contagious by the attitudes and output of the workers, or perhaps they were just frightened menials who wouldn't dare oppose the Field Marshal. However, even though he held great power, he didn't strike me as the dictator type.

Alrik grabbed my hand and began to guide me in the direction of one individual; the one person there that he wanted me to meet.

"Valentine, the man standing over there is the lead mechanical engineer and the heart of this oasis. Without him, none of this would have been possible. His abilities are extraordinary. Come, I will introduce you."

We walked to where this wonder man was crouched over, with sparks flying as he welded a hinge onto one of the intricate panels.

"Dr. Carson!"

At first the man didn't turn around. Then Alrik lightly tapped him on the shoulder.

"Dr. Carson!"

At that, Dr. Carson turned off his welding gun, placed it on a bench, lifted up his mask, and looked right at Alrik with a big smile. It was apparent by his response that he and Alrik were friends. At first, he didn't notice me, but once he did, his entire countenance changed. One after the other, Alrik introduced us, not aware of the striking distressed looks that we both wore as we exchanged glances.

"Valentine Brannigan, I would like to present Dr. David Carson. He is from, where did you say? Long Beach

… California. He came all this way to help us in this project, and I am very grateful! David, you have probably heard of the Brannigan family. This is the late Magnus Brannigan's daughter, Valentine."

This was not Dr. David Carson … this was Carson York, Adina's husband, my uncle, who died many years before I was born! Poor Carson! At first, he was speechless. It was all he could do to stare down at Alrik's hand holding mine, then follow the line of my arm up to my face. With the darker navy tulle partly covering my eyes, I could tell by his initial reaction that he believed me to be Adina. Upon examining me more closely, particularly my body and shorter stature, he let out a sigh of relief that I was not her.

"Are you quite well, Dr. Carson?"

"Yes, sorry, I'm just a little tired."

"Of course, you work too hard!"

122

Carson looked at me in the same manner which

Malachi did when beholding the shoe that he had never

made. But Carson's gaze of displeasure intensified when he

spotted the butterfly brooch fixed on the lapel of my suit

jacket. He had seen this permanent fixture of Adina's, and

knew that it didn't belong to the lookalike stranger that

stood before him. I could tell that he was consumed with

fear. Fear for Adina's safety, wondering what could have

possibly happened that would have caused her to give up

her beloved brooch. He was without words, and didn't even

know where to begin. My entire presence obviously

unnerved him greatly, and I didn't blame him. Honestly,

that made two of us! In a million years, I would have never

expected to see him either. Although I suppose I shouldn't

have counted on anything less. From the moment I arrived

here, I had experienced one surprise after another; being in

Friedlich at the same time as Adina and Malachi, taken by

the Gestapo, and now meeting Carson. So my *shock value*

was certainly not as intense as his. It was obvious that he was searching for words, something that would break the awkward silence.

"That is a lovely brooch, Miss Brannigan. I've only seen one other like it."

"Thank you. Yes it's rare to be sure, it belonged to my aunt. As a matter of fact, kind of a romantic story actually. She came all the way across the country to marry a man she had never met. They only knew one another from letters and pictures. She took a bus out to meet him and told him that he would know her by this butterfly brooch which she would be wearing on her lapel. It belonged to her grandmother, and was very precious to her. She wore it all the time."

Carson's mouth dropped open, as he turned as white as a sheet. Again, the same kind of reaction I got from Malachi. He didn't look relieved, but worried. He knew the story I spoke of, and like walls crashing down around him, I had heedlessly invaded the most personal part of his life that a stranger had no right to know. How I wish I could have told him who I was, and that I was only here to help. Instead, I obviously stirred a tumultuous flame of curiosity within my uncle that would surely make him seek out the truth, especially given the information I had revealed about the two of them. Convinced, even for that one moment that I was Adina, here in this highly secretive place, in the company of another man no less, must have caused a wink of insanity and an immediate fear for his, as well as Adina's safety. Yet judging by the look on his face, it wasn't a moment of madness at all, but more one of heartbreak. I knew Adina and Carson's background, how much they adored one another, and even the fleeting second of thinking that she was here with Alrik must have pained him greatly. I'm sure it didn't help that Alrik was extremely good looking and known for taking any woman he wanted. Perhaps Carson had initially concluded that Adina and Alrik had found one another while he was away.

Carson seemed paralyzed where he stood, and couldn't stop looking at me. Alrik took notice of the obvious doting and became irritated.

"Do you know one another?"

"No!" Carson stated in a rather irritated manner. "She just resembles someone I know."

Obviously annoyed, Carson instantly began checking his watch, completely distracted by the time of day, and his earlier cheerful smile had all at once been replaced by a somber constitution.

I quickly found out that Alrik was a touchy-feely sort, when out of the blue he turned towards me and began running his fingers over the contours of my face. His stare was intense, so much so, that they made both Carson and myself very uncomfortable.

"Well, my dear Fräulein, it appears that you have one of those faces, a lovely face."

"What a curious thing to say, Field Marshal Richter! Whatever do you mean?"

"Please, call me Alrik. It is as I said, you just have one of those faces."

His comment left me feeling ill at ease, and I would soon find out that his perplexing remark somehow bound me to the shadow of one who imprisoned his heart.

The longer we stood there together, the more ill at ease Carson became, all the while consulting the timepiece on his wrist, and growing more and more anxious. Alrik became irritated with my uncle's strange behavior.

"Is there somewhere you need to be, Dr. Carson?"

"Actually, I could really use some time away. I'm not feeling very well. I'd like to spend the day in town and be back tomorrow."

Alrik looked perplexed, as he had never seen Carson act this way, and had certainly never known him to request time off, especially so early in the day.

"Of course! You work too hard, and far too much! But I will expect to see you first thing tomorrow morning, yes?"

"Yes, of course!"

I regretted the extreme suffering that I had caused Carson. He was clearly panicking, and couldn't get back to Friedlich to check on Adina quick enough. Maybe the light in all of this darkness was that, in addition to forewarning Malachi, maybe I was here to caution Carson as well. If I could somehow protect both of them, this journey would be well worth the craziness that I had encountered thus far. I was encouraged, even excited at the thought of doing something that would not only change *their* lives, but also Adina's. Her days and years would have been so much more joyful if Carson would have been by her side. I imagined a world of the two of them returning home from Germany *together*, and the regret over Malachi, gone.

The problem, however, was when and how would I be able to talk to Carson? I couldn't tell him right now, not in front of Alrik, and not without the Tempus Vector close by. No, now was not the time. Calling to mind that I too would be returning to Friedlich very shortly, perhaps I could go and talk with him before leaving to go home. But until the frame was once again in my possession, I found myself in a catch-22, and it would be a foolish venture to say anything. This was a frustrating dilemma.

Alrik, obviously uncomfortable with the interaction between Carson and I, took my hand, prompting us to leave. This entire situation was so surreal, and I was completely at a loss as to Alrik's fascination with me. He acted as if he knew me in an intimate way, as if we were a couple, which was absurd. He had seen Adina days ago, and yet I was the one picked up. But why? What was his interest in me? In her? As I continued thinking about the craziness of it all, I became even more determined to return to Schuh Coffee, retrieve the Tempus Vector, talk to Malachi and Carson, finish this thing, and go home. I wanted to go home and see Carig. I already missed him, and hated being away from him.

"Safe travels, Dr. Carson!"

Carson responded with a grieved nod and dismal farewell.

"It was a pleasure meeting you CARSON ... I mean Dr. Carson."

When I said his name, his real name, I believe he heard Adina in me and knew something beyond his understanding was happening. Alrik took my hand and we walked away. I had to take another look back to see Carson, as it could very well be the last time I would ever lay eyes on my long lost uncle. As I did, he stood watching

me leave with a look of confusion on his face. It was

apparent that I was leaving him with a burden of

uncertainty and suspicion.

"Do the people who work here, also live here?"

"Yes, most of the time. Periodically we do allow

them to go and spend time with their families."

"What about Dr. Carson - does he have a family?

Do they stay in your house?"

"Dr. Carson has no family here, but goes into town

when he needs to get away. I have heard rumor that he has

a love interest in town. Perhaps his desperate need to leave

had something to do with her.

"Now back to your question, Fräulein. Yes, the

workers live here. Each person has been given their own

personal bungalow behind the farm, where they are treated

very well. It is most comfortable. They dine together at

every meal in an eating house right outside of their accommodations, and have become a very close team of extraordinary people. I have hired one of Germany's best chefs who creates nothing less than a masterpiece for each meal. The people who work for me are extremely valuable individuals who know their jobs well, but there are a few who have become cherished acquaintances. While I expect their best, I also *give* them the best. They are well cared for and are invaluable commodities to the future of Germany."

"Commodities?" I thought to myself. That was a very strange way to talk about a human being.

"Thank you for the grand tour. I must say that I am extremely impressed and overwhelmed by what you've done here!"

"You are very welcome! Before we go, Miss Brannigan, may I extend an invitation to you? I would be honored if you would spend the remainder of your holiday here with me. I would very much like to know more about you."

I tried as best I could to react to his proposal as if I were flattered. His request would need to be handled delicately, making him believe that, as much as I appreciated his offer, I would have to decline, but possibly return another time.

"How kind Alrik, thank you! But maybe another time. I really do have to get back to America. Business waits for no woman!"

I pointed at the exit door. "Shall we?"

Obviously disappointed, he opened the door, allowing me to exit before him.

To my dismay, zealously waiting right outside the door was Officer Sauer, along with his faithful duo. He was disturbingly cheerful with a satisfied look on his face that reminded me of a cat who had ruthlessly devoured a canary. He knew something, and whatever it was practically caused him to burst out of his skin. Excitedly pulling Alrik aside and bending towards his ear, he quietly mumbled only a few words.

I studied Alrik's face to see if I could read his reaction, but he showed no emotion at the news and only looked straight ahead as if he were in deep thought. I didn't know him well enough to be able to interpret his detached response, which for me, was torturous, leaving a sinking feeling in the pit of my stomach. I wish I could have known what he was telling him. Had he discovered that I was not Valentine Brannigan? I'm certain that bit of information would have overjoyed Halag. I wanted to run, but there was nowhere to go. Like always, I had to stand there hiding my fear, not letting on that I was afraid of being found out.

Chapter 5

KARUSSELL

"Even the muscle tone was impressive on these white and cream
war horses, draped with armors of gold and pastel saddles."
~Benidette Hammell~

It was all I could do to remain calm as Sauer, who

obviously detested me, continued filling Alrik's ear with

more information, all the while scowling in my direction as

he spoke. Curiously, Alrik countered back with quick

dialogue that I couldn't make out. The most alarming but

peculiar detail of the entire interaction occurred as Halag

walked away. He practically marked me a target out of the

corner of his eye with a harassing wink and a smirk. Alrik

warily circled back to where I stood, failing to make eye

contact with me, almost as though he were ashamed or

embarrassed about something. As he opened my car door, I

couldn't help but notice the glowing trickles of sweat on his

brow, encompassed by glaring guilt. As he slid into the

driver's side, he pursed his lips to speak. It was obvious there was something that he wanted to say, or maybe in this case, confess, but he remained silent. In one swift move, he turned on the ignition and began to drive. After only a short distance, we carelessly stopped in the middle of the road, and then he hesitantly looked in my direction.

"Fraulein … I have some bad news!"

"What is it?"

"The bridge that you crossed to get here ... has collapsed. I am sorry to tell you that, because of this there is no way for you to get back to town. Dolph Bridge has been in place for over two hundred years and it is our only connection to the town of Friedlich. Until it is repaired, you will have to stay with me."

"Are you really trying to convince me that there is no other way to get back to town? Are you *serious*?"

"Of course I'm serious. Why would I say it otherwise?"

"Unbelievable! Alrik...you know what? I have the distinct feeling that you're trying to keep me here. Is there something going on that I should know about?"

"Of course not! I have instructed Halag to assemble a construction crew immediately to repair the damage."

"Damage? It seemed very sturdy when we crossed it earlier. Take me there! I want to see it for myself!"

"As you wish, Fräulein."

The entire way there, Alrik made every attempt at conversation, but I was beyond angry and couldn't even look in his direction. Just the sight of this double-dealing roadblock who was trying to prevent me from fulfilling my task made me want to spit nails. I knew that this setup was an intentional act meant to keep me here.

As we pulled up to the riverbank, I was overwhelmed with crushing disappointment at the state of the bridge, or rather, the now gaping chasm of impassable swells. It wasn't just damaged, it was completely ripped out and gone. I was no expert, but it looked to me that this beautiful landmark was purposely demolished, leaving no evidence that it ever existed. They stood together in their lies, but I knew that this was done by human hands, certainly not by an act of God. Even if it would have collapsed by some strange fluke of nature, there would be fragments of foundation left behind, but there was nothing. I didn't know *how* they did it - but they did it! To add to their foul brew of deception, it just happened to be perfectly orchestrated *today,* of all days ... while I'm here ... on this side of the bridge? The entire production was clearly instigated by Alrik, and initiated by Halag.

I needed to calm down and think clearly, so I walked down the length of the river to be by myself.

Although Alrik allowed it, he along with the others kept a watchful eye on me from a distance. Despite my frustration, something occurred to me as I faced this unexpected fork in the road. Perhaps this truly was a stroke of divine intervention, and Halag and Alrik were merely pawns of a bigger plan. But as for me, I had a choice to make. Rather than causing a scene, I would make the best of this setback and have faith that *here* is where I was meant to be.

While observing the rushing water's white-tipped billows, I recalled a brief but insightful entry in Adina's journal. She wrote it after returning from what she called "the most difficult journey thus far" where she had been pressed by difficult and unforeseen circumstances. Through it all, she stated that she was stretched to the point of breaking, but she was irrepressible and didn't break, she grew. Not until she surrendered rather than battling for her own way, did she become an invaluable instrument of the solution. Adina was far wiser and more patient than myself, and I only hoped that I could be more like her. I would be lying if I believed for one second that this idea of yielding would come easy to me. I knew myself better than that, and before letting anything or anyone break me, I would pick up a sword and fight. This battle, however, could not be won with a sword in hand, but with a wisdom and intelligence to outthink my enemy. For now, I would comply with my circumstances and refuse to be smothered by my own doubts. "Don't overthink, Beni. One day, one hour, one minute, one thing at a time!"

Just as quickly as I had resolved to surrender, I was immediately struck by thoughts of Carson. Staying here would allow me another opportunity to speak with him. I only hoped that Halag would leave me alone. I had a horrible feeling that investigating me, or rather Valentine Brannigan, was at the top of his list. If he scratched past the surface, he would surely find out that the real heiress was at home in New York, and would have never ventured over to this country.

While contemplating Halag, I hadn't realized that Alrik had walked up behind me and gently placed his hand on my shoulder.

"Are you ready, Fräulein? I assure you that your stay will be most enjoyable."

"Well, since I have no choice, Field Marshal Richter, I accept your invitation."

He reacted like a child getting his own way, obviously delighted, almost giddy. Once again returning to the car, we drove back to his grand estate.

By the swift response and readiness of the staff, it seemed as though there must have been a system in place where an alarm sounded the moment a car descended the driveway. Like clockwork, all of the servants were once again standing out at attention, waiting to greet us. I wondered if this was a common occurrence when anyone came, or if it was just for my benefit. I looked at Alrik with a slight grin, honestly about to break out in laughter.

"Um, Prince Alrik, I have a question for you."

He looked at me unamused by my humor.

"Why did you call me prince? I am not royalty!"

Again, I smiled, slightly laughing.

"Are you making fun of me?"

"No, it's just...I'm sorry, never mind."

"No, please tell me, why is this so amusing?"

"Well, do you make your servants come out here each time you come home? I've read about such things in books, but have never seen it; and when I have read about it, it was more of a royalty thing."

His offended countenance softened, and he came very close to me, slightly smiling. Once again he felt at liberty to enter my space, making me feel most uncomfortable, and whispered in my ear.

"Valentine, this is Germany, and I am the Field Marshal, not a prince. The servants' personal greetings have always been a tradition in my home. I am sorry if it offends you."

"It doesn't offend me, it's just not necessary. I mean, certainly not for me."

When I once again walked into the marble-covered entry, Alrik motioned for the brown- haired, heavyset maid to come and show me to my room. He told her exactly which room to put me in.

"I am Gerda. I can help you."

She definitely meant it when she said that she would help me. Before making our way up the stairs, she and I played a quick exchange of tug-o-war with my suitcase, until I finally relented and let her carry it. Between her stout physique and bustling disposition, if I would have allowed it, she would have carried *me* under one arm and my bag under the other. She was greatly mistaken though if she believed for one second that I wanted to be treated like a delicate flower. Maybe that's what other women around here aspired to, but not me. On the other hand, it was clear that her authoritative attitude when it came to me especially, was pleasing the master of the house, securing her position at the Field Marshal's estate.

My chamber was located in the west wing, facing the back of the house, which had a glorious view of the forest in the far distance. I opened the door that led out to a spacious balcony that overlooked trees for miles. The immediate back area that surrounded the house was filled with gardens, gazebos, and half a dozen sitting areas.

From down below, I heard the joyful giggles of a little girl. Wearing a baby blue dress, and a bouncing headful of curls, she held her arms straight out and began spinning in circles until she was dizzy and fell down. The instant she tumbled, I noticed Alrik reach down and sweep her up in his arms, hugging and kissing her. As he sat her down, she got up and ran and laughed, calling for him to chase after her which he did with great joy. "Vati, Vati!" It was very sweet and unexpected. I didn't realize that Alrik had a daughter, but I could clearly see that she was his joy. Unsure of what had become of the little girl's mother, the abiding sadness that I saw in her father's eyes suddenly made sense.

As he held her, several gardeners came out to where they were standing and peeled back a wall of tarps covering a magnificent full-sized carousel. It reminded me of the one in Bar Rousse Park that Adina would take me to when I was a little girl, only this one was much more elegant and sparkled like a shiny new ring. I thought I had seen everything, as I had gone to school with many wealthy girls, spent numerous weekends at their estates, and seen many sumptuous things. In all that time though, I had never

seen a full-on carousel in someone's backyard.

As I turned around and took a more thorough look

at the room that I would be staying in, I was struck by its

flamboyant beauty. Like everything else here, it was

exquisite. The elevated ornate ceiling lined with panels of

gold was lavished with a crystal chandelier hanging in the

center of the room. The walls were pale yellow with a

cream-and-black designed carpet atop wooden floors. The

gold filigree bed was spread with satin cream and black

velvet pillows. On the windows were white sheer pleated

shades that allowed soft hues of light to enter the room. It

was lovely.

Not realizing that I had been assigned my own

personal servant, I was startled to see someone standing in

the shadows. It was the same woman that showed me to my

quarters, and apparently, she had been waiting and

watching me the entire time. It wasn't until she sneezed that I even noticed her.

I could tell that Gerda spoke very little English, so our communication began with a visual presentation revealing the highlights of my quarters. Even with the extravagance of brilliant glass bottles filled with exotic perfumes that sat on the dressing table, and the mahogany box that overflowed with jewels, she seemed most excited over the wardrobe and its contents. She opened the doors wide like a hostess on a game show, revealing dozens of beautiful gowns, and then told me that they belonged to me and to pick one for dinner.

"For you, for dinner ... uhhh five o'clock, yes?"

"Um, sure. I will be at dinner at five o'clock, but I won't be wearing one of those dresses. They don't belong to me."

All I could think of was that those dresses, along with everything else in this room all the way down to the bristles in the hairbrush, once belonged to the well-taken-care-of Mrs. Field Marshal. Assuming the personal property of Alrik's former wife, or the little girl's mother, was both weird and uncomfortable. I pointed at my suit that I was wearing.

"I'll just wear this, ok?"

"No, no, no. Beautiful dress you will wear, yes?"

I had no doubt that she had received precise instructions and was trying to follow them to a tee. Poor thing was obviously terrified of failing, and didn't want to get in trouble because I refused to follow orders, so I just agreed to disagree, which she seemed to take as a yes.

"Thank you, Gerda."

"Ok, I come back and check on you soon, yes?"

"Ok, yes."

148

Finally, I was alone. This one single day seemed the longest of my life, full of unexpected and unknown events, and I was exhausted! With an overall feeling of fatigue, it became difficult to keep my eyes open for another minute. The soft and inviting bed seemed to be calling my name. I decided to take a short rest on the luxurious satin cover, and shut my eyes for a few minutes before I had to get ready for dinner. Regrettably, my idea of a short catnap turned into a deep sleep with no chance of waking me. Supposedly Gerda tried rousing me for dinner, to no avail. My lethargic state probably stressed out the poor girl. She had no idea that waking me was not always an easy task. In any case, I ended up sleeping the entire night, and when I did awaken, not only was I tucked in beneath the comforter, but I was no longer in my blue suit. Someone had changed me into a nightgown, but I had no recollection of who it was. I sat up, feeling a bit hungover, and assumed the feeling was simply due to all that I had been through with traveling and all.

From the other side of the room I heard the sound of water sloshing. Gerda had filled a bath for me, and was bent over the tub stirring in a delicious-smelling salt. I walked over to where she was, unintentionally startling her.

"Good Morning Gerda!"

"Good Morning to you, Fräulein!"

"I'm so sorry about dinner - I hope that was ok?"

"Ok, yes ok!"

I wasn't sure she knew exactly what I was saying, but she pointed at the tub and then grabbed my shoulders and nudged me behind a dressing screen where a robe hung.

"Thank you, Gerda."

I kept peeking out from behind the screen, waiting for her to leave, but she just stood there waiting for me to come out.

"You don't have to stay, you can go thank you."

I wasn't sure what she was waiting for, but it appeared that she had every intention of bathing me, which was out of the question. As lovely as a bath sounded at that moment, and as cushy as this experience was turning out to be, I wasn't here on holiday. My ultimate goal was to talk to Carson, and then find my way back to Malachi... back to the Tempus Vector.

Finally, after I refused to disrobe, Gerda left the room and, most importantly, left me on my own to bathe. I let my robe drop, immersing myself into the fragrant steamy water. Oh how I loved baths, and this one was perfect! I ended up soaking for far too long, and when finished, I was greeted by a smorgasbord of delicacies that Gerda had arranged for me. The silver tray was brimming with goodies: a pot of tea, toast with butter and marmalade, cheese, sausage, and grapes. Since I was all but starving to death, I didn't hold back and ate every last morsel.

Now that I was full and ready to get this day going, I began sorting through the wardrobe, looking for something to wear. All that I found were endless dresses, slips, and undergarments; all utterly useless items. I was thankful that I had a few of my own things, minus my queen's bra. My tendency to overpack had paid off in this instance as I had thrown in a pair of black slacks, a white blouse, and black flats which would be perfect for a day of exploring. My feet were still throbbing after hours of high heels, making me even more thankful for a comfortable pair of shoes.

As I made my way downstairs, I was unaware of how late it was until I heard the clock toll eleven. Between my absence at dinner and my tardiness this morning, they would surely add *lazy* to the already negative opinions they held about Americans.

I tried to be as quiet as possible, and yet Alrik was there waiting for me as soon as I opened the front door.

"Good morning, Valentine. I expect you slept well?"

He was not wearing his uniform like yesterday, but instead was decked out in riding clothes.

"Yes, I slept very well, thank you! And thank you for breakfast - it was delicious."

"Of course. So where are you off to?"

"Well, since it looks like I missed out on the riding, I guess I'll just go and explore the area .... see what I can find."

"Tonight I will be entertaining guests, and if it's not too forward, I was hoping you might be there as my, well, my companion."

"Companion, eh? Well, that's a first. I've been asked to be someone's date, but never their companion."

I couldn't help but smile from ear to ear as his seriousness somehow made me laugh. Not a making-fun-of kind of laugh, because rarely do you meet someone who is so dangerously solemn as he was. There was something in his eyes, a longing, even a bit of desperation of sorts in the way he asked me.

"Well, I guess since I'm here I may as well. I really didn't bring anything to wear for such an occasion. If I could get into town, however, I could possibly find something."

"Actually, fräulein, I have had something *special* made for you to wear. It will be brought up to your room later. Until then."

Just as before, he kissed my hand, and walked away.

Finally! Now that I was alone, I would try to find Carson. Unfortunately, the moment I started off on my own

I was confronted by the same two guards from the previous day. I tried to ignore them and pass by quickly, hoping that my indifference might discourage them from following me. Sadly, I was their mission, and they stayed on me like two dogs on a fox. My grand ideas of exploring had just been squashed by the Field Marshal's babysitters. It became unmistakably evident that I was not a guest here like Alrik had implied, but instead a prisoner. A guest would be allowed to roam about unaccompanied ... unguarded. They were so intent on keeping a watchful eye on me that they assigned not one, but two guards on my behalf. I knew then that my only way of getting out would be a strategically planned escape, and I hoped that somehow Carson would be able to help me. I felt if I could just talk with him for a few minutes, that he could help me figure out another way to get back to the town. Surely there was another way.

I strolled to the back of the house in order to get a better look at this German countryside estate which was even more exquisite up close. Everything about it was beautiful and quite excessive, especially for one man and his daughter. I couldn't help but be intrigued by Field Marshal Richter and this awe-inspiring villa that he called home.

Continuing on, I passed through all of the patios and headed toward the forest.

As I was about to enter into the thicket of trees, the guards stepped in front of me, and simply said, "No!"

When I looked over to my left, I saw the bungalows where Carson and the other scientist probably stayed. The outside of their quarters was lined with armed guards. It looked as though *their* freedoms were limited as well. I raised my arms mocking my two guards, as if I were under arrest, and then turned once again and faced them.

"Ok, ok, I won't go in there! Listen fellas, maybe we started out on the wrong foot. Why don't you tell me your names?"

Positioned like two pillars, with solemn and fixed stares, neither said a word. To be perfectly honest, I was unsure if they could speak at all. Their girth and size, which they had in spades, was no match for their lack of human element.

"Let me guess….Abbott and Costello? Laurel and Hardy?"

Nothing! No response whatsoever, not even the tiniest grin. This duo of doom who also lacked a sense of humor, plagued me with their dullness. It was difficult to tell if my cheeky comments phased them in the slightest. Nevertheless, I had to keep reminding myself that my foolhardy approach would most likely not serve me well in this place, and I needed to be careful.

On my walk back to the house, I unmindfully

glanced up to the balcony and noticed Alrik looking down

at me. I returned his menacing scowl with an icy stare,

believing that my boldness would embarrass him and make

him look away, but it didn't. It was obvious he wanted me

to be aware of his undivided attention. While glaring back

at him, I pointed to each of my guards with a disagreeable

look on my face, and then gave him a taunting and

facetious thumbs up, so that he would know that I did not

appreciate his security detail. Upon witnessing my scoffing

display, he surprisingly seemed to chuckle and rather

enjoyed my displeasure, which was the opposite reaction of

what I was looking for. Dispensing with his games and

blatantly looking away, I glanced back in the direction from

which I'd come, trying to familiarize myself with the vast

grounds and compose a mental picture. At some point, I

would revisit those bungalows ALONE so that I could find

Carson, and have a private conversation with him.

Continuing forward while still looking back over

my shoulder, I was confronted by, and nearly collided with,

quick-paced staff members who were diligently preparing

for the evening's events. I immediately became outraged as

I observed countless trucks moving in from all directions.

Ironically, even though the bridge was out, they were

somehow able to bring in mass deliveries of food and

supplies, and dozens of cases filled with every kind of

alcohol known to man. My suspicions about Alrik's bogus

story of "no way in and no way out" was confirmed. Unless

of course, these were flying trucks that somehow soared

over the vast ravine. He had lied to me, confirming what I

already knew to be true. Not only had he gone to great

lengths to keep me guarded, but I had the distinct feeling

that my captivity was pre-calculated and deliberate. He had

planned this masterful performance for the past week, ever

since he saw me, or Adina that is, walking down the street.

Feeling like an insect tangled in the center of a sticky web, I broke away from my keepers, hoping that they would allow me to roam free, unwatched. Even though they were hindered by a uniform, heavy boots, and a rifle, they barreled after me like two German tanks, making their capture appear practically effortless. It was the first time I had seen any sign of life from either of them, as they were quickly on my tail. But as for me, I could feel the ever familiar "cut and run" character trait rising up within my spirit. The feeling of being cornered and the desperate need to escape had once again possessed me. If I would have had the Tempus Vector in hand at that moment, I would have grasped it tightly and disappeared forever. But that was not the case, and I could no longer succumb to my childlike temperament. I was in the here and now for a specific reason. This wasn't about me. It had never been about me.

Blinded by unmindful fury, I found myself at the front entry of the house, and quickly stormed up the stairs.

160

Whatever the reason for any of this, I was upset and just

wanted to be alone in my room, but my timing was about as

perfect as a broken clock, for at the same moment that I

was raging up the stairs, Alrik was coming down. He threw

out niceties in my direction as I continued rushing past him,

intentionally not saying a word and deliberately not making

eye contact.

"Are you well, Fräulein?"

Quickly walking on, I continued in silence ... he

knew exactly what was wrong. I refused to give him the

satisfaction of an answer and I returned to my room.

Pacing from one end of the chamber to the other, I

attempted to come up with a plan or some kind of next

move. Staying focused and being alert had always been

who I was, and had always worked well for me. It may

have been my imagination, but this time attempting to nail

down a plan of action left me feeling fuzzy-headed and

confused. I was reminded once again of the whole "surrender" thing, and how Adina truly didn't become effective until she learned to surrender the outcome of her journey to divine wisdom rather than her own. Instead of hopping back into my boat of self-sufficiency, I would have to learn to go with the flow, clarifying every step that I would take, and each word that I spoke through a filter of discernment. Even though I knew what I needed to do, all of these thoughts circling around in my brain only frustrated me more. It was like a sea of blank elements that I was supposed to piece together and make sense of, but at this point, I wasn't sure about anything! My problem seemed to be that one moment I was all on-board with the "surrendering to a higher plan of action," and the next, I jumped right out of the boat, and commenced floundering in my own shallow pool of reasoning. Why couldn't I be more like Adina? She always seemed so sure of herself, so mature. I decided to cling to the reality that she probably

162

wasn't always so "on the ball," and that there was hope for me yet.

It was obvious by the industrious preparations taking place throughout the estate that this would be no small event. Taking into account the mile-long dining room table filled with gold and burgundy place settings, and the unusually large number of chairs being assembled for the orchestra, not to mention the ample amount of food and liquor that was being delivered, this would surely prove to be a night overflowing with crowds of people. It would also be the perfect backdrop for my escape back into town. I knew that if I could at least have the safety net of the Tempus Vector in hand, I would feel more at ease. The way things currently stood, with one single word or fulfillment of a task, I could be stuck here for the rest of my life, which was not sitting well with me at all.

During the dancing, and of course, the vital business of the evening, I could easily get lost in the throng and disappear before anyone knew that I had gone. Now that I'd seen where the bungalows were located, I would go there first and find Carson. Hopefully, he'd be able to help me, but I would have to remain discreet since he was the only American in his group and was probably being watched closer than the others. I certainly didn't want to do anything that would bring negative attention to him. Actually, my hope was to accomplish the opposite, that somehow I would be able to prevent his tragic ending.

I trusted ... I hoped, that he'd be there. For all I knew he could be back in town with Adina. And then there was the delicate matter of my complicated explanation of who I was, and why a woman who mysteriously looked like his wife and was in possession of her brooch had arrived from out of the blue. This was far too much information for me to work through at one time. I made a decision right then and there that I would deal with each event as it came.

Out of the corner of my eye, I noticed a soft pink evening gown hanging on my wardrobe. The sleeveless top was made of pink studded lace, and the bottom of the dress flowed freely. I didn't even want to think about how they figured out my size. Sitting below the dress was a wooden shoe box. When I noticed that the box said "Coffee," I was elated. It was the first bit of hope that I felt since I arrived here. When I opened the box, there sat a pair of matching pink shoes. Knowing that frivolous shoes were not the kind of thing that Malachi spent his time making, I deducted that his hand must have been forced, and the thought of it grieved me.

I had seen this box before; it was identical to the one in Adina's chest, the one that held the Tempus Vector. I wished this one had the frame in it as well. I would feel so much better and would have so much more confidence if it was with me. Every thought that I considered, every plan that I made seemed dashed and clouded by the fact that I

165

was separated from the frame. Just the sight of Malachi's name on the box somehow filled me with courage though. No matter the consequences, I was resolved to complete my task.

As I looked closer, I noticed that sticking out of one of the shoes was a piece of paper - a note from Malachi. It was vague, to say the least, most probably just in case someone other than myself got ahold of it.

Please enjoy these handcrafted shoes that were custom made just for you and designed to take you wherever you want to go. There are many unknown truths that you will learn on that path - remember, you are but a vessel, not the power. You may only bring about change where change is required ... let nothing hold you back! You know, and have heard, that all things come to an end, as will this.

I had to read it over several times before I truly

understood what he was trying to tell me. Hmmm, these

shoes will take me where I want to go. "Unknown truths!" I

had heard that term before from Carig. The unknown truths

were unwritten facts, even obstacles, that the Carrier of the

Tempus Vector would come to discover with experience. I

already knew that my life was a vessel being used to

execute a specific task, but what I didn't know was that I

would only be able to bring about *required* change, not of

my choosing or wisdom. The note, even though vague,

made me feel so much better. All of this was not just on my

shoulders, but there was a wisdom greater than mine that

had a plan. I had been so afraid that I would do or say the

wrong thing at the wrong time. Malachi was telling me to

just go for it. Nothing that I would do or say would bring

about change unless it was meant to be. I knew that

whatever my purpose or responsibility in all of this, even

though I wasn't sure what it was yet, in time I would find

167

out. I took great comfort in his words, suddenly sensing an added empowerment, boldness, and confidence that I hadn't felt before. I wasn't going to make the wrong thing happen, which removed a huge amount of pressure.

Just then, I heard a knock at my door. Gerda had returned.

"Come in!"

"Hello - no sleeping. It is time to get ready for party!"

She walked me over to the screen and handed me the robe.

"Go!"

I took off my clothes and changed into the robe. When I came out, she called me over to the vanity and told me to sit down on the stool. I was finding that Gerda was quite bossy. The vanity table was filled with brushes and hair pins, perfume bottles, and make-up. She looked at my

168

pearl and aquamarine necklace that was hanging around my neck.

"So beautiful!"

"Thank you."

"Now, I fix your hair!"

"That's ok, I can do it."

"No, no, no! I must do it!"

"Ok, Gerda, fine."

For the next hour or so, Gerda worked on my hair. I was glad that she kept it down. I think after she started working on my thick mane she realized how many hundreds of pins it would require to keep my hair up, and so she figured long smooth curls would be best. Honestly, it suited both me and the dress better anyway. Impressively, she applied all of my make-up as if she had done it many times before - much heavier than I liked it, to be sure. It was done well, until her unfortunate final finish of Poison Pink lip color that made my already full lips take over my face. Before I could stand up, she dabbed each of my wrists and behind my ears with an unfamiliar spiced fragrance. Once again I was prodded, this time to go behind the dressing screen where, I slipped on the pink evening gown while Gerda zipped up the back. The dress was alluring and flowy, but nothing like what Adina could make. Rushing over to the shoebox on the floor in front of me, Gerda gently slipped the beautiful shoes on my feet that Malachi had crafted. I remembered what he said in his note, "They will take you where you want to go!" Just to amuse myself, I clicked my heels together, but nothing happened. Laughing at myself, and noticing Gerda's perplexity, I told her that I guessed that's not what he meant.

Before going downstairs, I walked out onto the balcony to get a bird's eye view of the party. I saw dozens of people already standing around waiting for dinner. This was going to be uncomfortable ... I had to keep my mind thinking about who I was, Valentine Brannigan, and try to recall any and all information that Rae had told me. Anything I didn't know, I would just adlib.

As the door opened, my room filled with the clamoring sounds of people who were ready to party and were well on their way to utter drunkenness. Being the center of attention was never my ambition, and until now, not an issue. But because I was an American-made heiress, I was about to be thrown into the main event of the evening, battling a brood of twisted thinkers. The thought of contending with this group of pompous windbags who aspired to bludgeon the world with tyranny and swastikas, was mind-boggling.

I took a deep breath and made my way into the hallway and to the top of the stairs. As I descended the marble staircase, there was Alrik waiting for me. He was wearing his black formal uniform, and if I were being

171

completely honest, was overwhelmingly handsome. I only

wished that it was Carig waiting for me instead. My heart

ached for him, and I missed him so deeply that twinges of

loneliness rose up from my throat, filling my eyes with

unruly tears.

In a most provocative and inappropriate manner,

Alrik followed every move that I made and every curve of

my body as I approached him. I not only felt uncomfortable

but somehow guilty for purposely walking into the center

of his attentions. He didn't even know me, but it was

obvious that he was infatuated with the stranger who stood

before him. He walked up the remaining two stairs to meet

me, and then took my hand.

"I couldn't wait one more second to be near you, to

feel my lips touching your hand once again."

As he kissed my hand, he inhaled ardently as if his

next move might be tasting my skin. Alrik had been very

forward before, but at that very moment as we stood together on the stairs, he elevated his affections to the next level. Standing at the bottom of the stairway and surveying the crowd of strangers, I noticed at least half a dozen women who were glaring daggers in my general direction. Apparently, they had come here for the sole purpose of spending the evening with the esteemed Field Marshal.

As he continued fervidly caressing my hand, completely indifferent to those who were watching, I had had enough and was embarrassed by the gathering attention. Pulling my hand away from his mouth, I continued moving forward. Not allowing my disinterest to discourage him, he once again took my hand, intertwining his fingers with mine as we entered the festivities. Even in the midst of the crowd I could still feel his eyes on me, and then he put his mouth to my ear.

"You are a vision, Fräulein!"

He kissed my cheek, and lingered at the curve of

my neck, feeling very comfortable being so close. He spent

the next half-hour or so walking me from one person to the

next, introducing me to his friends and colleagues as the

American heiress, Valentine Brannigan, not once letting go

of my hand. Most attendees had already heard that there

was a celebrity in their midst, and were very curious about

the visitor from the west. I could feel myself growing more

frantic with every introduction, fearful that I would be

found out.

When the dinner bell rang we were all escorted into

the formal dining area. As the double doors were opened by

two seasoned looking butlers, I was taken aback by the

beauty of the room. The walls from floor to ceiling were

covered in gold baroque that was inlaid with mirrors,

making the entire room glisten like diamonds. Still holding

my hand tightly, Alrik escorted me over to my seat which

was positioned at the opposite end of the table from his,

and next to his uncle. Although relieved to be free of Alrik's grasp for a time, the idea of sitting next to an entirely new group of people who would be filled with questions unnerved me. Hesitantly, I opted to feed his ego and make him believe that I preferred to be seated next to him.

"Alrik!"

"Yes, Fräulein?"

It was so noisy that he put his ear to my mouth, to better hear me.

"Why am I all the way down here? I don't know anyone. I would really rather sit by you."

He immediately turned his mouth to my ear and whispered back his reply.

"Fraulein, my chair has been intentionally placed, as it was my desire to have a perfect view of you for the evening. I would much rather look at you than anyone else."

He made his way to his seat, greeting his guests along the way while also watching me out of the corner of his eye. I didn't even know what to say. I was dumbfounded by his flirtatious stalker comment.

Most of Alrik's guests spoke German, so at first my interaction with them was limited. That is until they decided to speak in broken English, as they were very curious about me. Every chair was filled except for one, which I thought to be rather curious. It was obvious that this was the social event of the season, or rather a mandatory affair where non-attendance was viewed as unacceptable. As a place setting had been arranged, I assumed that someone was either running late, or had the nerve to not show up for such an illustrious event. Another very evident observation was that this group, including the women, drank like fish. They far exceeded any party experience I had while at college; the wine was flowing like water. But apparently this was not unusual behavior for them. It was impossible not to drink, as servants were ready to refill every time a sip was taken. It was unsatisfactory that any glass should be empty.

Sitting next to Alrik's uncle, Klein Richter, brother of Alrik's father, was quite an experience, and the fact that he spoke English was both a blessing and a curse. When I first sat down, Klein was distracted by a silver tureen of beer cheese and pumpernickel. While in the middle of melodious sounds of gratification over his seemingly favorite appetizer, he turned and looked at me, and without warning, spiraled into a choking frenzy; something overcame him the second our eyes met. He coughed and sputtered for the next few minutes until he caught his breath, and then bellowed out for a refill. Amongst the commotion, Alrik raced over to check on the well-being of his uncle.

"Are you alright uncle?"

When finally settling down, Klein didn't respond to his nephew, but looked right at me in a frightened manner and said only two words.

"A ghost!"

"I beg your pardon!"

Alrik quickly stepped in and announced to everyone that once again his uncle had drunk far too much, and now was beginning to see ghosts. Everyone laughed and quickly dismissed Klein's normal lunacy.

For the next few moments, Klein sat in silence and then said the most curious thing to me. He told me how pleased he was that Alrik had found someone that complemented and suited him so perfectly … whatever that meant. Surely he wasn't talking about me!

After that strange episode, Klein returned to his normal jovial and funny state, forgetting where he was and thinking nothing of pulling the female servants into his lap

every time they walked by as if he were in a brothel, which

apparently was a common occurrence. The more he drank,

the louder he became, spilling everything that was on his

mind. Even though he was an obvious drunk and carouser, I

liked him. Like Alrik, there was a sweetness to him that

somehow didn't belong in this place.

I thought this a perfect time and person to ask about

Alrik's wife to find out what their story was. As he rambled

on, I began to more clearly understand who Alrik Richter

was and why he behaved the way he did. All that I had seen

thus far was his ability to manipulate anything and anyone

in order to get whatever he wanted. But as Klein carelessly

spilled the sordid details, I discovered that the man who

Alrik once was, died with his wife. I was both saddened

and moved by his life story.

Caprice Richter died five years ago due to

complications during childbirth, and the loss of her nearly

ended Alrik. She was the love of his life. As I attentively

listened to their love story, it made me think of Carig and

ours. Like our story, their childhood friendship grew into

love. Caprice, however, was at a disadvantage being the

daughter of the estate's gardener who had moved to

Friedlich from Paris when she was a child. As children she

and Alrik played together, but as they grew up, Count

Richter, Alrik's father, could tell with each passing day that

their affections for one another were growing stronger and

stronger. Unfortunately, he had absolute ideals about

Alrik's future, especially when it came to the elite Richter

bloodline. When it came to mixing the inferior with the

superior, Count Richter was highly opposed, and continued

to dig in his heels, refusing to allow his son to associate

with, let alone have intimate relations with, someone such

as Caprice. Alrik was sent away to the finest schools in

Germany, purposely meant to keep the two of them as far

away from one another as possible. His love for her though

was unceasing and stronger than any objection that his father had. One day, unbeknownst to his father, Alrik came back to Friedlich and secretly married Caprice, concealing it from everyone. The happy couple living in a cottage in the woods outside of Friedlich were the best memories that Alrik had ever experienced. Caprice was playful and full of life, completely different than anyone he had ever known before. Those few months they spent together were perfect. When they discovered that Caprice was pregnant, they approached Alrik's father in hopes that he would accept her now that she was carrying his grandchild. Unfortunately, his fury grew even darker at the news, and he made it his life's mission to destroy all three of them. Making their lives completely miserable and full of unending stress during her pregnancy, he partially accomplished his objective, as Caprice died after giving birth to Annaliese. Alrik was so broken afterwards that everyone who knew him feared he would never recover. It was apparent that even Alrik's uncle was troubled over the cruel actions of his brother and the horrid trail of consequences that he had left behind. To this day, Alrik blames his father for her death.

"So, where is Alrik's father?"

Klein drank the last gulp of his wine in an effort to numb his pain.

"I would say.... burning in the pit of hell, Fraulein Brannigan! Enough of this talk! Now, tell me, do you know who all these people are that are sitting around the table?"

"I don't. I have absolutely no idea who they are!"

"Well, let me ask you this.... what color uniforms do you see these men wearing?"

As I looked around the table every other chair was filled with a man dressed in sharp black with emblems and trims of red and gold, all except for Halag. He wore a dark olive green uniform, not nearly as impressive as the others.

182

"Very good, Fräulein. Now, being that you are from America, do you know by these uniforms in whose company you sit?"

For whatever reason, he felt the need to ask questions of me that I most certainly wouldn't know and then found great pleasure in answering his interrogation.

"These men are of the highest ranking German officials in the country, Alrik being the foremost of them all. Each of them carry great power and authority, and answer to none but Hitler himself."

As I looked around, I was disturbed at being in the same room with some of the most twisted minds in our world's history who would eagerly serve a madman. I was immediately sickened, either from all of the wine or the thought of the company I was in. But then I looked down at Alrik. He seemed different than the others. He had a kindness in his eyes. I honestly couldn't imagine him purposefully hurting anyone. After hearing his story, I was saddened for him and the calamity that had plagued his life. I found myself staring at him without realizing it as I played his tragic love story over and over again in my mind. At the same time, his gaze never broke from mine.

After our exchange of fond interactions, his wanton stare remained constant. The customary over-consumption of house wine didn't help matters either, but only increased Alrik's fixation on my every move. His constant attention was imposing and inappropriate. Although he was unaware that I was a married woman who loved and adored my husband, his hapless captivation somehow originated long before my arrival. For some strange reason, he was enamored with me - why I didn't know. To make matters worse, audacious intoxication set in motion his true feelings, making each breath he took an evident craving for my attention. I couldn't take it another moment, so I excused myself from the table to go out and get some fresh air. When he saw me stand up and walk out, he arose to go with me, but was forced back to the table by Fraulein Ursula Hildegard, daughter of the Empire Leader of the SS, who apparently had been positioning herself to fill the highly coveted position of the new Fraulein Richter for years. Alrik was uninterested, but needed to keep up good relations with her father, so he opted to stay.

Quickly walking through the ballroom where the orchestra had already begun warming up, I arrived at the back of the house where I was greeted by the gold and mirror-lined carousel, lit up and glorious, shining brilliantly upon every turn. Due to the attendees that were present, it was apparent that high-level precautions had been taken to keep them all safe, and me from leaving. Far beyond the populated areas of the house which were intentionally left dark, were shadows of armed guards lining every border of the property. In their darkness, they were able to keep an effective watch on those of us who stood within the light.

185

My idea of escaping tonight, just disappearing into the twilight unnoticed, would never work. This safeguard strategy of using the element of night for cover left the partygoers in clear view, like a lit up aquarium in a dark room. Because there were so many guards, compounded by the fact that I was completely unfamiliar with the surroundings, it would certainly lead to a failed attempt at breaking away. I would either need to wait until later tonight or tomorrow to contact Carson and hopefully, he would be able to help me. Not only was he brilliant, but he had been here long enough to know how to get in and out of this place.

As I once again became captivated by the glistening turns of the carousel, I noticed one other person standing on the other side who was just as captivated by the lights and sparkles of the gilded rotation as I was. Alrik's adorable daughter, looking like a little angel in a lovely white dress.

186

I walked out to see her, as she was standing alone looking up at the grand ponies.

"Hello! What's your name?"

The little girl didn't answer me, and looked scared, since I was a stranger.

I knelt down and pointed to myself, "My name is Valentine!"

She was adorable with a head full of beautiful blond curls, and stunning blue eyes like her father's.

"Do you want to ride? How about I ride with you?...on the horsey?"

She reached up her arms for me to pick her up, which I did, and sat her on the pony with the pink saddle. Directly next to her was an identical pony, only with a blue saddle, which is where I sat, keeping my hand close by to prevent her from slipping off. The attendant who was standing by for the evening, started it up once he saw that we were ready.

Slowly the carousel began to turn, playing a German waltz. As we continued spinning round and round, I put my head back looking straight up at the elaborate features. I was moved by the beauty and the amazing craftsmanship that it displayed. Each horse was magnificently handcrafted to look lifelike, not missing one intricate detail. Even the muscle tone was impressive on these white and cream war horses, draped with armors of gold and pastel saddles. Above their heads were golden cherubim blowing battle horns, making ready the skilled herd. But the details that struck me the most were the realistic eyes of the beasts, which were intense and focused on the anticipated battle. Most horses on a children's carousel would have more cartoon-type features, but these were different.

The girl's enthusiastic laughter declared her love for this merry-go-round, thrilled by every moment of the ride, never wanting it to end. I couldn't help but laugh with her … her joy and her merriment were contagious.

When I looked up, Alrik was just standing in front of the carousel, his eyes following the two of us with great intensity. Catching the attendant's attention, I asked him to stop as I slipped off my horse, then lifted Alrik's daughter from hers. She immediately ran to her father and pointed at me telling him that my name was Valentine. With a big smile, I walked over to where they were.

"Yes, I am Valentine … now what is your name?"

She plunged her head into her father's shoulder, hiding her face from me.

"That's ok, you don't have to tell me."

"Her name is Annaliese."

"My, what a beautiful name. A beautiful name to go with such a beautiful little girl."

Right away, Annaliese's nanny came out to take her to bed. But before she did, Annaliese tugged on my dress. I bent down to look at her eye to eye. She wrapped her arms around my neck and gave me a kiss on my cheek.

"Well, thank you for that. You have sweet dreams, Annaliese."

Alrik came over, took my hand, and helped me up.

"You have a beautiful daughter, Alrik."

"Yes, she is!"

I could tell by the way he looked at her that she had stolen his heart.

"And that....wow, is a magnificent carousel. Annaliese seems to love it!"

"Yes, I had it made for my wife years ago. When she died, I had it completely covered.... I couldn't stand to look at it."

The grief in his eyes turned to joy when the conversation shifted toward his daughter.

"But Annaliese, she's such a curious girl! She wanted to see what was hidden for so long under the tarp. When I finally unveiled it, she wanted to do nothing but spend her time on the horses.... even naming each one. This now belongs to her. She is all I have that means anything!"

I walked over to him and put my hand on his shoulder.

"Alrik, I'm so sorry for all that you've been through, I truly am!"

Relishing my kind words that were laced with sympathy, he grabbed both of my hands and pulled me close to him. Then placing his head to my chest, he nestled

closer with a deep longing to be comforted, so I

compassionately returned his embrace.

"Everything will be ok, truly it will!"

He continued holding me, not wanting to let me go.

As terrible as I felt for him and for Annaliese, I was not the

answer to his troubled past and loneliness, so I took a step

back and pushed him away.

"I think we need to go back inside, with your

guests...they'll be wondering where you are."

For a moment I didn't think that he had even heard

me, but then he agreed while slowly releasing me from his

embrace. He kissed my hand, and then slid his fingers into

mine. Together, we walked back into the dining room, once

again capturing the crowd's attention. Only this time, they

looked at us as if we had been up to no good. As Alrik once

again placed me at the end of the table, he gently kissed my cheek and returned to the head chair.

There were several things that had altered since walking out of the grand party. For one, dessert was now being served, delicious looking creme brulee with berries for everyone. For everyone except an obnoxious drunk and disorderly imbecile with the initials "HS" who was demanding berry scones, which were quickly brought in and placed in front of him in an effort to appease his agitated melodrama. As the dessert wine was being poured into each glass, Halag elevated his desperate need for attention by grabbing the bottle from the waiter. I watched in disgust as he recklessly guzzled the bittersweet, washing down each bite, and staring straight ahead as if he were alone in the room. The sad thing about it all was that no one paid too much attention to his actions, as if they were used to it and no longer shocked by his extremely rude manners.

The second change that I notice was that the empty chair

was now filled. To my great surprise, it was Carson.

Chapter 6

SECRETS AMONG THE DARKNESS

"I just can't believe it, and why would I go on a plane without Adina?"~Carson York~

Carson was placed on the opposite end of the table

from where I was sitting, right next to Alrik. I couldn't

seem to stop myself from staring at him. Hearing endless

accounts of this incredible man, and thinking about the

many years I watched Adina hold on so tightly to him,

made me excited at the thought of being a part of his life, if

only for a little while. I honestly never imagined in a

million years that I would have the privilege of not only

meeting him, but of also having a relationship with him.

Yet here I was, only a few feet away from my uncle, my

uncle who died over seventy-five years ago. All I really

wanted to do was just sit and talk with him to get to know

him, and him me. He was just as Adina had always said.

His smile and mere presence lit up the room! It wasn't

simply his alluring smile, but every word he spoke captured his audience with his charismatic insight and thoroughly handsome mannerisms. I am certain after one look into those eyes filled with kindness, Adina must have been hooked. There was one other thing that I didn't expect, and that was such a friendly relationship between Carson and Alrik. It was clear that their rapport was that of a highly respected friendship. It was obvious that they genuinely cared for one another, and over the past few months had certainly developed a kinship of brotherhood. Of course, it made sense that Carson was seated with Alrik at the head of the table. He had a way with people - it appeared that people enjoyed being in his presence.

Once again, I was regrettably positioned by Klein, who seemed delighted that I had returned to his company. He had obviously overindulged in the spirits of the evening, and his now tasteless jokes and insufferable behavior proved to be an excruciating experience for those seated around him. They also seemed more than delighted upon my return, in the hopes that I would take on the role of the keeper of the intoxicated.

In a slurred, barely coherent voice, Klein turned all of his attention on me.

"You're just in time for dessert, Fräulein. Are you feeling better?"

"Yes, the fresh air was just what I needed!"

Alrik seemed to enjoy watching my interaction with his uncle. Trying not to make it too obvious, as I was right in Alrik's line of vision, I attempted to make eye contact with Carson, but he was preoccupied with the many high ranking guests who were fascinated to hear about the progress of his latest achievements with the greenhouse experiments. I continued glancing in his general direction, but it almost seemed he was avoiding any kind of visual communication with me on purpose. Who could blame him? After all, he had no idea who I was, let alone that we were related. Looking at this situation from his point of view, my presence probably made him feel extremely vulnerable - my looking so much like Adina and all. Here he was, trying to serve his country in a very dangerous undercover position, and along comes a woman who looks just like his wife, wearing a butterfly lapel pin identical to hers. Not only that, the first time he saw me, Alrik and I were holding hands. I'm sure the whole thing threw him for a loop. With all of this in mind, I decided to cut the poor fellow a break and just bide my time until we could talk. Meanwhile, unbeknownst to me, Alrik had noticed my continual observation of Carson and became annoyed at my fascination with him.

Once the orchestra began to play, everyone stood up and made their way into the magnificent ballroom. Without announcement, I looked up and both Alrik and Carson were standing right by me, and my new best friend, Uncle Klein.

"Valentine, you remember Dr. Carson?"

Finally making eye contact with Carson, I was met with an apprehensive regard.

"Yes, very nice to see you again Dr. ...Carson. I'm glad to see that you made it back from town."

He took my hand and kissed it.

"It's nice to see you as well. Yes, it was good to get away and see the city!"

His eye was immediately drawn to the pendant around my neck that Adina left for me to wear at my wedding - the something old, and something blue. Of course, Carson knew it as the ring that Adina wore when she married him. His face became red, and I could see by his clenching jaw that he was not only bothered, but extremely upset, maybe even a little concerned for Adina, hoping that she was alright, but because of the company around us, he couldn't say a word. His posture did say: Who are you, and what in the hell is going on?

"What a lovely pendant! So rarely do you see that particular combination of pearls and aquamarine. Are you fond of pearls?"

"I do like pearls, but it was actually my aunt who loved them. This belonged to her. It was once a ring."

Carson looked at me fearfully, unable to make any sense of my response. I believe his intention was to catch me off guard, but it was I that continued taking him aback. Alrik, even more annoyed over our interaction, opted to interrupt the tension-filled conversation with a spin on the dance floor.

"Fraulein, would you care to dance?"

"Of course!"

He took my hand, and we proceeded to walk out onto the ballroom floor. It might have been my imagination, but the intensity of the music rose the moment the "Field Marshal" stepped foot onto the floor, as if a king had arrived. With each turn on the floor it was difficult not to notice Carson's worried and sorrowful expression as he seemed so alone and in a state of bewilderment. I tried to think of how Adina would handle this situation. I did know one thing, she would not be happy with me if I left Carson in the dark and feeling confused.

With each pass by him, I mouthed the words, "Ask me to dance!" Once again, I knew that this would place him in an awkward and dangerous position. But being that it was almost impossible to have any alone time where someone wasn't watching me, and more than likely watching him as well, the dance floor seemed like the only practical chance we might have.

"So Valentine, when you are not traveling around the world and working for your family company, what do you do with your time?"

201

"Well, I love to read, but I also love to ride horses."

I had to think quickly - my roommate, Rae, and all of her family were horse people. When I visited them, we would go out for entire days riding over the hills and mountains surrounding their ranch and stables. With a little push from Rae, I even joined the Riders of Yardley. Our team of endurance riders trained on some of the most difficult terrain, and then competed with other schools in our conference. Rae was a rider, and so was her grandmother Valentine, who also attended Yardley.

"Really, what is your favorite novel?"

I nervously smiled at him hoping he wouldn't ask me a question that I couldn't answer with ease and confidence.

"Well, it's so hard to pick just one, but I will forever be in love with *The Count of Monte Cristo.* I've read it so many times, that I practically have it memorized."

Looking straight into my eyes, he surprised me with a familiar text that I knew so well, which also seemed to sum up the scars embedded deep within his soul, that were made obvious through the pain in his eyes.

"'Moral wounds have this peculiarity - they may be hidden, but they never close; always painful, always ready to bleed when touched, they remain fresh and open in the heart.'"

My heart broke for him. He seemed almost out of place, almost as if he didn't belong within this people group. His heart was openly kind, and freely worn on his sleeve. The passion in his words made me believe that he couldn't possibly be too invested in the goings-on of the German movement. He seemed the type that would be forever happy just to spend a quiet life with the woman he loved, cherishing her always, whispering romantic sweet nothings in her ear. He was definitely a romantic at heart, a "lover not a fighter", even though he hid it effectively beneath his stern exterior.

"Alrik, how wonderful. You are familiar with the Count as well? I've always loved that excerpt, but find it so sad. Do you know others, or did you memorize that piece for any particular reason?"

"I too read that many times as a boy, with my mother - she loved Edmond Dantes. Sadly, I watched her escape into stories such as this. It was the only place where she was happy. All she ever wanted was to be loved, but my father was incapable. What does one do who has so much love and passion to give, but is bonded to another who is cruel and unfit to return such sweet affection?"

"I don't know, what?"

"Well, in the case of my mother, she did not escape into the arms of another, but to the tattered, tear-stained pages of a book, making herself part of a happier ending.

Finally one day, it was as if her grief enveloped her so completely that she was never able to return."

"I'm so sorry, Alrik. That must have been horrible."

"Yes, the two people I loved most in the world were destroyed by the same man."

With eyes that were both vacant and desperate, he pulled me closer.

"Fraulein, that's why I can't, I can't let you..."

Before he could finish his statement, Carson reluctantly walked over to where we were dancing and asked if he could cut in. It was obvious by the look on Alrik's face that he wanted to say no, but like any gentleman, he smiled and agreed.

"Of course...I'll be back in a few moments."

With arms still around me, he gave me a prolonged kiss on my cheek while cautioning Carson with an icy stare.

Carson caught hold of me, and quickly whisked us off to the other side of the room, as far away from Alrik as he could get, as questions came flowing out of his mouth.

"I don't really know where to start, but who are you, and what are you doing here? Where did you get the butterfly brooch and *now* that necklace? I know who they belong to, and it's not you. I know that you're not Valentine Brannigan. I've seen pictures of her, and you look nothing like her. Do you know what they'll do to you if they find out you're lying? I have been wracking my brain trying to figure out what this is all about, and I have no idea. This whole thing is so strange."

I struggled to say anything at all. Here I was with my Uncle Carson, who I had never known, and he had never known me.

"Carson, I …"

"And how do you know me?"

"Ok, listen! I'll explain - I never thought in my whole life that I would ever meet you. But … oh gosh, how do I tell you this? Carson, when you first saw me, who did you think I was?"

I could tell that he was reluctant to say anything. He didn't trust me, and I didn't blame him.

"Carson, we don't have very much time, and what I'm going to tell you will be very difficult for you to believe, but just try. My real name is Benidette Hammell. My maiden name is Crawford."

He just stared at me, still so confused.

"Adina is my aunt, and I am your niece. She practically raised me."

"Adina? You know Adina?"

"Yes, I know her very well! She's my aunt."

"That's not possible! She's too young to be your aunt, and she has no nieces or nephews!"

"You're right, she doesn't have any nieces or nephews - not yet! I can't explain it right now, but just know that I am speaking the truth."

Neither of us realized it, but we had stopped dancing in the middle of the floor, just talking intently, unaware of the couples whirling around us. It was a very sweet moment for me, but Carson was still in a state of unbelief, while also trying to deal with this holy mess of information.

"I know that I should think that you are absolutely crazy, but for some reason, even though it makes *no sense whatsoever,* I somehow believe you. I don't understand it, but like most mysteries that confound ordinary thinkers, the proof of you stands here before me."

Carson's eyes became enkindled with excitement, as if he were beholding a notable scientific discovery. I watched as his guard of uncertainty came crashing down, followed by newly identified questions and a fervor that rose up from his heart about his one and only niece.

"By what means do I find myself holding onto and looking into the eyes of one who was shaped out of nowhere?"

Together we laughed at his far-reaching challenge, but like any person in his methodical world of one and one equaling two, he next answered his own question.

"You are an unexpected and unexplainable component which rarely happens in the world of science and engineering. But I'm not like most in that field. My mind has always viewed things in a more *unconventional* way. What's happening here is perplexing, like the idea of a man walking on the moon, but somehow seeing Adina in your eyes makes all of this bewitchingly logical."

His face was beaming almost like a proud father, and I was able to experience firsthand the amazing tenderness that captured Adina's heart.

"It is wonderful to meet you, Benidette, my beautiful niece who looks so much like her *beautiful* aunt. Golly kiddo, I nearly had a heart attack when I saw you yesterday! I was afraid for Adina, and I couldn't get to Friedlich fast enough to check on her."

"I'm so sorry, Carson, that must have been awful! And you're right! War is coming, and you and Adina should leave. But there's one more thing you should know about Adina."

Carson's face turned dim the moment I presented a threatening statement that included Adina.

"When Halag found me in town, he said that they had been watching me for a week - but I just got here yesterday. They weren't watching me, they were watching Adina. I fear that if I hadn't come here when I did, they would have eventually found her. I won't be here much longer - she just needs to be careful who sees her."

I could tell that this information bothered Carson greatly. But one thing I knew to be a fact about Adina was that while in Friedlich she was never taken captive by anyone, and worked the remainder of her time here in Malachi's store.

For the next few beautiful moments, we were allowed to enjoy one another's company. He was one of those people who couldn't help but smile, even when the world seemed harsh and unfair. His expression of tenderness was as much a part of him as his warm and joyful heart. I too fell instantly in love with him. Without making a scene, Carson squeezed my waist, wishing that it could be a great big hug and that instead of this hidden conversation, we both wished that time could stand still just for us.

Suspiciously monitoring our interaction, Alrik could feel the intensity of our conversation from where he stood and perceived it as flirtatious. Remembering the other day and how Carson and I looked at one another, he felt that there was something between the two of us. Becoming enraged at the thought, he marched onto the dance floor in an attempt to interrupt our discussion.

"Well, you two seem to be getting along very well! Do you even realize that the music is still playing? I understand that you are both Americans and must have many familiar things to talk about, but it is unacceptable to stand in the middle of a ballroom and engage in conversation rather than dance. It is quite rude!"

It was obvious that Alrik was upset, and I needed to suppress the flames. Poor Carson was already overwhelmed by the information that I had just shared with him, and I could tell he didn't know how to respond to Alrik, so I had had to think quickly.

"Actually Alrik, our talk did get a little heated because Dr. Carson here seems to believe that the steel panels that our company provided in the building of the Titanic were of inferior quality, and the reason for her ruin."

I looked up at Carson trying to make a bit of a scene.

"You know what, Dr. Carson, Brannigan Steel has been fighting those false accusations for years now, and quite honestly, I don't appreciate it at all. My father was so confident in the product we provided, that he sailed and died on that vessel. Do you think he would have even boarded the ship if he believed it was made of inferior steel?"

Carson looked at me completely stunned, and covered his mouth with his hand in an attempt to conceal a slight grin, as my actions were unexpected but most clever. Bowing his head and clearing his throat, he offered up a most humble apology.

"Forgive me, Miss Brannigan; I didn't mean to offend you!"

"Well, next time you need to get your facts straight before you challenge me. That is if we ever talk again!"

At that, with my hands shaking and heart practically beating out of my chest, I turned around and walked away from both of them, hoping that my performance cleared any thoughts of anger or suspicion that Alrik may have felt towards Carson. Leading Alrik to believe that I was

offended and resentful towards Carson created a safer and

more ideal situation for my uncle. It was best that he didn't

believe that we were on friendly terms at all.

I was, however, completely disappointed in myself

with what I had said to Carson, or rather what I didn't say.

My first interaction with him could have very well been the

last time I would ever see him, and I didn't even warn him

about what would lead to his death. All of it was just so

much harder than I thought it would be. How could I tell

him that he would die here? Maybe my quick bit of wisdom

that war was coming and he and Adina should leave right

away made an impact. I must admit, I was amazed that he

accepted as truth, the weight of information that I had just

told him. *That* ... in itself ... was miraculous. After all, my

story, this journey, is an unbelievable paradox, that's just

too crazy for anyone to think true, and I had no idea how he

would respond.

When the evening finally concluded, I was glad to be out of the room full of people and finally by myself - this was all too much. I felt I was just existing here, not accomplishing a thing. Making my way once again to the carousel, I stepped up onto one of the magnificent white horses. I couldn't help but admire the spectacular craftsmanship, done to perfection, not lacking even one detail. There were only two people I knew who could sculpt something like this out of wood, and that was Carig and his grandfather, Killen, before him. Brushing my fingers over the wooden creation, I missed Carig so badly that I couldn't bear it. I didn't want to be here anymore; I wanted to be with my husband. It made me sad to think that this is what our life would be like from here on out. I couldn't even imagine what he was going through right now. I hoped that what he said about time was true, and that only minutes had passed for him and he wasn't feeling the excruciating pain of days gone by. With all that had happened so far, it actually felt more like weeks to me, and I was tired and ready to go home.

Thoughts of him filled me with joy and made me smile at everything I saw. The glorious golden ballroom along with general exquisite surroundings made me think of Carig. Everything beautiful made me think of him. I wished he were here to see it - he would appreciate the genius of the artisans.

Without warning, a familiar but terrifying voice roused me from my deep thoughts of Carig - causing my heart to sink.

"Well, Fräulein, you seem to be getting along quite nicely having twisted Alrik around your little finger."

"Why, Mr. Sauer, what a displeasure to see you again. You know, I was noticing that you were the only one sitting at the table not wearing a black uniform - is there some significance to that?"

I wasn't really sure of his ranking, but I could tell by the refinement of the black and red uniforms, along with the embellishments that adorned them, that those who wore them far out-ranked this horrible man in green. Unfortunately, I knew that once the hateful words came pouring out of my mouth that I really should have just kept quiet. Halag was like a time bomb, ready to explode at any moment, and my insulting words had just set him off. He became infuriated and scurried over to me like a rat, standing face to face with me.

"You! ... Fräulein, are trouble! I knew it from the first moment I laid eyes on you. Something about you is not right, and I intend to find out what it is!"

He stepped up onto my horse and grabbed my neck, pushing my head into the brass pole. His grip became tighter and tighter.

"Stop Halag, I can't breathe!"

Even though I tried pushing him away, his strength was too much for me, and his fury had come unleashed. As he continued holding my neck, he got right in my face spewing words of venom.

"I despise you, you Americans who think you're better than everyone else. There will come a day when you and everyone like you will bow down to me!"

I couldn't breathe, I couldn't make a sound - I could only faintly hear what this crazed maniac was hissing at me.

His grip only became tighter as I tried to peel back his fingers, and I could feel myself dying. The pain in my throat and the burning sensation within my lungs began to fade. This was it, I would die here and never see Carig again. As the lights from the ballroom dimmed, in the far distance I could hear Carig calling my name. His voice turned into the sound of waves roaring on the shores of Bar

Rousse. I could see him coming towards me, he was running, still calling my name, but before he could get to me a wave came and swept over me and everything went dark.

It wasn't until Alrik and Carson reached the scene that Halag relented.

"Stop, get your hands off of her! My God what are you doing? What have you done? You are finished here!"

As Halag pulled his hands away, I slipped off the horse and fell to the ground. Halag only smiled at Alrik as if he were quite satisfied with himself. He seemed to find pleasure in this destructive deed, as he hurled threats of exposure toward Alrik.

"You idiot! You know and I know, that *I* will never be done here. You owe me! You will always be indebted to me…. remember, cousin, I carry your secrets!"

Alrik paid no attention to his words, but in a rage, grabbed his neck and pushed him down to the ground. Like a mad man, he began hitting him repeatedly until his face was completely bloodied and unrecognizable. Even when Halag was unconscious, Alrik didn't stop.

Carson ran over to where I was lying, and tried to revive me.

"Miss Brannigan, Miss Brannigan!" Then whispering in my ear, "Benidette, please wake up!"

Carson called frantically for Alrik.

"Alrik, stop! She needs help right now! She's barely breathing!"

Just then two guards ran up to where Alrik was kneeling.

"Get this animal out of my sight! Lock him up, and don't let him out until I say so."

They grabbed hold of Halag and dragged him away, leaving a trail of blood behind. Alrik ran over to where I was lying.

"Carson, go into the dining room and find Dr. Ottoman."

A few minutes later, Carson and the doctor came rushing out. Dr. Ottoman bellowing out orders to Alrik and all of those standing around. Alrik quickly swept me up and carried me through the ballroom full of people who were shocked by the outrageous events that had just taken place, and by the looks of the bruises on my neck, assumed that I was dead or close to it. Whispers of Halag's name rose up from the crowd, saying that Alrik's insane cousin had finally gone too far.

Step by step, Alrik carried me up to my room, the whole time saying over and over again, "You'll be alright … please no, not again … not again!"

Dr. Ottoman made his way into my room carrying a large black leather bag, followed by two of the housemaids with arms full of the doctor's requested supplies. Alrik wanted to come in, but the doctor told him to wait downstairs and he would send for him later.

"I insist, Ottoman! I want to be in there!"

"Alrik, no! I can't promise anything, and her injuries are severe."

He placed his hands on Alrik's shoulders, speaking firmly to him.

"This is not a good place for you; it would be too hard. I will call when I know anything. Please let me attend to her - we must get ice on her throat before it closes completely. If that happens, there is nothing I can do!"

With those parting words (words he had been shaken by before), he stood out in the hall and watched the door close in front of him. Even though considered ill-mannered, Alrik never returned to the party but was seen

frantically riding off on his black horse.

Dr. Ottoman did everything he could to save me,

even offering up pleadings to God to spare my life,

assuring Him that Alrik would never survive losing

another. Unbeknownst to me, I was unconscious for days

that were dotted with a few touch and go episodes. Once

the doctor had done everything he could, Alrik came and

stayed with me, never leaving my side.

When I woke up, I didn't know where I was. All I

knew was that my neck and throat were throbbing, and I

could barely move my head, let alone swallow or speak. It

was dark except for one candle burning on my side table.

Because of the breeze from the partially open door, the

shadow of the flame was dancing on the walls. Aside from

the pain of my swollen throat, I was freezing. As I reached

up to determine the extent of my wounds, all I could feel

were ice packs fixed to each side of my neck. Even though

I was heavily covered with blankets, I was still so cold. I tried to speak, but nothing came out. For an instant, I thought I heard Carig's voice, and I was relieved that I was home. With everything within me, I tried to call out his name.

"Carig!"

"I'm here, Fräulein!"

"Carig!"

When I finally made out the face in front of me, I was profoundly disappointed because I saw that it was not Carig, and I was not home. It was Alrik. All of this was real, and I was still in Germany. According to Alrik, I had been out cold for the past three days. I couldn't say a word, my throat had been crushed and was still badly bruised and swollen. I turned towards him and found him looking at me, deep in thought.

"Valentine, the last time I sat at a bedside it was my wife's. She had suffered many days of painful labor. There was heavy snow that night. As a matter of fact, there was so much snow that the doctor couldn't get here until it was too late. Hour after hour I listened to her scream, holding her hand, trying to ease her pain, but there was nothing that I could do. When the doctor finally arrived, our daughter had been born, but Caprice had lost too much blood, and I sat here, just as I am with you, and watched her take her last breath. When she died, the person I was died with her. For months I wouldn't even look at Annaliese, it was just too painful."

My heart ached for him; he still carried such immense grief. The tears that ran down his face were tokens of his broken heart. I just continued listening as his sadness turned to joy the moment he laid eyes on Annaliese - she became his purpose for living and carrying on. His whole face lit up as he spoke of her.

"These days of watching you unconsciously suffer and fighting for breath, so reminded me of that night, but you are still here with me, Fräulein. There's something I need to say - I wanted to say it when we were dancing. The very moment that I saw you, I wanted you ... I wanted you here with me. In my whole life, it was only Caprice until you."

I knew then I had to say something. I didn't want to be the source of any more pain for him; he'd been through enough. I tried to speak out, but still, nothing came out.

"Please, Fräulein, just listen. Please don't go back to America; stay here with me. Be my wife. I will love you forever! I know it's been just a few short days, but somehow I loved you even before you came here. I know that makes no sense, but when you appeared it was like magic. Now, just please know that if you say yes I will spend the rest of my life making you happy."

He bent down and kissed my forehead.

"You sleep now, and I'll check on you in the morning."

He left the room, and I laid there feeling like I had made a total mess of things. What in the world was I here for, and how was I going to get back to the Tempus Vector? Just then, I heard the balcony door open, and a rush of wind filled the room.

Remaining still, I looked to see who had come in. I was afraid that it might be Halag come to finish what he had started.

"Benidette!"

I tried to look at who was calling my name, my real name. It was Carson. He hurried to my side, looking down sadly at what had happened to me.

"Benidette, I had to come and make sure you were ok. Can you talk?"

228

I motioned "no" with my eyes.

"Ok, well you not being able to speak will not make this easy, but I have to know more about you, what's going on that brought you here, and how you got here."

I sat up holding my throat in pain as the ice pack fell. The look of horror on Carson's face confirmed the fact that my throat looked as bad as it felt.

"Dammit to hell, they ought to shoot that man, he's out of his mind. This is not the first time he's hurt someone. Not too long ago, he shot one of the scientists that I worked with. He was brilliant. Halag accused him of trying to escape, but he had been given permission to leave and go see his family. It's only because he's Alrik's cousin that people look the other way when he does such things. But this time, as far as Alrik is concerned, he went too far. As long as I've known him, I have never seen Alrik this angry. I'm so sorry for all of this."

I motioned for him to get me a piece of paper and pencil. Maybe I couldn't speak, but I could write. I wasn't going to hold anything back, just like Malachi said.

"Ok, Benidette."

I wrote down for him to call me Beni.

"Alright, Beni ... how is it that you are Adina's and my niece?"

I am the daughter of her youngest brother, Rich Crawford.

"The Rich Crawford who's a baby?"

Yes.

"Have you and I ever met before?"

I just didn't feel ready for what I was about to tell him.

No, we have never met.

Carson looked perplexed.

230

"If you are my niece, wait, tell me first, how did you get here?"

I have a calling on my life that gives me the ability to go to different times in history and correct events that are flawed.

"So you ... came here from another time?"

I nodded yes.

"What year are you from?"

2016.

"What? 2016? That's impossible!"

I could tell that Carson was completely stunned, and absolutely wouldn't believe any of this if the evidence of me wasn't before his very eyes.

"That's impossible, it's impossible."

I took his hand and squeezed it, letting him know that it truly was impossible, but it's real, and I was really here.

"Why haven't you ever met me? If Adina raised you, why am I not there too?"

I closed my eyes and took a deep breath. Carson sat back as he could tell I was struggling to answer his question. It occurred to me that if he was the reason that I was here, once I told him, it would be time for me to leave. Only since I don't have the Tempus Vector, I would be stranded here for the rest of my life. But I had to tell him, I may not have another chance. It was a risk I would have to take.

Carson, you....

Oh my gosh, I couldn't even write it! I scratched out all of what I had written, and took a deep breath. Having to tell him this, made me completely emotional. My eyes filled with tears, and my already throbbing throat tightened even more.

You die here - you never come home.

His jaw dropped as he read my words, and he just looked at me, so completely shocked at my revelation.

"How? When?"

I only know that it's sometime around October, 1941 on a plane - your plane crashes. Carson, whatever you do, don't get on the plane then.

"I just can't believe it, and why would I go on a plane without Adina? So Adina makes it out, right? Did she remarry?"

Yes, she makes it out, and no she never remarried. Carson, you were the love of her life. She spent her entire life loving you through serving others. She lived an amazing life - you would have been very proud of her. I would always ask her why she never married again, she was so young when you died. She would just tell me that

there was only you.

Carson was so moved by Adina's faithfulness to him that just thinking about her put a huge smile on his face.

"So Beni, you're my niece. I don't understand all of this, but thank you. Now kiddo, how can I help you?"

I had to leave my things in town. I can't get home without them. Is it true that the bridge is the only way back to town?

"No, there's another way. I'm going back to town in a few days on a truck that picks us up and brings us back. We have to get you on that vehicle. I'll work on it. In the meantime, I've been hearing things, things about you. Alrik has every intention of you staying here. Is it true he wants to marry you?"

I frantically tore into my reply, as this was weighing

so heavily on my heart.

Yes, Carson it's true. But I'm married. I have a

wonderful man at home who's probably thinking I'm never

coming back. I have to get back to him.

"Well, we have to get you out of here before it goes

any further. And Beni, we have to get you out before they

find out that you're not Valentine Brannigan."

I felt such a sense of relief that I had someone to

talk to, and someone that I knew would help me.

By the way, how did you get up here?

"There's a trellis of roses that climbs all the way up

to your balcony. It wasn't that bad except for a few

puncture wounds from the thorns."

For the next few hours, we sat and conversed about

Adina and what her life was like after Carson died. Once he

left, I felt so sad. He was wonderful, just like Adina said. I regretted deeply that he had not been part of my life, and then I was grieved because even after I told him about the plane crash, I didn't feel the urge to return. It appeared that his death was inevitable, and nothing that I would do would change that. All I knew was that Carson was not the reason that I was here.

Not only did I feel saddened about saying goodbye to my uncle, but I couldn't help but be bombarded with thoughts and memories of my years with Adina that should have included Carson. His death was senseless, and these two amazing people deserved to grow old together. Tragically, she left Germany alone, forever parted from Carson. Although she missed him terribly, she rose up from the ashes of her grief and lived an extraordinary life. But she didn't stop there, she, in turn, poured into my life, and without her, who knows where I would have ended up?

I became so emotional just thinking about her and how she impacted my life. I wanted to see her so badly, to wrap my arms around her, one last time. To my dismay, this desire was quickly squashed by an awareness that the task that included contact with Adina had already come and gone. There was only one thing left to do, the only thing to do! I would honor her with my life calling and become the woman that she always aspired for me to be.

After he disappeared from the balcony, I just laid in bed. My neck was in excruciating pain. Luckily though, he left just in the nick of time. For as soon as he walked out, Gerda came in with new ice packs and some pain medicine that Dr. Ottoman had left for me.

"Oh, Fräulein, poor, poor, girl!"

She poured a spoonful of the medicine, gently holding it to my mouth as I struggled to swallow it, and then she replaced my ice packs.

"This will make it all better, yes?"

I just looked at her and smiled.

"You sleep!"

After she left the room, my mind was too busy thinking to sleep. The harder I tried to relax and rest, countless thoughts began bouncing in a thousand different directions.

Suddenly, from out of nowhere, something very weird occurred. Although strange, it was a familiar feeling that I had experienced once before while lying in a coma the days following my run-in with the Devil's Knuckles. But ever since then I had believed it to be a dream. Just like before, a rustling but warm wind filled the room, quickly extinguishing my only source of light. With that current of air my eyes closed, and my body became paralyzed. The only thing that I could feel was the throbbing pain in my throat. I could hear nothing but the wind, although within it I could feel a presence standing beside me, and I was afraid. I attempted, to no avail, to open my eyes, to move my arms, my legs, but I remained numb and helpless.

238

Within the lively twists of the gale moving through the room, I heard a voice weaving in and out of the threads of an unfamiliar tone, awakening the promise that I was not alone. Without warning, all of the warmth of the wind encircled my throat. Then as quickly as the gust came, it stopped.

When I opened my eyes, the room was just as it had been. Even the candle was still lit. I wasn't sure what kind of medicine had been given to me, however, the effects of it made me not only hallucinate but also caused temporary paralysis. Whatever it was, it miraculously seemed to ease the pain in my throat.

Feeling almost hyper and anxious, I felt an overpowering desire to get up. Being that it was quiet in the house, and everyone was asleep, I decided to take a look around. This was my chance to explore undisturbed. Every moment of every day since being here, I'd been guarded. Even though I'd been instructed by the doctor to keep the ice packs on my neck, I removed them, slipped my finger through the loop of the brass candleholder, and quietly crept my way out of the room.

Chapter 7

THE HALL OF CAPRICE

"So many things had aligned perfectly in order for this place to be discovered, by me, a sojourner who unearthed a phenomenon of sorts." ~**Benidette Hammell**~

Greeted by suffocating darkness as I stepped out of my door and into the hallway made me rather uneasy. Not only was the darkness overpowering, but being completely unfamiliar with the enormous estate and the twists and turns of the maze-like corridors compounded my fears. Only the glow from my candle lit the way for my prompted journey down the pitch-black hallway. I wasn't exactly sure what I was looking for, but for some reason I felt compelled to continue. It appeared that I had purposely been placed in a location of the house that kept me conveniently separated from the main affairs of the household.

I quickly discovered that this enormous residence was a labyrinth of hallways, leading into more rooms than I could even count. Weaving my way through passageways of unimaginable darkness, I turned a corner that I believed connected me to a long hallway that led toward the front of the house. Only the shadows of night lay before me - so I thought. But then, unexpectedly, down the center of the hallway I noticed a small fragment of light beaming through a crack onto the floor. The golden sliver glow ahead became my beacon that directed me through the somber corridor.

It seemed to take forever to finally reach that light, as I was distracted by the unfamiliar and haunting sounds of a settling house. Creaking noises rose up with every step forward, making me long for the safety of my room. The journey was slow-moving to be sure. The frequent pauses became a perpetual merry-go-round of hoping and praying that I wouldn't see anyone standing there, as it would most certainly scare me to death. In all of the great novels that I had read over the years, being on the edge of my seat was never a source of enticement. Knowing the outcome, knowing that Edmond Dantes and Mercedes would once again find one another and live happily ever after, was where I liked to be. It was comfortable and predictable, unlike this already-terrifying experience filled with darkness and the unknown. The cloudiness of night, along with the flickering of my candle, ignited my imagination which in turn played disturbing games with my eyes, projecting the ghost-like shadow of Halag's face constantly before me, haunting me.

When finally I arrived at the origin of the light, I was met by two massive paintings hanging on the wall adjacent to one another. With only a tiny crack separating the two, it allowed the sliver of light which had become my guide, to escape the confines of the wall and slip out onto the hallway floor.

From what I could see, each painting was of a single horse - one black, one white - rearing back on its hind legs, front legs tearing at the heavens. Each stallion, set in frames of brilliant gold, was facing the other in what seemed to be an irony of opposites, both longing for one another. Touching the works of art, I could tell that they played on the wall, obviously not mounted securely as normal frameworks of this magnitude should be. As I put my fingers in the small gap between the two paintings, I was able to pull them apart. They surprisingly became a gateway to a place that was not meant for just anyone to find. Much to my delight, I discovered that each simply served as a sliding entry over an opening which hid a passage that would lead into a secret room. It was strategically hidden so that no one would ever discover its location unless they were walking down this hall at a precise time - *only on a night with a full moon, and during the moments when the lunar dawn rested over this room,* setting it aglow, and sending a beam of light onto the hallway floor. So many things had aligned perfectly in order for this place to be discovered, by me, a sojourner who unearthed a phenomenon of sorts.

The rumbling and creaking that resulted from the apparent disuse of the rolling doors echoed off the walls, and I cringed at the thought that someone may have heard the unusual noises, most certainly alerting them to my nocturnal activities. I stood frozen in place with my eyes shut, afraid to even take a breath for what seemed like an eternity, listening for the bustling of footsteps coming my way. But to my relief, only silence filled the air, and as far as I could tell, no one had heard and no one was coming. With a sigh of relief, I looked inside the unknown, realizing one thing for sure, I was stepping into something mysterious and most definitely off limits.

Initially I was taken aback by the primitive and eerie flight of stairs that was set before me. Based on the decor in the rest of the house, this small section certainly did not fit with its almost barbaric and gothic-type entrance, that made me question what I would find next - so I mentally prepared myself for the worst. If not for the beautiful warm light that practically called me here by name, I may have assumed that this hideous stone cubby may very well be the hidden entrance into a room of unimaginable evils.

The small cave led to a steep flight of stairs that was surrounded with jagged gray stone walls, blanketed with cobwebs which stretched from one side of the room to the other, seizing the light and transforming themselves into strands of pure gold. Taking my first step up, I was forced to break through the meshing of webs, trying to ignore the fact that spiders lived among the threads and I had just disrupted their bliss. Before going any further, I turned back around, and as carefully and quietly as possible, closed the two doors back together, and began my ascent up the stairs.

Arriving at the last step, I would have thought I had been lured into a dead end if not for glass inlays set within a wooden paneled door, allowing light to shine through the panes, which continued to give me vision forward. The door was more cupboard-sized, causing me to crouch down and slide through to the other side. The unusually small entrance ended up being only one of hundreds of panels into the room of light.

As I pushed open the panel, the darkness was instantly gone, and the night was shining like the day. This was not a place to fear as I had previously believed, but a haven. There before me was a great wall of windows that covered the center section of the house; it was magnificent and beautiful. This room, or great hall, was located at the very front of the estate, on the very top story, seemingly built on as an afterthought to the rest of the house. The bottom portions of the windows were made of clear beveled glass; the top sections were also beveled, but stained gold. The moonlight permeating the room was filtered through the golden panes, creating a gilded effect across the entire span. The walls were elaborately carved with inserts of teardrop-shaped crystals placed within each paneled section, setting the room aglow with beams of reflected light moving in all directions. Although the room stood still, the movement of light reminded me of the carousel, and with every turn of light, the marble statues hidden within the cavities of the massive pillars located in the middle of the room appeared to patrol my every move. The black and white checkerboard floor cloaked within the gilded rays, created a path that seemed to push me forward, awakening my already curious mind.

Proceeding down the long hallway, the golden room unexpectedly revealed itself to be a historical family gallery brimming with paintings of Alrik's lineage. The vintage attire worn by his ancestors, along with the archaic painting styles and techniques, dated them to be at least two, maybe three hundred years old.

Although the room was spacious and grand, the untoward entrance route covered in cobwebs revealed that it had been some time since anyone had visited this hidden chamber. More than likely, this great hall was *only* for the private use of the master of the house. Except for the sliver of light revealed during a full moon, no one would ever know it was here. It was a miracle that I found it.

To my immediate right was an array of prominent portraits of men and women who were significant in the history of this family. One after the other laid claim to be the master matriarchs and patriarchs of their time. As I moved forward, I saw what appeared to be a portrait of Alrik as a young boy sitting in between his mother and father.

Until this very moment, I hadn't really experienced the power of being consumed by a story so clearly embedded within a portrait. Pen and ink had always been my source of imagination, but the image of the family now before me was a heart-wrenching tragedy playing out before my very eyes.

Alrik's father bore a scowl of cruelty, while mother and son wore fearful and somber expressions. Alrik's cherubic face spoke a thousand words, with eyes that longed to please the tyrant, while still naive in his hopes for love and acceptance which would never come to fruition. His mother's hand held Alrik's tightly as if to say, "I'm here and everything will be all right." Her worn face that was once joyful and full of life, spoke volumes about the years of maltreatment. Yet no longer was she fearful for herself alone, but now also for the life and future of her precious son. She was half wishing she had never brought him into this miserable world of suffering, and was dying inside at the thought that he may become a clone of his wretched father. Her unceasing love for him was so powerful that I could sense the distressing affliction in her eyes, and practically hear the supplication of her heart echoing throughout the halls imploring him, "My dear son, you are not your father. Choose to never walk as he has walked - be a man filled with love and compassion for others. Always choose love."

With those words resounding through my mind, I was moved with compassion and grief at their torment. My heart was broken for both of them. Since arriving here, I seemed to be in a constant state of sorrow over the welfare of my new acquaintances, and it was eating me up inside. Perhaps this is what Malachi meant in his diary entry that said,

"The Carrier will at times find themselves lost in the brokenness that surrounds their journey. That comes from a caring heart that is more concerned for the happiness of

251

others than their own. You will not be able to fix sorrow. It

is, and will always be."

The next painting was of Alrik as he is now, young

and handsome, sitting on a black horse just like the one in

the hallway. He looked perfect, like a god. But the one

thing that stood out to me was the expression on his face.

He was clearly happy, and staring at someone or something

that brought him incredible joy. Perhaps it was the portrait

that sat right next to him - a woman on a white horse

swiftly riding through the forest. It was like looking into a

dream. Her snowy-colored dress and long brunette tresses

flowed freely in the breeze. The horse ran with such grace

and elegance, that its hooves barely touched the ground.

The next painting was of the same woman, at least I

believed so as I still couldn't make out a face, only this

time she was walking alongside her horse in the middle of a

meadow. After that point, every portrait starred this same

faceless person, all captured at a distance, not up close like the others in the previous hall.

I had a strange feeling about what was coming and then experienced a deep-seated urgency to turn around and walk out, which I chose to ignore. This venture was risky to be sure, but the idea of leaving was unthinkable - without a doubt, I knew that I was supposed to be here, and I prayed that I wouldn't be found out.

Reaching the end of the gallery, I came upon a closed door, and carefully and slowly turned the handle unsure of what was on the other side. As I peeked through the slightly opened door, all I could see was darkness. Once again taking up the candle and holding it in front of me, I entered the room. Very quickly I realized that this space was an extension of the other, minus any windows. It was completely enclosed, while also covered in paintings, all of the same woman. The walls were filled with various sizes of portraits of her, and her alone, which unlike the other, appeared to be more of a shrine than a family gallery.

Nearing the end of this smaller chamber, I all but stumbled over a dark wood and leather lion chair that sat directly in the center of the room. The chair faced a wall that was covered in a magnificent-sized portrait of the same mysterious woman who was now sitting beneath a lovely old oak tree. Her ample smile set the tone for a face that was overflowing with happiness and joy as her hands were gently placed on her pregnant belly. When I saw the unqualified look of love on her face, not only for the blessing within her but for the love of her life who stood before her, one word came to my mind - complete. At that precise second in time, her life was perfect and complete; not one fraction of an ounce could have been added to make it more absolute.

Stepping closer to examine the portrait more thoroughly, I noticed a familiarity with each line and curve of her face. However, not until I studied her eyes and her mouth did I feel like a ton of bricks had just come crashing down upon me as her full being came into focus. At first I thought that my eyes were playing tricks on me. After all, the only light in the room was my one small candle. Gasping for air, I couldn't believe what I was seeing in the picture! It was me, or what looked like me, and I was altogether gripped with fear! Beneath the painting I noticed a lengthy inscription titled with the name Caprice Richter. Struggling to read the rest of the inscription, I only wished that my German was a bit better. Thankfully, I was able to understand the written word more effectively than I could speak it.

To the captor of my heart, In life you gave it perfect cadence, but in death it ceased and has refused to strike another movement apart from its cherished companion. When we meet again, my lovely Caprice, if I should be allowed to be with you again where the angels dwell, I beg you bring life once again to my heart. Nonetheless, it will always belong to you.

Caprice Richter, Caprice? This was Alrik's wife who died while giving birth to Annaliese. The resemblance between the two of us was uncanny! It all started to make sense now. How Alrik acted as if he knew me the moment he laid eyes on me, not to mention his irrational and instantaneous love for me. I was convinced that he believed that I was her. The whole thing was so bizarre and completely unbelievable.

This idea that he had conjured up in his mind reminded me of a scene from a disturbing stalker movie, which I would never watch because the whole idea scares me to death. Basically, I was in the middle of my worst nightmare - shaken by a man who believed that I was his dead wife. I began to piece together the clouded reasoning behind this complex dilemma of mine, and why Alrik would blow up a bridge in order to keep me here. If he allowed me to leave, he would be losing her all over again.

I felt both sorry for him, and fearful for myself at the same

time.

Making myself comfortable in the chair where

Alrik had most likely spent many an hour staring up at the

one who made his heart beat, I gained a whole new

perspective of the surrounding area. For some reason, I felt

as though this chair had been the one witness that could

testify of the many sorrowful hours he grieved and

despaired over Caprice.

I continued scoping out the dimly lit room. At first,

I didn't notice, but on the opposite side of the room in clear

view from the lion chair, was a display of exquisite gowns,

all perfectly placed on dress forms and encased within a

row of standing glass enclosures. Around the neckline of

each fashion hung complete sets of jewelry, and at the base

of each gown, sat a pair of shoes. Not only would Alrik

allow the painting to consume him, so to find even a morsel

of peace, but he granted permission within the confines of his mind for the gowns to transform what *"was"* into a motion picture of nostalgia. Time would most certainly stand still within the walls of this alcove, as he would watch shades of her draw near to him fashioning each garment, feeling that it would be acceptable to never breathe again as long as he could be near her.

The longer I sat there, the more powerful their love for one another became, and I could feel it consuming me. As I studied each figure arrayed in elegance, I couldn't help but pause at one particular case - the one that held a breathtaking sapphire gown and sat a bit higher than all the rest. It seemed to hold some significance over the others, and I could feel its story capturing my attention. Time certainly did stand still! I couldn't really say how long I peered into the shimmering sea of blue, but without realizing it, I became lost in their love affair. I could see Alrik's face as he watched her walk down the stairs of this house wearing the lovely blue gown, neither their hearts nor their eyes ever parting from one another. Perhaps this was the night that he would announce to the world that not only was Caprice his wife, but that she carried their child. Before I knew it, tears of grief were running down my face. I felt his pain. It made me think of Carig and how devastated I would be if I ever lost him. I didn't know how Alrik could stand this place, or the memories that were locked up here. The powerful emotions held captive within this room were too intense for me, and I was just an outsider looking in, or was I?

Being here made me feel vulnerable and helpless, on the brink of being consumed by a huge wave. For that moment I didn't just get lost in their story, I became the story. I didn't just imagine seeing Caprice walking down the stairs, I felt I *was* Caprice. They were *my* eyes that were fully connected with Alrik, and his with mine. I was overwhelmed with sadness for him, and I was moved by his undying love and loyalty for his departed wife.

This entire experience was too much. I would surely lose my mind if I didn't leave now and shake off the ghost that had all but possessed me. I couldn't stand feeling so vulnerable and anxious, and this place felt like a trap that was trying to convince me that I was someone other than who I really was. Reminding myself that none of this was my life, but only a moment in time, prompted me to remain steadfast and hold on tightly to the real me.

The intense feelings that I had shared in my mind a moment ago with a man I hardly knew, made me long for Carig. I wasn't sure what emotions I had just experienced, but one thing I did know, Carig was the love of my life and nothing would ever change that. Yet I couldn't help but feel that for a sordid few moments, I had been unfaithful to him and it grieved my heart.

Just the thought of Carig reset my resolve. He knew and supported this life calling of mine, and because his thoughts never left me, and he was waiting in that third story room for me to come back, he was my reality and my home, not this.

Although it had only been a few days, I felt that I had been on this journey forever. I could see what Adina meant when she wrote about how easily one can get lost in another world, forgetting who they are, even why they are there. It was time for me to go. I had become too preoccupied with things that did not pertain to me or my calling. I needed to get back to Malachi, and warn him about what was coming. Once I told him, it would be time for me to leave. Because I left the frame with him, it was waiting for me there, and I would be able to go home immediately. All I needed now was for Carson to let me know his plan to get me back to Friedlich.

As I stood up to leave, I came across a small table that almost went unnoticed as it was also made of scrolled gold, and blended in perfectly with the surrounding walls. It would have remained unseen if not for the scarlet glass box sitting on top of it. The red box was etched in decorative gold. Inside, I could see papers folded, with a ring sitting on the top of the stack. I knew that I should leave, but I had come this far and my curiosity got the best of me.

The box was made of what looked to be a very thick and weighty leaded glass, one like I had never seen before. I lifted up the hefty latch, and first caught sight of a stunning gold and ruby ring sitting on top. My guess was that it belonged to Caprice. It was a very large oval stone encased in a cage-like setting, that was heavy and cumbersome. Even though the stone and setting were quite large, the band was sized for a delicate finger.

Setting the ring on the table, I picked up the

obviously important documents encased in heavy blue-

colored paper, resembling a *Last Will and Testament*. Upon

opening the thick stack, they appeared to be exactly that,

except the title at the top was not listed as a will, but held

an entirely different title, one which I had never heard of

before: *Contra-Pergarora Kaution*. I knew *contra* implied

to be against something and *kaution* was the German

translation for *caution, or to be careful of,* but what was

Pergarora? "Pergarora, Pergarora?" I continued

whispering the word to myself, hoping that the repetition

would somehow jog my memory of German vocabulary.

Startled by a familiar voice from behind me softly

pronouncing the word in English, I felt as though I would

die where I stood.

"It's Purgatory, Fräulein!"

My heart stopped at the sound of Alrik's voice. I had been caught red-handed, not only invading a room that was hidden but also in possession of his personal papers. I wasn't just casually holding them, but I was studying them, trying to figure out exactly what they were. I wondered how long he had been watching me. Slowly turning around, I wasn't sure what expression I would encounter, but the second I laid eyes on him, I knew his inner thoughts as I observed both pain and heartbreak running down his face. Holding my throat, and trying to utter an apology in spite of my damaged vocal cords, proved an impossible task. My throat felt like it was on fire, but after a few attempts, I was able to mutter a low, breathy response.

"I'm so sorry, Alrik. I couldn't sleep, and when I saw the light coming from this glorious room, I had to see what was in here. But I shouldn't have looked at these papers. They were none of my business, and even now I have no idea what they are."

I was so embarrassed, which only made my

nonsensical chatter continue.

"Honestly, I know so little German that I couldn't

even read them, and well, here you go. I don't need to see

them!"

I stood there with my arm outstretched, trying to

give them back to him. He did nothing except just stand

there looking at me, still shedding tears, which is

something I would have never expected from him.

"Alrik, are you ok? Why don't we go upstairs and

get out of this room?"

"No, Fräulein. Stay here!"

His tone was firm and demanding, almost as if it

were an order not a request. He stood completely

motionless, just staring up at the picture of his wife with

such sadness. From where I was standing, I could actually

feel the heaviness of his despair and loss. Alrik was

265

completely mesmerized by the image of Caprice, while at the same time pouring out his heart to me. I couldn't help but ache for this broken man before me.

"Have you ever done such horrible things that you feel there is no redemption for your soul? I ... I have done such things. My sins are greater than most. Caprice was not only beautiful to look at but her heart and her soul were pure. The call of her life was to love even the unlovable people, such as my father. She spent her life doing what was right and good, blessing all of those around her. She was far too good for me, yet she chose me. To this day, I will never understand why she loved me, and I will never understand why God took her instead of me! Every moment that I was with her I could see glimpses of heaven - she brought beauty and light to my life. Since the moment that she died, I have been in darkness. All I want is to see her again - that light, that light that rescued me from darkness. I know that my beautiful Caprice dwells in heaven."

Turning around, he looked at me.

"I want to be where she is, and would do anything to get there."

He grabbed the papers from my hands, holding them to my face with a crazed look and fire in his eyes.

"These were purchased with a great price; they are my Purgatory Papers, my escape from hell. I knew... I know that I can never get to heaven on my own, which means I will never see Caprice again, and that will never do. I can't accept that. These serve as my assurance that when I die, I will not spend eternity in Purgatory, but will be with Caprice in paradise."

He paused for a moment, almost as though he forgot what he was saying, even where he was.

"You saw the paintings of the two horses on the wall upstairs? They are Chariot and Atlas, and are the guardians of this room, only allowing entrance to those who belong in this place - you, Fräulein, were meant to be here."

His conversation made me feel completely unsettled. Every word that flew out of his mouth made me realize that his grief was yielding irrational behavior with a hint of madness, and I was frightened. My first inclination was to run away from this place as quickly as possible, but since that was unthinkable considering my highly guarded surroundings, and the fact that Alrik was borderline disturbed, I would need to handle this situation delicately.

He continued spilling fragments of their love story to me, while barely looking away from the all-consuming painting of his wife.

"Chariot belonged to Caprice; they grew up together. He was born sickly, and my father wanted him shot. He said that the white foal was flawed and worthless. Caprice begged for his life and told my father that she would care for him. Reluctantly he said yes, assuming that the colt would never survive. In payment for food and medicine for young Chariot, my father insisted that Caprice shine his boots each day in exchange for the needed provisions. Every night he would leave them at the front door of the servant quarters, and they were expected to be shined and delivered back to his closet before the sun rose the next morning. She would stay up late every night polishing them to his liking and then delivered them faithfully to his valet each morning. My father was a bastard, making her work for years doing such a menial task, when his wealth was so immense. It was simply a game of power to him - it was uncalled for!"

He hung his head low as if he were ashamed.

269

"But I was just as much at fault. I should have never allowed it."

I watched as Alrik's face became red and irritated at the thought of his father, and then his head fell forward, followed by a deep breath.

"It was a godsend for everyone the day he died, but I have no doubt that hell became an even darker abyss the day he arrived."

He paused, not saying a word, and then his entire countenance changed as he spoke emotionally about Caprice.

"She named him Chariot as a promise from her to him that someday he would grow strong enough and big enough to carry her wherever she wanted to go. And so it was, her beautiful white Chariot was nursed to health and grew to be a strong stallion who loved Caprice. When she died, Chariot vanished into the woods never to be seen again by any of us. As she was dying, he could hear her screams of agony, and cried in unison from afar. He knew…. he knew the moment she died, for it was at that instant that he tore out of his stall, and ran into the woods. The carousel was meant as a gift to my beautiful Caprice; a place where she and our precious newborn baby girl could spend time together. But as it turned out, it became a monument to her and to Chariot instead. The horses are exact replicas of her prized stallion. She was an excellent rider; she and Chariot were like one being when they were together as if they read one another's thoughts. Like her, he was a picture of beauty and grace."

Alrik stopped talking for a moment, just looking down at the ground and then he chuckled as tears ran down his face.

"Caprice was filled with life and fun - something I had never known until her. Every time she pulled on her riding boots, she would sprint to where I was, and jump into my arms and say silly, nonsensical things that would always make me laugh. She was always catching me off guard with her terms of endearment. Things like 'Most powerful Pharaoh, fetch me my Chariot?'"

He let out a sigh of happiness as if he could feel her arms around him even at that very moment.

"Atlas and I would ride alongside them for hours. It was like heaven here on earth. Caprice on her white stallion was like watching an angel flying through the air. She was my life, my joy."

Just then he picked up her ruby ring, holding it between his fingers, raising it to his lips, and kissing it with his eyes closed as if it that small memento was really her. I had no idea what to say that could possibly make this situation better. After all, the grieving process had never ended for him; it had become a way of life.

"Alrik, I am so very sorry. I wish there were something that I could say or do. I know that it has been difficult here without Caprice, but look at how you have been blessed, with Annaliese I mean. I can tell when I look at her that her mother was beautiful in every way. And I see that same overflowing joy in Annaliese. But you know what else I see in her? You! I see you in her eyes and in her smile. She's breathtaking, really! And in regard to how bad you are, or what you've done in the past, don't you know that every single person in this world has done bad things? Everyone! But I can tell that you have a really sweet and caring heart. All the things that you've done wrong, you need to let them go, and forgive yourself, it's in the past. People in general are just flawed, but many times beauty comes as a result of our mistakes. If you don't let go of the mistakes of your life and forgive yourself, you will forever be walking around in chains that have been forged by your own hand."

With tears streaming down his face, Alrik walked over to where I stood and held my face in his hands, looking intently into my eyes.

"Thank you, Fräulein, for your words of kindness."

Then completely unexpectedly, he kissed me, and I pulled back quickly.

"Alrik, no!"

Letting out a heavy sigh, he came once again close to where I was standing.

"Fraulein, I know why you're here. You were sent here for me, but I don't know if you realize it yet or not. You have been sent here to fill this gaping hole in my heart, and fill me once again with joy and a purpose for living, a second chance. You are my second chance. I knew why you were sent here from the moment I laid eyes on you in Friedlich. You have been sent to be my wife, and the mother that Annaliese has never known."

I was filled with fear over his words to me! Three times he told me that I had been sent here for him, as if he knew. But what did he know?

He took my hand and placed the ruby ring on my finger.

"Marry me! Let us not put this off any longer. I believe you feel it too."

I had made a huge mistake in comforting Alrik. My compassion only added fuel to the fire, and now I was standing in an impossible situation.

"Listen, Alrik, I am not Caprice. I was not sent for you! I don't know what you mean, or where you got the idea that I'm here for you. I…. I have someone back home who I'm in love with, and he loves me. He'll be waiting for me."

I took the ring off of my finger and held it out to him.

"I can't take this. This ring should go to Annaliese, not me. Alrik, I can't marry you. I have to go home, do you understand?"

My throat was on fire, and with each word my voice became softer and harder to understand.

"Caprice told me that someone would come so that I wouldn't be alone, and that I would know when she did. From the moment I saw you, Fräulein, I knew you were the one that she described. I just don't think that you know it yet."

He walked back over to me and took the ring, placing it back on my finger.

"Come, my dear, you need your rest."

"Alrik, I'm going to put this ring back in the box, and you can save it for Annaliese. Do you understand me?"

He ran over to the box, slamming his hand on top of it.

"No! The ring is yours, and you *will* be mine."

"Please listen to me! I am not Caprice. I am Valentine Brannigan from America, remember? I'm just here for a short time, until the bridge is repaired. I'm not staying!"

He turned around and looked at me, obviously upset as I could see the veins bulging in his forehead, and his jaw clenching. Standing only inches from my face, and holding onto my shoulders, he asked the question that I had hoped never to hear.

"Who is Valentine Brannigan?"

"I... am... Valentine Brannigan, you know that!"

He reached into his trouser pocket, and pulled out a folded piece of paper.

"According to this newspaper article that Halag found, you, Valentine Brannigan, are back in New York, getting married this coming Saturday. I am looking at the picture of you and your fiancé. You look nothing like this picture. Either she is a fraud, or you are. Something tells me that you, my dear, are an imposter, and everything that you have told me is a lie. So, tell me, who exactly are you? Are you a spy? Have you come here to steal my work?"

"Steal your work? Are you kidding me? I didn't come here to see you or your work at all! I was forced to come here, remember? Until Halag brought me here, I had never even heard of you. Since you really have nothing to do with me, and I have nothing to do with you, I demand that you let me go!"

"Fraulein …? Well that's funny, I don't even know your name … Whoever you are, you are in no position to make any demands. You say you're from America, but as far as we can tell, there is no record of anyone of your description from America traveling here. There is no one and no country looking for you. Whether you like it or not, you have become my permanent guest."

Chapter 8

THE SACRIFICE OF ESCAPE

*"You are here now. Heaven has come to me. You are the
fulfillment of my wishes and desires."*
~Alrik Richter~

My worst nightmare had become a reality. I had a

pretty good idea what had happened. After staying by my

side for the three days after my near-death experience with

Halag, Alrik was summoned to the cell where his cousin

had been placed. While there, Halag's informants delivered

the findings about the real Valentine Brannigan, complete

with the New York Times article about the upcoming

wedding of the century between the famous steel heiress

and Roland Davenport, including an entire page of

engagement photos. Just the thought of him seeing that, and

this charade that I believed I could pull off, made me feel

so stupid for my impersonation. I'm pretty sure that I went

in the wrong direction with that whole thing; no wonder

Malachi was shaking his head in shame at me. I guess I should have just given him my real name from the get-go, but it didn't feel right at the time. This whole idea of being given wisdom when I need it was very confusing.

Upon hearing the news, Alrik wanted to immediately confront me. When he came to my room and discovered that I was gone, of course it made me appear all the more guilty in his eyes. "A spy, definitely a spy!" he most certainly thought. All of this information, mixed together with the range of emotions that had obviously risen as he observed me sorting through his Purgatory Papers, multiplied by the jaunt down Caprice Lane, made him see red.

I knew what I had to do! My next move was imperative to my survival here. I had to calm him down, and it wasn't going to happen by arguing with him about staying or leaving. Adina, my pillar of wisdom, always told me that "a kind word turns away wrath." That's what needed to happen right now. I needed to calm his wrath and play along with his game until I heard from Carson, and could escape back to town.

Hateful scowls and stares like daggers flew at me like a lightning bolt to a metal rod. His cheeks were flushed and his breathing elevated as he awaited my response to his accusations. This predicament was going to send me down a path that I had hoped I would never have to submit to, but it was the only way. As I walked toward him, all I could think was, "Please forgive me, Carig."

I slowly walked over to where he was standing, looking deep into his eyes with a goal of captivating him with my seductive gaze.

"Alrik, I'm so sorry. I never meant to upset you or lie to you. The truth is, I was scared. Halag burst into the shoe store where I was shopping and started treating me like I was a criminal. I wasn't doing anything wrong, just shopping. I thought if I gave him a name of someone famous he may recognize that he would let me go, but he came in with the intention of finding and taking me because you told him to. Am I right? So in reality, you were not honest with me either. And then on top of that, you accuse me of infiltrating your home, trying to steal your secrets?"

My response made him calm down a fraction from his heightened state.

"Yes, you're right. The moment I saw you I sent Halag after you, and ordered him not to return without you."

"Well then, I'd say we're even ... maybe we can start over?"

I reached up and held each side of his face, and then ran my fingers over his mouth. While I caressed his lips, he began kissing my fingers one by one, and then I ran my hand to the back of his head and pulled his mouth towards mine, offering an unexpected encounter of our lips.

At first he seized my shoulders and pushed me away, just looking at me with anger smoldering in his eyes. But after only a few seconds, his rage melted away and he grabbed and kissed me back in a most fervent and aggressive manner. It took everything within me not to push him away and wipe the taste of him from my mouth in disgust. I was aware that it was me who instigated this toppling of dominoes, but I hated it, I hated him, and I hated that I was put in this situation. His hands slid down my shoulders, to my arms, and onto my hips, where he grasped my nightgown in an attempt to do away with the silken nuisance. Pushing me over to the table with one arm, and then with the other, in one swift movement he swept everything off the surface, including the scarlet box that violently shattered against the wall sending the Purgatory Papers flying along with it.

"Alrik! What are you doing? Your beautiful glass box, your papers!"

Deafened to my pleas, he lifted me up onto the table, making it a platform to render the most intimate part of himself and take from me what only belonged to Carig. In one quick act of passion, I watched the documents flying in all directions, validating that the Purgatory Papers that he had relied on for his salvation and his doorway to Caprice, were no longer needed. I had become his redemption.

At my words, he wildly kissed me again, and held me so tightly that I could barely move. It was as if every feeling and emotion that he had possessed since Caprice died, had right then and there been unleashed, sending him into an unchecked frenzy.

"You are here now. Heaven has come to me. *You* are the fulfillment of my wishes and desires."

I couldn't just lay there and allow his lust to go any further - I had to stop him before it was too late!

"Alrik, wait. Not like this."

"No, Fräulein, I want you now. I want you like I have never wanted anyone before. Please, please, don't ask me to stop!"

He continued moving forward, his passion being just as powerful as his anger.

"Alrik, I said no, not here. Please, just wait!"

"Wait until what? Don't ask me to wait ... no more waiting!"

"Please, Alrik, just stop - wait until we're married."

Taking a step back, he smiled like I had never seen from him until now.

"You want to marry me?"

"Yes, I want to marry you! But Alrik, I'm not Caprice, you know that right? No one, including me will ever take her place. And do you even realize that we have only known each other for a few days? This, all of this is moving *way* too fast. I think there is a lot we need to talk about first. You don't even know who I am. I think we need to get to know each other, don't you? I'm not sure what kind of women you're used to, but I don't just go around having sex with people! This may sound very cliché, but I am not that kind of girl!"

He half smiled at me, obviously not used to anyone saying no to him.

"So, if you, Fräulein, are not 'that kind of girl', why would you tell me, after only knowing me a few days, that you want to marry me? Is that what 'nice' girls do?"

Little did he know that I only said it to save myself from his advances, and to give myself more time to find a way out of here. I was confident that I could carry on this convincing charade for the one more day until I would leave with Carson and then never return.

"Well, I guess I was just thinking that you would make a wonderful husband! You have a very kind heart, and honestly, I think you're hot, so there ya go!"

Alrik laughed out loud at my comment and once again moved close to me.

"Thank you, Fräulein, for your kind words. You are remarkable, and you seem to describe the person that I desire to be. I will love you forever, no matter what! Tell me though, what do you mean when you say I'm 'hot'?"

He felt his forehead and cheeks.

"I mean, I did get rather excited and heated for sure, but no one has ever called me hot."

I guess I didn't even realize what I had said, and to whom I said it, it just came out. I chuckled under my breath, and smiled at him.

"I'm sorry, Alrik, I shouldn't have said that to you. I mean it's a good thing really. In California it means you are very handsome, you know like so good looking that you're too hot to touch, I guess?"

He was well pleased with my opinion about his looks.

"Aww, so you think I'm handsome ... you think I'm hot?"

This conversation had gone on long enough, and it was well past time to change the subject.

"So, back to getting to know one another - first of all I want you to know that I am no spy, just a traveler."

"So, Fräulein, the story you told me about having someone back home, that's not true either, right?"

Oh God, Oh God, what should I tell him? If I tell him the truth, he still won't let me go. If I lie, making him think I would be with him may cause him to ease up on the reins and give me enough space to escape.

"Well, actually, I do have someone back home, but it's nothing too serious. Besides, I'm here now, with you."

He came over and kissed me again, and as his lips touched mine he spoke words that followed his breath into my mouth.

"He's not hot like I am then? I've wanted to taste your lips from the moment I saw you. *This... us,* must happen soon. You may not know me, nor I you, but somehow my heart and soul have known you for ages. For when the eyes of my soul saw you for the first time, my blood furiously thundered through my veins, making a heart that had lain dormant for so long finally begin to beat again. So tell me, my beautiful mystery guest, what is your *real* name?"

"My name, my real name is Benidette.... Crawford. My friends call me Beni."

He wrapped his arms tightly around me, and I was afraid! Not because of actually fearing who he was, but for the unruly feelings that were stirring within him. I feared that I would be unable to manage the Pandora's Box that had been unsealed by my presence.

Just as I predicted, he became consumed by his desires and emotions, and began caressing each curve of my body through my gown, completely absorbed as his breathing once again elevated.

His soft and gentle words of love, laced with a fragrance of spice and leather, suddenly sparked a memory that had long been hidden in my mind. I knew that I recognized his face the moment I saw him. But now, as my senses stirred in unison, they brought to life what I had once thought to be the dream of a little girl, and I viewed him in a completely different light. My now vivid remembrance of a mysterious old gentleman in an overcoat was revealed before my very eyes. As if lightning struck, it all came together. The words were the glue that fused together the memory that was splintered in the corner of my mind. I now remembered where I had seen him - those eyes, that voice, the white horse. He could tell that my thoughts were elsewhere, and took a step back and looked deeply into my eyes.

"Are you alright, Fräulein?"

"Yes, I was just remembering an old friend that I met many years ago, who reminded me of you."

"Ah, I see. Well, he must have been 'hot' then, yes?"

I couldn't help but laugh at his surprising sense of humor.

"What an adorable laugh you have Benidette….Benidette."

He took my hand and kissed it, and then held it gently.

"So, you are Benidette Crawford. It's my great pleasure to finally meet you!"

"You as well, Field Marshal Richter."

It had been years, but I remembered. He was "the man at the train station." Thoughts of my encounter with the old gentleman over eighteen years ago, opened the floodgates of memories. Memories of Adina, and how it was she who intentionally brought me to meet him.

Chapter 9

THE WHITE HORSE

"Her name is Lily. She is an intelligent and mighty war horse who holds great wisdom. Keep her close. Her heart fears nothing, and she would gladly give her life to guard yours."

~Alrik Richter~

Having such a tumultuous childhood, until Adina stepped into my life that is, left certain events hidden within the confines of my mind until this very moment. Since that time, I hadn't given my youthful happenings another thought. After all, I was only seven, and those days were both challenging and wonderful at the same time. Even though I craved the attention and love of my father, I was constantly left disappointed by him. His selfish existence revolved around nursing his own wounds of loss and pain, paying no attention to those of his only daughter.

That September, he informed me in his usual insensitive way - as if he were giving information to one of his employees rather than his daughter - that he would be traveling through Europe for the next three months for work, and would be leaving me with my nanny during that time. I pleaded with him to take me with him, but he responded to my tears with a quick reminder that things had changed, life was hard, and I needed to grow up. I begged him to at least let me go to Bar Rousse and stay with Adina. He quickly shut that door, with a stern "not a chance!"

My nanny at the time, Miss Becky, was kind and wonderful, but when my father requested that she take care of me for the next three months, she knew what needed to be done, for my sake. After all, what kind of father would leave his daughter alone with the nanny for the holidays? She refused, telling him her plans wouldn't permit such a commitment since she would be going to stay with her daughter during that time. To this day, I believe that Adina and her ever-present generosity was somehow behind this arrangement. Becky relied on every penny she earned, and it was very unlike her to turn down extra work. Her refusal left no time for my father to find another nanny, and no other option except to send me out to stay with Adina. At that point, I really didn't know her very well, but this first experience with her, Mari, Killen, Uncle Wil, Aunt Angelina, and of course, my real home, Bar Rousse, Maine would be the beginning of the happiest memories of my life. Quite honestly, it was the *real* beginning of my life.

Adina made all of the arrangements with my third-grade teacher, promising to tutor me through October, November, and December. On our way to the airport that day, there were no words of love from my father or even the slightest hint of heartache. Never once did he mention that he would miss me or count the days until we were together again. Instead, he was consumed by one phone call after another, at which time I was warned not to make any noisy interruptions, "or else." When he did throw a word in my direction, it was only to speak harshly about Adina and

295

how she had a lot of nerve trying to butt into his life. But I paid no attention to him. I was excited and couldn't wait to see her again, and to see Bar Rousse for the first time.

All I had ever known was Southern California, and I couldn't even imagine this new place that seemed like another world. I only knew it by the few photos pasted in a book that Adina had sent me. Arriving in Bar Rousse made me feel like Dorothy Gale stepping out of a black and white existence, and into one filled with life and color.

It was ironic, both the first and last time I arrived in Bar Rousse was in October, the month of the esteemed Catwalk Masquerade Ball. Both times were not only memorable occasions for me but gloriously life-changing. For a little girl who was raised without a mother, watching Adina in all of her glamorous splendor preparing for the ball was such a thrill. Images of her stunning gold lamé gown flashed through my mind and made me smile a bit. She was her own person, and it was always her intention to stand out from the normal black and white attire of the evening. Oh how I begged her to let me go with her that night! If she could have, she would have, but this event and all of the uppity-ups wouldn't stand for it. She promised me though, that someday I would get to go, and when that day came, she would make a most unbelievable dress for me to wear - which she most certainly did. The night I attended the Catwalk Ball, she not only fulfilled her promise but it was that night that I fell in love with Carig. Even now I could see him standing there in his tuxedo with eyes as green as my gown.

That Halloween was the first I had ever known; filled with childlike fun, just as it should be. Making me long for the next October, *or anything* that would include Adina. Until that point, I had only known this night of Hallow's Eve confined to a gated community, saturated with the rich and elite who panicked over the idea of children walking on their grass. Costumes were but a

297

contest between overbearing parents with the goal of creating cookie cutter ensembles, no weightier than a bunch of paper dolls, and completely absent of imagination. But this Halloween was quite different than any I had known - it was carefree and magical.

A few days before the big night, Killen drove me to the Farmer's Market on the outskirts of town. As we pulled up to this colorful fall garden filled with acres of vegetables and scarecrows, he put me in a wheelbarrow and told me that I had now become the Pumpkin Seer, whose job was to choose just the right pumpkins to display on Halloween night. Heeding his instructions to watch and listen carefully as we wheeled through the pumpkin patch, only selecting pumpkins that called out my name, filled me with wonder and curiosity. I just giggled and told Killen that he was so silly, that pumpkins couldn't talk.

"Aw, you betcha they can, Lass! These are no ordinary pumpkins! These here are Harvest Pumpkins.

When I was a lad, there was many a scary night when the glens were cloaked in fog so thick ye could cut it with a knife. But lo and behold, when the skulls of the harrowing gourds were aglow, they shone like the sun through the gloom. Nothin' could get us while they flamed. They held a great power that will protect us on the night of All Saints - keepin' the bad spirits away from our home. Now lass, we need a barrowful to keep the lands safe. So you stop talkin', and start listenin'. Not with only yer ears, but with yer soul, and tell me which ones. Ok then?"

For hours I would put my ear up to the pumpkins and close my eyes tightly, listening for them to call my name. As I pointed them out, Killen would gather them up, placing them carefully in the cart. His belief in these harvest pumpkins was so convincing that I believed it too, and to this day I can actually remember hearing the quiet whisperings of the pumpkins calling out my name with hopes of being chosen as the centerpiece guardians of

299

Adina's lands. By the time we were done the barrow was piled high with pumpkins, and I would proudly sit on top of the dozens of soon-to-be jack-o-lanterns.

Once we returned home, Killen and Mari began the grueling process of cleaning and carving the symbols of protection. Not only were pumpkins used to guard the house, but in addition, turnips were hollowed out and placed on the window sills. Never for one minute was I afraid that an evil spirit would ever come near our home. Killen made sure that we were safe.

The morning of Halloween, Adina took me into town to Uncle Wil's store. Wil loved Halloween, and had an entire section of his store filled with all sorts of vintage masks and costumes that he had collected over the years. Uncle Wil was just a big kid himself who had fun playing jokes on others more than anyone I knew. It was his goal to scare as many people as possible on this day by wearing the scariest and most grotesque mask he could find. All throughout the day he would hide behind the rows of goods, popping out at the most unexpected moments in order to make the biggest impact possible. Poor Mrs. Elizabeth Pennycook with her nicely stacked handbasket filled with groceries, nearly had a heart attack when he snuck up behind her as she was sorting through the sweet potatoes.

His fun was simple but thrilling, and I loved every minute of it. Aside from his array of masks, from the prettiest of princesses to the most grotesque demons, pirates, and fairies, he had boxes upon boxes of clothes and costumes of every kind. The cases of orderly disorder were located at the opposite end of anything normal, and the topsy-turviness of it all became my playground. Although I liked the idea of being a beautiful princess, and even pretending to be Adina at the Catwalk, I was drawn to the mask of an old wrinkled woman, mixed it with a long red skirt, white blouse, and black corset, and wielded a broom handle for a sword. I became an old pirate woman. To this day, that was by far the best Halloween I had, or would ever have. During those three months, I fell in love with Bar Rousse and Adina. Along with Wil and Angelina, Killen and Mari, I had found my family. Each of them loved me unconditionally, and when Carig came along, he made my family complete.

The day after Thanksgiving, Adina woke me up early with the surprise of a train ride to New York City. The weather had turned cold, but that was not going to keep us from shopping. She bundled me up in a black and burgundy tweed coat and matching hat that Adina, of course, had made specially for me. On the way to the train station, it started to snow - something I had never seen before. The beauty created during the fall and winter in Bar Rousse, made me a lover of these two seasons.

The ancient-looking train station blanketed in white reminded me of an old movie, something rather mysterious filmed in black and white, with steam rising up from beneath the great belly of the locomotive. Boarding the train, we walked down a narrow aisle until we arrived at our seats. Adina placed me on a booster seat by the window so I wouldn't miss a thing. I didn't know it yet, but this would mark the first of our many shopping adventures in New York together. Who would have known that in two short years I would be living at a boarding school in the "Big Apple," and Adina would take this exact train there to visit me on a regular basis?

After a short ride, we arrived at one of the stops along the way. Most people who were traveling to New York stayed on the train, waiting to once again start moving. But not us.

"Come along, Benidette, there is someone who wants to meet you."

I asked her who it was, but she didn't answer me. I may have only been a little girl, but I knew enough to know that the only people I knew in this area were in Bar Rousse, yet there was someone who wanted to meet me. I was quite curious about who this stranger might be, and what their interest was in me. She told me it would be a very quick stop, since the train would only be there for a few minutes.

As Adina and I departed the train and stepped onto the platform, I watched as she looked all around her, obviously not spotting the person we were waiting for. But then in the distance, I saw a tall man in a hat and overcoat slowly walking towards us. I held Adina's hand a little tighter, the closer he came. I was scared because I didn't know who he was, and wondered why he wanted to see me. There wasn't a lot that I remember about that man except his tired blue eyes, his wrinkly face, and his unusual accent.

He knelt down before me and said, "So, you are Benidette Crawford, it is my great pleasure to finally meet you!"

He extended his hand to shake mine, and then took my hand and kissed it lightly. He was the first person who had ever kissed my hand. I asked him why he talked so funny, and he told me it was because he was from a place far away where people talk a little differently.

I then wanted to know the name of the place he was from. His eyebrows furrowed and he sadly said, "Friedlich, in Germany - very, very far away."

I felt uneasy in his presence as his gaze never left mine. I kept looking up at Adina, not knowing what to say. He then reached into his coat and pulled out a white horse, hand carved out of wood, and handed it to me.

"This is for you, Fräulein. Her name is Lily. She is an intelligent and mighty war horse who holds great wisdom. Keep her close. Her heart fears nothing, and she would gladly give her life to guard yours."

Looking up at him, I smiled. He was the first man that I could ever remember speaking to me as if he cared about me. "Thank you, sir. She's so pretty, but my name is Beni not Fraulein."

He chuckled at my reply.

"Yes, you are most certainly Beni. Goodbye, Benidette. I hope to see you again someday."

Looking at Adina, he tipped his hat, told her that he was forever grateful, and I watched as he turned around and walked away. There may have been more that he said to me, but that was all that I could remember. Now I knew, that kindly old man with the white horse was Alrik Richter, the man standing before me now!

After reminiscing about the memory of my train station encounter with the older version of Alrik, I had an entirely new perspective of him. The man before me now had blue eyes that still danced when he smiled, and the only lines on his face were the appealing dimples that were far from being a flaw. All I knew was that at some point in his future he would figure out that I was from another time, and would search for me as a child. That still left the question however, of whether or not I would ever make it home, or if I would forever be here in this time with a man who was not my husband. At this point, I couldn't let myself think too much on it. I had to stay positive and know and have faith that the Tempus Vector brought me here for a reason, and would once again get me back home.

Alrik stood close to me, holding my shoulders and caressing my arms.

"I love you, Benidette! Benidette, Benidette, that name suits you, Valentine never did. Tell me you love me too - I need to hear you say it!"

I couldn't stand this. I didn't want to say it, because I didn't love him. The struggle within me was excruciating! As a matter of fact, I felt fury rather than love in my heart. I hated my calling; I hated the Tempus Vector; and if I could ever get back home, I promised myself that I would never leave again. This was it. Nothing was worth this pool of lies that I found myself drowning in! How would I ever be able to look Carig in the eye? He would never understand. Even I didn't understand. I knew though that Carig trusted me, and would know that I'd only do what was necessary to get home.

Escaping was my number one priority. I had to keep my head above water until then, which would mean making this whole charade work. If I didn't transform myself into a believable character, one who loved this stranger, I feared that I would be trapped here forever. I was counting on Carson to come through for me, but until that happened this act would have to be flawless, every part of it.

Remembering the instruction of my theater teacher, Miss Paszkowski, "Wrap your mind, your heart, and your soul around your character. Become your character so deeply that you practically forget who you really are! Convince your audience as if your life depended on it, as if they are a jury deciding your fate! Only then will you be a star that outshines all of the others." I knew that my heart belonged only to Carig, and this was only survival, nothing more. If the tables were turned, I would want him to do whatever was necessary to come back to me.

"Who am I? Who am I?" I thought to myself. "I am Benidette Crawford in 1940 Germany, standing before a man who says he loves me, and needs me to love him back. Right now, I am here, and will never get back if I don't become what he wants me to be."

I closed my eyes, putting my hand on his chest and inhaled so deeply that I almost choked with the words that came out of my mouth.

"I love you, Alrik! I've been trying to push you away, but I can't do it anymore!"

It was done. I had said the words out loud that he so desperately wanted to hear, and he believed me. My execution was flawless, putting him at ease and making him feel free to reveal his heart to me. Funny, saying it wasn't nearly as difficult as I thought it might be. For some unknown reason, I couldn't help but care very deeply for him as well. He had a heart that would be very easy to love. "When Caprice died, my heart seemed to have stopped beating; like it had turned to dust inside of me. But you Benidette, have made my dead heart beat again."

It was difficult to comprehend the words that he was saying to me; he hardly knew me. I felt that he was most likely in love with the idea, or even the look, of me, and he wasn't holding anything back. I couldn't deny that Alrik was charming, and had a gift for saying all of the right things. Even the strongest and most dedicated individual would have a difficult time ignoring him. His allure went much deeper than his charm, and he was exceptionally attractive in every way. With every word he spoke, I had to make a conscious effort not to permit him to lure me into joining him in his enchanting notions.

I felt that I had been fighting a battle since the moment I got here, but now it had turned into a war for my soul and my allegiance. Clearly, there was a devil on one shoulder whispering that it was ok to forsake what I knew was right, and on the other was an angel reminding me who I really was and whispering echos of Carig's name in my ear. While in front of me an attack had commenced with weapons of charm and tenacity, like thunder rumbling across the heavens, the candidness of Alrik's incredible words of love, with eyes that looked right through me, left me searching for a stronghold of my own.

Aside from the guilt of kissing another man, I felt horrible at the hurt that I would inevitably cause Alrik;

wounding his kind heart. And then my abandonment would most probably ruin him completely.

"Alrik, I think I need to lay down - I feel a little dizzy. Do you mind?"

"Not at all, Fräulein. Let me help you. But before I take you back to your room, please ..."

Alrik got down on one knee in front of me, with the ruby ring in his hand.

"Please, please, be my wife!"

He took my hand, and slipped the ruby ring onto my finger.

"It's too much, Alrik, I don't need such a ring. This belonged to Caprice. Please, save it for Annaliese - really."

When I took it off and handed it back to him, he stood up, looking straight into my eyes.

"Someday if you like, you may pass it down to her, but my beautiful American girl, it is yours, and it was meant to be on your finger. All I care about is that you are by my side always; that you will be my wife. So, Benidette," he said in fervent desperation, "marry me!"

"Yes, Alrik, I will be your wife."

Chapter 10

THE RIDE

"The sun, now sitting on the water, made me miss Carig terribly, and wish that I was home. Everything beautiful reminded me of him." ~**Benidette Hammell~**

Alrik was so delighted at my response, that he picked me up and swung me around.

"You have made me so very happy, Fräulein! Thank you for saying yes. I promise, I promise to spend the rest of my life making you happy!"

I was not feeling the same enthusiasm as the blood rushed quickly from my face, and I became lightheaded and nauseous.

"I think I'm gonna be sick!"

I couldn't take it anymore! I was trapped in a place where I didn't want to be, had almost been killed by strangulation, and now I felt like I was dying from the inside out, choking on my own deceit and lies. It was too much. Before I even knew that I was going down, everything went dark, and Alrik caught me before I hit the floor.

I woke up to the sensation of a cool cloth bathing my face, and the soothing sound of humming.

"Oh yes. You ok-k now, yes? I be back, Fräulein!"

Hildegard had only one speed which was "panic mode." I could feel the anxiety radiating from her, simply being next to her. As my personal attendant, she had obviously been put in charge of nursing me back to health. The moment I awoke, she quickly sprinted out of the room to inform the master of the house that I was awake. A few minutes later, he glanced around the corner, standing at the doorway looking over at me. When I opened my eyes, he was the first thing that I saw.

"How are you feeling, my love?"

Slowly sitting up and looking out the balcony window, I wondered how long I had been out. Time was ticking. I could feel it in my soul.

"I'm fine. What time is it?"

Alrik grinned and chuckled.

"Why, do you have plans?"

"No, I just didn't know how long I've been asleep."

"You have been asleep for only a few hours, but there is still much day to be had, unless you are still feeling poorly and prefer to stay in bed."

The thought of staying in this room, or even this house, all day did not appeal to me at all.

"How does some fresh air sound?"

"Fresh air? What did you have in mind?"

"Yes, well, I was thinking ... if you're up to it, that we could go for a ride."

"A ride, as in a car?"

"Well, I was really thinking that Atlas needs a good run. You can ride with me, if you're not feeling well enough to handle your own horse. You mentioned that you had ridden before, are you accomplished?"

"Yes, I can ride, and I think I can handle my own horse."

He had no idea, but was soon to find out, that I was an excellent rider. At the Yardley Academy I competed in endurance riding. Many a long weekend was spent riding through the hills of the Brannigans' vast property, and I soon became the one to beat.

"That sounds like a brilliant idea!"

"Very well. I will have breakfast and riding clothes sent up at once, and I will meet you at the front of the house at 1:00."

A few minutes later, Hildegard came in and concocted a pungent bath of salts and oils that most likely appealed to Alrik, but were definitely *not* my cup of tea. They were far too sweet for my taste.

"You don't have to put those in the water."

"Yes, okay-k, I must, thank you!"

I could tell that she was dead set on *not* disobeying any orders that were given to her, so I just smiled and thanked her.

"You go, take off clothes. I help you bathe!"

"No, really, I don't need help bathing!"

Again she looked at me as if to say, "Please don't argue or I will get in trouble. Just let me do my job!"

"Ok, let me get undressed."

She was clearly scared, and I didn't want to be the cause of any additional stress, or I feared that she would explode before my very eyes. I went behind the screen, took off my gown, and walked out and submerged myself in the lovely but candy-coated bath that Hildegard had worked so hard to make perfect. I closed my eyes, hoping to open them and be in my own bath in Bar Rousse filled with rose petals from Adina's garden. Yet when I did, Hildegard was standing there staring at me waiting for confirmation that the bath was acceptable.

"Wunderbar! Hildegard, danke!"

She gave me a huge smile, grabbing the sponge and bathing my back and arms, and then left me alone for a few minutes while she prepared my riding clothes. Infused by the aroma of sweet peas, it was difficult to think straight, let alone fathom that this time last week I was just about to marry Carig, the love of my life. I missed him so much, and with each passing day I felt as if I was drifting further and further away from him, feeling so empty without him. Only he could fill this ever-growing void inside of me.

"Hildegard, I think I'm finished. May I have a towel, please?"

She ran over holding a large fluffy towel and then threw it around my shoulders. As I dried myself off, she stood there ready with a white bathrobe for me to wear while I ate some breakfast. Still difficult, almost impossible to swallow, compliments of Halag, I was only able to eat a few bites, although the eucalyptus tea was soothing to my bruised throat. I hated feeling this way. Between sleep deprivation and lack of food, I felt weak and vulnerable. While competing at Yardley, at the end of a ride, exhausted and feeling that I couldn't go on, my coach would tell me that this was the time to be mentally tough and to not allow how I feel to dictate how I would perform.

Hildegard had laid out my riding clothes which were, to say the least, not exactly what I was used to. The camel-colored riding pants for one thing, were a bit baggier than what I normally wore, but along with the tailored

320

houndstooth jacket, white blouse, and yellow tie, it was

quite sophisticated and stunning. Slipping on the black

riding boots that I am sure once belonged to Caprice, I was

finally ready and made my way downstairs.

Chapter 11

PIGEONHOLE

"It's my Pigeonhole - this is where Papa says I'm safe."
~Annaliese Richter~

Arriving at the bottom of the staircase, I heard

sweet music coming from a room hidden beneath the flight.

When I looked inside, there sat Annaliese singing out loud

as she was joyfully involved in her own little world of

accessorizing her truest companions. The nook was

completely filled with dolls. Dolls of all shapes and sizes,

clothes, and accessories. It was the ultimate playhouse. She

seemed to be quite comfortable in that miniature alcove, as

if she spent many an hour there. The Richter estate was the

size of a hotel, and yet Annaliese chose this small safe

cubby beneath the stairs as her locale of choice. The entire

octagon-shaped room was covered in white paneling from

floor to ceiling. The surface of the upper section exploded

with chiseled thickets and flowering vines that had

322

seemingly barged in from the outer gardens. The bottom

panels were in window-like sections, enchanted recesses

that revealed colorful fields of painted florals. A long

wooden dowel extended from one end of the room to the

other, packed tightly with satin hangers, draped with tiny

clothing. Rows of shelving were stacked to the left of the

door, all covered with petite-sized shoes in every color

under the rainbow. Practically every inch of the faux

greenhouse was filled with Annaliese's most precious items

and toys, including two rose-colored hammock cradles that

were suspended from the ceiling. But there was one

particular item that stood out from all the rest. A miniature

carousel, that was an exact duplicate of the one that stood

in the back of the house. These small prancing horses

became a hazy daydream of that memento once held. This

oddly shaped hideaway beneath the staircase was like being

in another world.

Her bright eyes widened when she saw me standing

at the door. In one quick leap, she jumped up and grabbed

my hand, pulling me into her world. Plopping down atop a

large pink satin pillow, she patted the area right beside her,

instructing me to sit and join her in this fantasy world of

dolls. She made me responsible for dressing Anna with the

long brunette hair and deep blue eyes, insisting that Anna

and I looked just alike and she was now my baby. Of

course Annaliese took care of Inga, the doll with golden

locks and blue topaz eyes. She was filled with stories about

her adventures with Inga, and spoke passionately about

their close calls, running from the witch and into the safety

of her magical garden. Each word she spoke and every

expression that dawned from her dancing eyes reminded

me of her father. I related to her constant story-filled

chatter, only my tales originated from the people and places

in the photos hanging on Adina's wall. Annaliese made her

way to the rack of beautifully handmade tiny dresses,

324

choosing a blue one for Inga, and a yellow one for Anna.

We sat there together dressing our dolls, and brushing their

hair. She was in her own world, telling a story one moment

and singing a song the next. She seemed to love the fact

that someone was taking the time on their own initiative to

sit and play with her.

"My goodness Annaliese, you have a beautiful

voice, and you speak English so well. I wish that I spoke

German half as well as you speak English. Who taught you

to speak English?"

She stopped and looked at me shyly, out of the

corner of her eye, "It's a secret. I have lots of secrets! Do

you know how to keep a secret?"

I was more than intrigued by her response.

"Yes, I am very good at keeping secrets. Would you

like to tell me yours?"

"It's *secrets,* Fräulein. I have more than one!"

"Ok, Annaliese, I would love to hear your *secrets!*"

"Well, first sing me a song!"

"Alright, what song would you like for me to sing?"

Annaliese shrugged her shoulders, as if to say she really didn't care... just sing! The only song that came to my mind was Adina's favorite that she always played on her record player, but quite honestly, I wasn't even sure it had been written yet. I guess it didn't matter, Annaliese would never know.

"Gonna take a sentimental journey, gonna set my heart at ease, gonna make a sentimental journey, to review old memories. I got my bag, I got my reservation, spent each dime I could afford, like a child in wild anticipation, I long to hear that 'all aboard.'"

I couldn't help it, but with each word of the song that came out of my mouth, tears followed. I seemed to have a love/hate relationship with this golden oldie. On one

326

hand, I loved it, it was Adina's theme song. On the other hand, it was a bitter reminder that she was gone from my life forever, and I missed her more than words could say. As I continued singing, the words of the song came alive like never before, and I slowly realized that due to my travels, it spoke to me in an entirely different way than it ever had before. This was not only Adina's song, it was her life. A sentimental journey. But now it was mine. I had now started down this road of sentimental journeys that would change my life forever. Until this very moment, I didn't understand how much the experience was weighing on my heart. No wonder Malachi never married, and Adina never remarried. The road I'm on would require actions that certainly would not encourage wedded bliss; the sacrifice would be too great for anyone to overlook. My heart was breaking inside as I sang.

Annaliese could see that I was upset, and she came over and adoringly brushed my hair.

"What's wrong with your singer box, Fräulein? Did you hurt it? It's ok, you don't have to keep singing. I'll tell you my secrets."

Between my tears and my beat up vocal cords, the song didn't come out very well, and Annaliese could tell that something was wrong. My hoarse, raspy voice sounded like I'd been a chain smoker for the last fifty years.

"Well......I have two tutors for English. One of them teaches me to speak and write English, and the other one teaches me how Americans live. Papa says maybe one day we will live in America, and he didn't want me to feel different and not get along with people who live there."

"Why would you move to America?"

Once again she shrugged her shoulders, probably not even knowing the real reason behind why they would go.

"Well, Annaliese, I'm sure American girls would love you! I mean, I'm an American girl, and I like you!"

"I like you too, Fräulein, and I am very happy that you will be my new mother!"

I couldn't believe that Alrik had told her. Now I wouldn't only be disappointing Alrik, but also Annaliese. I know how it felt to lose a mother, and the hope that Adina brought into my life gave me purpose. When I left, this young girl would have no one.

"Annaliese, you have a wonderful father - he loves you very much!"

"I know! Papa doesn't call me Annaliese, he has a special name for me."

"Really, what is it?"

"He calls me his little Pigeon."

"Pigeon? I like that name!"

She smiled and told me that this little room was her very own special place.

"It's my Pigeonhole - this is where Papa says I'm safe."

"Is there a reason you're not safe?"

Again, she shrugged her shoulders, either not knowing the answer to my question, or choosing not to answer. She was very smart for one so young.

"So, Fräulein, do you want to know my other secret?"

"Yes, tell me."

"I have a magic door that takes me to a beautiful place, and when I go through the door, my Papa said that even though I will go through a long dark tunnel, when I get to the other side, there will be a beautiful garden, a secret garden, and that he would be waiting for me on the other side."

Her talk of a secret door and garden, sparked my
curiosity, but I tried to stay cool so that she would tell me
more

"What a wonderful thing, Annaliese. How kind of
your papa!"

"Yes, he is my favorite person in the whole wide
world. He loves me no matter what."

"I can tell that he does. So, do you want to tell me
the rest of your secret?"

"Hmmmm, that's all the secrets I have!"

"Well, I mean, where is this magic door?"

Annaliese pointed to the wall where the rack of
shoes hung.

"Over there. Do you want to see me open it?"

"Well, if you want to."

She walked over to her racks of shoes, and on the bottom shelf was a small pair of wooden clogs. When she stepped down on the pair, they lowered in unison, causing the loud clicking noise of an inner latch to unhitch from inside the wall. In turn, the entire panel swung wide open revealing Annaliese's secret corridor. The engineering of this secret get-away was brilliant, and perfectly concealed beneath the bands of shoes. No one would ever know this airtight and seamfree panel was a doorway. It was obvious that it was created as an undetectable escape route, something that Alrik believed may someday be necessary. All that I could see as I examined the web-filled opening, were stairs extending straight up and curving to the right, then total darkness. Just as Annaliese said, it was dim and narrow, a very scary course of escape for such a little girl. No wonder he had to reassure her of a beautiful garden at the end. This so called "magic door" was a private passage that most likely led to the outside of the house. Alrik had enough wisdom and insight to know that he needed an escape plan in place if the upcoming war took a wrong turn.

"This is very special! So, you've never been through the magic door?"

"No, but Papa said if any bad people ever came in the house, that I should go through it and he would be on the other side waiting for me."

I quickly closed it, and picked Annaliese up and held her.

"You know what, Annaliese, everything will be all right. You have a wonderful papa, and he will always make sure that you are safe. I can tell that he loves you so much."

Annaliese loved to be held, and hugged me back so tightly. Hearing someone clear their throat, I looked over and saw that Alrik had been standing there watching our interaction.

"Come, my love! Our horses are on their way."

He walked over and kissed Annaliese on the forehead.

"My little Pigeon, we will be back very soon."

Before I left Annaliese and her room of dolls, I noticed how happy she was watching the two of us together. It was a look of contentment from a little girl who longed for both a mommy and a daddy. I felt bad as it seemed that she was often left behind, most often in this room.

"I will see you later, beautiful girl!"

The moment we walked out of the room, Alrik turned and kissed and held me as if he would never let go.

"Thank you for being so kind to Annaliese. Like her father, she already loves you ... she has struggled greatly not having a mother, but now you are here. Everything will be different now. Everything will be perfect, my love. Worry about nothing!"

Oh, if he only knew the things that were worrying me and what was to come, he wouldn't be quite so optimistic. After hearing Annaliese talk about America, and seeing the escape her father had created for her, I honestly didn't believe that Alrik was very confident in the leadership that was taking over his country and what the future held. People who believe fully in their cause don't create escape plans as he had so strategically designed.

Being met by an uncharacteristically warm day seemed to rejuvenate my weariness, and the sun shining on my face as we walked outside was glorious. In the distance, I could see two gentlemen leading saddled horses in our direction. The two royal-looking stallions were just like the pictures in the hallway that led to the Hall of Caprice, one white and one black. Alrik could see the curiosity in my face.

"Is that Chariot? I thought he was gone!"

"No Fräulein, this is Lily. She is now your horse."

"My horse - Lily?"

I instantly fell deep in thought, recalling once again the old gentleman at the train station with eyes filled with pain and joy. After all those years, he felt the need to meet me, and for the second time, give to me a horse named Lily.

I could see Alrik's mouth moving, but couldn't hear a word he was saying.

"Beni, Beni, are you alright my dear? Is something wrong?"

"No, sorry, I just remembered something."

Hoping he wouldn't ask about the scenario that had just played out in my mind, I turned my attentions to his noble stallion.

"And this must be Atlas?"

"Yes, this is my faithful Atlas."

I slowly approached Lily to introduce myself. As I extended my palm towards her face, she curiously captured my scent. As she nuzzled her head against my cheek, I couldn't help but to stroke her velvety white coat. We were immediate friends, almost as if we had known one another all our lives.

"Oh, you are so beautiful, Lily! Believe it or not my 'white war horse,' this is not the first time we've met. You and I are kindred spirits! But you are far more beautiful than your wooden look-alike."

She continued nudging her head in my direction, not wanting the comforting strokes to stop.

"Ok, Lily, of course!"

It was apparent that Atlas was protective of her, as he was uncertain about my presence, and was whinnying distressfully.

"Hello boy, don't you worry. I'll take good care of your girl!"

Putting my foot into the stirrup, I hoisted myself up onto the saddle with some unexpected assistance from Alrik as he gave me a swift push, seeming more than happy to make contact with my backside. I turned around with a surprised look on my face, but he seemed quite pleased with himself, grinning at me with an ornery expression of accomplishment. As Alrik mounted Atlas, we casually made our descent down the long driveway, making our way out to the forest which would lead to the open pastures of the Richter property. Once we had arrived at the edge of the grasses, Alrik asked once again if I was sure that I felt well enough to ride. I looked at him and smiled.

"Just try to keep up - hah!"

At that moment, Lily and I took off so quickly that we left the boys in our dust. Lily was an amazing beast and wicked fast. Alrik was more than pleased at my riding skills, and I was sure that he would by no means allow us to stay in the lead. But I had no intention of allowing the two of them to catch up and take the first position either. The grassy lands seem to go on forever. It was beautiful, and I felt better already. Somehow, out here in the fresh air, riding Lily, everything seemed ok. I felt empowered.

I was feeling quite accomplished at our ranking, until I realized after looking behind me that Alrik was holding back and allowing Lily and I to stay in front. It was obvious by the pained look on the face of Atlas that he was very unhappy to be curbed.

Impressed by what was ahead, I slowed down to a trot as I came face to face with an enormous and stately oak tree. This grand specimen was clearly hundreds of years old. But even more spectacular was the crystal blue lake in the distance. Something so amazing couldn't be ignored. I had to stop and take it all in. A few minutes later Alrik rode up to my side with a satisfied look on his face. With a huge grin, I teased the second-place horseman about riding so slowly.

"What took you so long, Tex? You ride as slow as molasses!"

Coming up closer alongside Lily, Alrik surprised me with his response.

"My dear Fräulein, it was my intention to stay behind you the entire time."

"And why is that, sir?"

"One simple reason really - the view!"

I tried to just discard his very male chauvinist comment, and change the subject.

"What is this place? Where are we?"

It truly took my breath away - so much so, that I almost didn't believe that it was real. I likened it to an enhanced photograph, but it was real.

"Alrik, I can't imagine that heaven could be more beautiful than this!"

Hanging from the limbs of the tree were silver lanterns attached with long pieces of silver chain that glimmered in the sun, making it appear that lights were raining down from the sky.

"Well, Fräulein, you are very close. This place is called Kristall Himmel. It means Crystal Heaven."

"Wow, what a perfect name! Thank you for bringing me here! I'm totally blown away!"

Alrik laughed. "Blown away, huh? I have never heard anyone talk the way you do. Is that how they speak in California?!"

"Well, honestly, I'm a little unique all the way around. So, do you come here often?"

"There was a time after Caprice died that I came here and stayed for weeks. It was the only place where I felt peace. I never wanted to go back to that house again. If not for Annaliese I would have never returned at all."

As we drew closer and dismounted our horses, we encountered a crew of servants awaiting our arrival, all of them dressed in white and completely at our beck and call. I was amazed that everywhere we went, even in the middle of this haven, servants were available and ready to wait on Alrik and take care of any need he may have.

A small table for two had been set up on the edge of the lake, and the tree was surrounded by white quilted spreads and dozens of pillows in all shapes and sizes.

"Hmmm?"

"What is it, Fräulein?"

"I thought we were just taking a leisurely ride - an adventure to see where the wind would take us, but you planned this whole thing, didn't you? Are you trying to seduce me?"

He smiled at me, answering with an alluring expression and crystal blue eyes the color of the lake.

"I, I only wanted everything to be perfect for you, that's all - and maybe trying to seduce you a little!"

"Oh, that's all, huh? Well, Field Marshal Richter, it would be difficult not to be wooed by beauty such as this."

"Oh my love, you have seen nothing yet. Come!"

Gently pressing on the small of my back, he guided me to the dining table which was set with colorful china that matched the bouquet of exotic wildflowers brimming over the edges of a silver vase. In a million years, how could he have known that these are my favorite flowers? I could tell that he would have never chosen such a bloom based on his own likes. He struck me more of a *refined* flower kind of guy, preferring a rose or gardenia. Simply a coincidence, I'm sure.

Within moments Lily and Atlas, along with all of the attendants, had left us. I had no idea where they had all scurried off to so quickly, but even more concerning was the fact that we were now alone, which was an unfortunate situation. Alrik was aggressive and accustomed to getting what he wanted; nothing like Carig. He wanted me and was going to great lengths to make sure that his efforts were successful. Purity and integrity were not on his resume, definitely not qualities that he lived by. Rather, doing whatever he had to do to get whatever he wanted was his calling card. Bringing me to this place in all its beauty was his idea of a brilliant attempt at the highest level.

"We will dine at sunset. Come, you should rest."

With no warning, he scooped me up into his arms, and carried me over to the aged oak, then laid me down atop the soft white blankets. He quickly positioned himself directly above me, placing a hand on each side of my head. Immediately sneaking out of his reach, I popped up into a sitting position.

As I looked around, minding my surroundings, I found that I had been placed in the center of his well-calculated lovers' lair, not unlike a monarch butterfly caught in a spider's web. He wasted no time edging closer to me, and then he lightly brushed the hair off of my neck, kissing my cheek and my ear. Not saying a word, he turned my head and gently kissed my lips. I slightly shifted away from him, looking out over the lake, trying to think of something, of anything, to keep him away from me.

"Alrik, do you suppose that water is very cold? I was thinking that I would like to go in and get my feet wet."

345

"Well, I think you may have to find that out for yourself ... allow me take your boots off."

Running his hands down my thighs to my boots, he slipped them off one at a time. Trying to ignore his forwardness, I stood up and pulled the leg of my pants up off my ankles, so not to get them wet. I took off my jacket, and untucked my blouse, then headed towards the water. Thankfully, Alrik didn't follow me in, and I could finally be alone; I only prayed that the water wasn't too cold.

I didn't want to be here, but it didn't seem to matter what I wanted, I felt completely bombarded with unwelcome circumstances. All I knew was that I had to get back to the house and prepare to leave with Carson. A more urgent matter at hand, however, was this - I was here, alone with Alrik which was a huge problem, and I had to create a way to pass the time without getting myself in trouble. I held my face and experienced a brief episode of tears, followed by a spontaneous laugh as I wondered out loud if he would be interested in an endless game of Scrabble.

The water was unbelievably clear and inviting, looking as though it had never been touched by man before. I knelt down, skimming it with my fingers, and quickly discovered that it was freezing cold, so much so, that I expected to see pieces of an iceberg floating by. I'm certain that when I asked Alrik if the water was chilly, he already knew the answer, but he just wanted to watch my reaction as I stepped into the frigid bath. I stepped one foot in, and its insanely cold temperature actually burned like fire, but I continued with no hesitation - no reaction, so as not to give Alrik any satisfaction.

The sun, now sitting on the water, made me miss Carig terribly, and wish that I was home. Everything beautiful reminded me of him. Mesmerized by the general splendor, and unaware of how much time had passed, I didn't realize that my feet had gone completely numb. But somehow, frozen feet seemed a better alternative than returning to Alrik's continuous flirtations; I just didn't want to fight that battle. His advances were surely going to turn into a situation that I couldn't control, and would regret for the rest of my life.

"Benidette! Come back! It's getting cold!" I heard him repeat several times over.

But even when he called out my name, I didn't turn around. I just couldn't do it anymore. I wanted to go home, and I once again teared up. For some reason, this whole experience had turned me into a blubbering ninny! Normally I never cried over anything, but recent events had left me teetering on the edge of irrepressible despair. One thing was for sure, I didn't want him to see me crying. Maybe I would just stay in here forever. I wondered if Adina ever struggled like this.

"Oh Adina, I've messed everything up! Just as you warned me *not* to lose myself, I can feel that I'm slipping away."

"Who are you talking to, my dear?"

I turned around and not only saw Alrik standing in the water with me but all of the lanterns in the tree had been lit.

"What is it, Benidette?"

"Alrik, your advances are making me uncomfortable; they're inappropriate. You may feel you know me, but you don't, and I don't know you. You're acting as though we've been acquainted for years. People don't just jump into a lifelong commitment on a whim. I need time to get to know you. Furthermore, I'm unsure about how things work around here ... I have no doubt that women are lined up to have sex with you whenever you want, but I'm not like them! And honestly, I would rather

349

stay out here in this freezing cold water than to worry about what you're going to do next."

"I thought you wanted me to. You are, after all, going to marry me?"

"Wanted you to do what? It's true, I did say that I would marry you, but that doesn't mean having sex first. It usually works the other way around, right?"

"Forgive me, Fräulein, I did not mean to make you upset. I would be lying if I tried to cover up the fact that I want you, now! But you, my love, have made the expectation of waiting a completely stimulating experience!"

My quest to stay pure until marriage seemed to have the opposite effect of what I was trying to accomplish. I was trying to discourage, not encourage. It seemed to up the game in his mind, leaving the smitten young German even more mesmerized and infatuated.

"For now, can we just take some time and talk and get to know one another here and now in this place?"

He looked at me in a non-expressive manner; it was difficult to tell exactly what he thought about everything that had just occurred.

"Alright, Fräulein, as you wish, but let us first get out of this water, you're shivering."

He picked me up and carried me, which I was honestly thankful for as I'm not sure I could have moved my frozen feet out of the thick mud. Trudging onto the shore, he sat me down, quickly ran over and picked up a pail of water that was sitting by the table, and began washing the mud off of my feet, warming them with his hands and breath. He then retrieved one of the quilts that was folded under the tree and wrapped it, and his arms, around me. For the next hour he simply held me against his warm, strong body, which I have to admit felt amazingly good. He made me feel safe.

"Benidette, I have never met anyone like you. I'm sorry for my untoward advances, and you're right, women do not generally deny me anything. Being unwed and of a high status has allowed me certain privileges with very few limitations. I take who I want, when I want without any contest. These women would do anything to acquire my status and wealth, but I know that's all they want. They use me, I use them. I thought that is just how it was. They love the idea of the Field Marshal title, but feel no love for me or Annaliese. It is all nonsense, and has left me empty."

Alrik held me even tighter, and whispered in my ear.

"When I saw *you*, it was different though. Different than anything I have ever known, even though my glance was only for a second. I felt your warmth - I could see your heart, and it called out to me. You are most pure, not like any other, and it is not my intention to spoil that."

For a moment, he lost his words.

"I would be lying however, if I didn't confess that my body burns for you when we're together and aches for you when we're apart. At this very moment, to be exact, there is fire within me that can be quenched in only one way. It is uncontrollable as well as uncomfortable. I can scarcely eat or sleep, so forgive me for wanting to touch you and be close to you at every opportunity. For me, Fräulein, this is very simple. When I saw you in town, I wasn't looking upon a beautiful stranger, but one who I have known my entire life, who was gone for a time but has now returned."

His words confounded me.

"But Alrik, you realize that can't be, right? We have never met until now. I know that I look like Caprice, but

I'm not, nor will I ever be her. I think I just remind you of her."

"No, I mean yes, you do look like her, but you're not anything *like* her, and she was nothing like you. She needed me desperately; you are much more independent, like a wild flower."

He chuckled as he said it.

"That's why I requested wildflowers be set on the table, because you, Benidette, are like a wildflower."

I was absolutely taken aback by his intuition of who I was. After our discussion, the rest of the evening was most enjoyable, and we were both able to open up to one another about our lives and our pasts.

My conversation with Alrik went well, and instead of the evening being awkward and stressful, it was quite pleasant. We sat at the table for two with the lights raining down from above, and ate dinner and talked for hours. He told me all about his upbringing in the finest military schools, and when he first met Caprice. Inevitably when he would speak of his father, he would look down as if he were uneasy and distraught, with a somber look on his face. He asked all about me as well. He was enthralled by the idea of having a girl there with him that was born in America, let alone, California. I told him that my mother died when I was young, and I too had a difficult father, was mainly raised by my aunt, and went to boarding school for most of my life. He and I had very similar childhood experiences, as a matter of fact, we were alike in many ways. Of course there were differences such as living on opposite sides of the world, not to mention our eighty some years difference.

Upon hearing that I was a professor of literature at a *real* university, he found it very difficult to believe that a woman would be allowed to have such a job, but appreciated my love for books. We even discussed Halag, and how he had always lived in Alrik's shadow - he and his

crooked and perverse heart. Alrik kept him around only

because it was his mother's last request that he always try

to help her sister's awkward son. He told me that it was

Halag who came alongside Caprice and helped her nurse

Chariot back to health. He was the one who stood by her on

those long nights of caring for a sick animal, and he would

often be the one to shine my father's shoes while she slept.

Halag loved her, but her heart from the beginning belonged

to Alrik. When Caprice died, Halag's heart hardened, and

his tinge of craziness turned to complete insanity. It seemed

strange that he felt that way about Caprice, but had such a

violent hatred for me. I didn't quite understand it.

The thing that Alrik told me that surprised me the

most though, was his hidden love of farming, and the

science behind it. His ideas were ages ahead of the time

that he lived in, and it was evident that getting caught up in

a war, and holding such an elevated rank, was not his

passion. Somewhat like me, he was also in bondage to his life calling.

As I continued enjoying the scenery around me and the splendor of it all, I couldn't help but tease Alrik about this "simple and unplanned" dinner by the lake, which was anything but a casual picnic. I asked him if he even knew what it was to be spontaneous. Course after course was served with the perfect accompaniment of liquor, wine, or champagne that complimented each bite. Since I was still unable to eat anything very solid, I drank far too much alcohol, which led to a relaxed and unguarded version of myself.

As he opened his life and his heart up to me, I discovered that there was a genuine tenderness within him. I was looking at a man who really only wanted three things in life: to love, to be loved, and to farm. He was, and had always been, passionate about farming, but his father never approved of such an occupation, and warned him that the task of farming was reserved for those of lower classes. He was definitely not the typical German soldier that history portrayed. I asked him how he felt about the conflict between Germany and the rest of the world, but I could tell he didn't really want to discuss it. Somehow I felt that the only reason he did many things was because of the expectations put on him by his father, and he continually responded to my inquiries by saying that he loved his country and would serve with his life.

I lost track of the time, but I knew it was late, and my fuzzy-headedness was an ugly reminder that I had far exceeded my limitations.

"Alrik, we should probably be heading back - I am so sleepy."

"What, California girls can't hold their liquor?"

"Well, this California girl can't. It only makes me tired and fairly worthless."

"Well, my love, why don't we stay here until morning, and then we'll ride back."

"Where will we sleep?"

Alrik pointed over to the white pallets under the oak tree. Normally, I would have insisted on just returning, but shamefully, I was highly intoxicated and needed to lay down.

"Oh, ok, well since it's there, why not?"

He watched as I stumbled over to the pallet, not very sure-footed. The alcohol seemed to be impairing everything from my feet up, and in all honesty, I was thrilled to not have to get on a horse right now. I must have looked ridiculous trying to make my way to the blankets.

With slurred words, I told Alrik goodnight.

"Goodnight, my darling."

I collapsed onto the pallet made of soft cotton and down. It felt so good to lay down and close my eyes. All that Alrik could do was chuckle at my struggle, and hope that I would allow him to share the pallet.

"Fraulein, may I lay down with you?"

Looking up at him, I believed it thoughtful that he would ask, and with my eyes closed and completely relaxed I told him yes.

"Ok, Alrik, but no funny business, alright?"

He laughed at my directness.

"Sometimes the things you say! I have never heard anyone, especially a young lady speak as you do. But ok my dear, 'no funny business', even though I'm, how did you put it, *hot*!'

As Alrik lay down beside me, his body felt so warm and comfortable. He pulled the comforter up over us and kissed my cheek.

"Sleep well, Benidette!"

Chapter 12

AFFLICTION OF ERRORS

"As he opened his life and his heart up to me, I discovered that there was a genuine tenderness within him. I was looking at a man who really only wanted three things in life: to love, to be loved, and to farm." ~**Benidette Hammell**~

I fell into a deep sleep, which led to a dream that seemed so real. I was standing on the shore of Pebble Cove looking out at the water and Carig came up behind me, enveloping me completely in his arms. I was so happy, so relieved to finally be back with him. I turned around so that I could see his face, his beautiful green eyes and strong chin, his auburn hair. I had missed every part of him, and at that moment all I wanted was to make love to him, to feel his body on mine. I had spent my entire life parted from Carig, and then after only one night together, we were once again separated. All I wanted was him! But even though I was standing in his presence, I couldn't open my eyes; I couldn't see him, I could only feel him and hear the sounds of the ocean. Finally, he was once again in my arms! Caressing his shoulders was thoroughly exhilarating, and stirred my imagination, causing me to continue stroking his arms and chest, as I made my way to his muscular thighs.

"I love your body, your taste. I've missed you so much. I thought I would never get back home. Make love to me, make love to me now!"

Alrik, suddenly alerted by my tempting request, heard my slumbering demands and attempted to wake me from my dream state.

"Benidette, I'm here - what do want, my love?"

"You're here? I'm finally back with you? Hold me tighter!"

He did as I requested and held me tighter, but then to his surprise, the trance that until now remained within my mind, became tangible. I turned around towards him, touching his face, his hair, and then his body. I continued kissing him. The experience I shared with Carig on our honeymoon night was still fresh in my mind, and I wanted it again; I wanted him right now. My eyes were open but empty as I was there with him in body, but in the bothy with Carig in my mind. To Alrik's great pleasure, I not only spoke words of love to him, but I began undressing him and kissing him seductively.

"I love you, I love you! I missed you so much! Make love to me - I want to feel your body on mine!"

Alrik, knowing that I was dreaming, was compelled at first to hold back, but as I assured him with my words, he was driven to take me.

"Do you really want me to make love to you, Benidette?"

"Yes!"

At that, he started undressing me as quickly as I was undressing him, but as a truth was spoken, everything quickly came to a halt.

"I love you, Carig, I love you so much!"

Upon hearing the name Carig, Alrik stopped and just looked at my face that was filled with so much passion and desire, but not for him, for another...one named Carig. In a few short seconds, his feelings had gone from ecstasy to torment. He knew that, even though I had never spoken again about the other man in my life, he was still very important to me, and the relationship between us was more than a passing one - it was truly love.

Brokenhearted over the encounter, Alrik's brokenhearted anguish soon turned to anger as he realized that Beni had once again lied to him. Although she was still asleep, he couldn't stand to look at her one more second. The thought of her with another man was too painful, so he quickly rose and stomped down to the shore of the moonlit lake, fiercely skimming rocks upon the smooth waters. His fury and his crushed spirit were too much to take. It felt like Caprice dying all over again. Falling to his knees, he raised his fist to the sky, and cursed the heavens.

"Why God, why would you allow her to come here only to cause such grief?"

He wanted to rage. He wanted to turn off all of his emotions and reclaim his place of security atop his ivory tower, this expanse of power that others feared. He was angry, and wanted to make her feel as miserable as he did.

"She doesn't know who she's dealing with! Doesn't she realize that punishment for lying to the Field Marshal is death by hanging? How dare she lie to me twice. Caprice, wasn't it you who told me that someone would come? You said that I would know her, but now I don't know anything. Am I forever destined to be alone?"

Like a stallion made of alabaster flames racing through the celestial sphere, a fiery white star unexpectedly streaked from one edge of sky to the other. Emotionally charged at the sight, Alrik instantly knew that this was a sign from Caprice. It was her way of telling him not to be discouraged and to know without a doubt that Beni was the one. She was the one his dying wife had foreseen coming, only minutes before she took her last breath. "Don't be sad my love, I will be waiting for you in heaven and watching you from the stars. This I promise you, another love will come. She will take away your loneliness."

He pleaded with her not to leave him, stressing that another would never do. He grasped her delicate hand with both of his, hoping and praying that if he held on tightly he could prevent her departure, or even better, go with her.

"Alrik, you will know her - you will see me in her. She will shoot into your life like a star with no beginning and no end."

Waking up to the sound of fussing and chomping horses, who were clearly irritated at being summoned to serve in the middle of the night, was not what I expected to see hovering above me at an ungodly hour of the night, especially after such a memorable evening. Atlas and Lily, along with Alrik, already mounted, were restlessly staring down at me.

"What's going on? What time is it?"

Expressionless, he simply told me that it was time to return to the house.

"I thought we were here until morning."

"Things have changed, we're going back now!"

"Ok, are you alright?"

"Fraulein, put your boots on. Lily is waiting."

Something had happened in the last few hours that had completely changed Alrik's demeanor. As I slipped my boots on, I smiled as I remembered my dream about Carig.

It was so real, and it felt so wonderful to touch him. Alrik

noticed my reminiscent smile, and gave Atlas a swift kick.

"Let's go!"

As I stood up and noticed my unbuttoned blouse

and undone pants, a horrible truth occurred to me. I knew

from experience that I was not only a very physical sleeper,

but I also had a tendency to walk and talk to extremes in

the realm of my subconscious. Ask anyone who had ever

been around me when I slept. There was even a time in

college when I woke up in the morning covered in mud,

and I had absolutely no recollection of what had happened.

All my roommates could tell me was that they found me

standing at the hallway door with a glazed look and muddy

boots. But tonight - what had I done? I recalled that I had

way too much to drink for my own good, but I hoped, I

prayed that we hadn't had sex. I have never been one to

wear my heart on my sleeve, but many times my heart and

my thoughts make a full debut while I sleep. But then it occurred to me, if we would have indulged in such an act, he certainly would not be sitting up on his high horse, perturbed with me. Obviously, I had said something that upset him, and because I was dreaming of Carig, my guess was that my words must have reflected it.

I mounted Lily, and followed Alrik through the dark night. I wasn't sure exactly what time it was, but I would imagine around two or so. I was sure that he didn't realize it, but I really did feel horrible for causing him grief. It was never my intention to hurt him, but it was better this way. I would be leaving very soon, and a hatred for me would make my disappearance much easier.

The ride back was made in silence. Alrik didn't say one word, and the hush of his displeasure was deafening. The estate had been locked down for hours. Everyone was asleep except for the statue-like guards who had been trained in the art of stationary vigilance. After putting

Atlas and Lily away for the night, we walked to the main

house. Still, he said nothing. I had hurt him deeply. I tried

not to care, but I did. He threw open the front door, which

in turn sent an echoing sound of thunder throughout the

house. Not unlike Alrik's darkened demeanor, the entry

was pitch-black. I could hardly see my hand in front of my

face. I heard him climbing the stairs, and held tightly to the

railing as I followed behind. All of the events of the

evening weighed heavily on me, and the ascension seemed

endless. Finally reaching the top, I turned right towards my

room, and he turned left.

"Fraulein!"

"Yes, Alrik?"

"We marry on Saturday. Everything has been set."

I spun back around in a complete panic. Either he

was bluffing just to upset me, or he had in fact arranged a

wedding behind my back. Nonetheless, he had totally

disregarded our earlier conversation about getting to know one another, and allowed his anger to send him spiraling back into his normal state of hard-heartedness. He was going to make this happen and had all of the resources to do it. I had to go. I had to leave here before this wedding could have a chance to happen.

Blindly entering my chamber, I lit the candle, setting my bedside table aglow. As I looked around the room, I noticed that Hildegard had earlier drawn a bath for me, assuming that I would be returning. The once steamy water had since gone cold. I couldn't help but feel chilled as well. A cloud of gloominess hovered all about the room, or rather, all around me. Being deliriously tired didn't help my feelings of hopelessness either. I felt paralyzed. My efforts thus far had been futile, not revealing an escape from this situation, but only leading to a deeper pit. This place! What was I even doing here? All of it was a burden too heavy to bear that was crashing down upon me, like a tidal wave, and all I could do was stand and watch it

destroy, not only me, but everything I held dear.

Not having the strength or energy to change out of

my musty clothes, I fell into bed hoping to ease my mood

with some much-needed slumber. When I laid my head

down, I heard the crunching sound of paper beneath my

pillow. Sweeping my hand under the down, I discovered a

folded piece of paper, and without knowing why, my

anguish turned to hope, as if light had gloriously broken

through my darkness. I couldn't unfold the mysterious note

quickly enough, but once it was opened, the illumination of

the candle revealed my long-awaited salvation. To my

great relief, it was from Carson.

Beni,

I've just heard that you and Alrik will

be married on Saturday. The entire greenhouse

staff has been relieved of work for the weekend

in celebration of the event. We will be leaving

on a truck Friday morning at 4.30 a.m. There

is a spot for you. Beni, this is your chance to

escape, but it will be very dangerous for both

of us. The truck will pick us up at the end of the

driveway.

I have put men's traveling clothes

under your bed. Wear them along with the hat.

Tuck your hair underneath so as not to reveal

that you are a woman. You will have to climb

down the trellis outside of your balcony. Be

very careful. Halag is out of confinement and

will be watching your every move. I will be

waiting for you on the truck. When you arrive

and get what you're looking for, leave quickly.

Stay here no longer!

I will be praying for your safe return!

Everybody knew but me! It disgusted me the way Alrik accused *me* of lying, pointing out the *speck in my eye*, while disregarding the *log* in his own. He was clearly demented. He, and everything that he stood for, was a lie, a sham. I had been blind to his preconceived agenda about my future here. Even Carson knew about the wedding, which meant everyone else did as well. At this point, all of the invitations had most likely been sent out, and every last detail down to his bloody boutonniere had been confirmed.

From the moment he entered my life, I had ceaselessly grieved over my choice lies. I felt them like scavengers, eating away at my soul - trying to convince myself that somehow God would use all of this for good, making something honorable out of my flawed compromises. But Alrik clearly justified his actions with selfish motives. Even though it seemed that I had created a big mess rather than correcting a flaw in time, I was reminded that it was not me who was a pawn in his game, but he who would soon find himself at the mercy of the Tempus Vector.

Carson was wise to leave the letter unsigned. Not only was he risking everything he had worked for by helping me, but his life as well. I kneeled down on the floor, feeling for the stack of clothes and a pair of men's boots underneath the bed. Just then, I heard the hallway clock chime four. I didn't have much time! Without wasting another minute, I put on the traveling clothes, boots, and the hat that Carson had left for me. Just as he had instructed, I tucked in my hair, trying to look as inconspicuous as possible. I would have to leave everything behind, even Malachi's suitcase and all of my belongings. That is, except my aquamarine necklace and butterfly brooch, which I buttoned within the inside pocket of my jacket. Besides my wedding ring, these two items were precious to me, and I refused to leave any of them behind.

The remainder of incidentals that I brought to the house would have to stay.

As quietly as possible, I opened the balcony door and carefully examined every direction so to be assured that no one near or far was watching me. As I looked over the side, it seemed much higher than I remembered, but it didn't matter, I had to hurry. Throwing my leg over the side, I placed one foot and then the other through the slats on the trellis. The boots were massive and kept getting stuck in the slats, but little by little I made my way down to the bottom. On the other side of the house I spotted two soldiers standing together talking and smoking, but facing my direction. I needed a diversion that would allow me to get past them and out onto the main drive. Risky to be sure, I picked up a small rock and decided to toss it towards the stable, hoping I would hit it and not them. Remembering what Wil had taught me about throwing a baseball, I reached back, and tossed it as far as I could. Amazingly, it hit the top of the next building over, and rolled down the back side, alerting them to toss their cigarettes and cock their rifles. When they took off running toward the stables, I raced toward the main road. I was sure that the crunching sound of rocks beneath my boots would surely give me away, so I quickly pulled them off, and began tiptoeing down the driveway.

Staying low and close to the shrubs would hopefully camouflage my escape. In the distance I could see headlights beaming from the covered truck waiting at the end of the drive. I was elated at the prospect of finally going home. I had everything planned out in my mind. I would walk straight to Malachi's, give him the warning about October 5, 1941, grab the Tempus Vector, and then finally go home and all of this world would be over.

As I moved closer to the truck, I was gripped with fear, and knew without a doubt that I was *not meant* to step foot on that vehicle. I still needed to find my way to

Friedlich, but *not* with Carson. I turned around and ran

back down the driveway away from what I had thought

would be my passage to freedom, when I heard Carson call

my name.

"Beni, Beni, where are you going?"

He stood there looking at me so confused, and then

sprinted after me. I turned around and held up my hand,

telling him to stop and go back.

"Carson, it's not safe to go with you. I'll have to

find another way!"

"Beni, it's all arranged, it's safe. Come on, we're

ready to leave!"

I didn't look back. I couldn't stand to see the look

on his face. Oh God, what should I do, what should I do?

Please give me wisdom!

For the life of me, I couldn't believe that I was

running back *toward* the house. Either I had lost my mind,

or there was a higher plan here. Not getting in that truck

was the first *real* time I felt an unmistakable pull of

wisdom, one that couldn't be ignored. I would move

forward in faith. I couldn't see a way, but that didn't mean

there wasn't one.

Upon entering the courtyard, I heard Lily

whinnying from inside the stables, the exact location where

I had thrown the rock only minutes earlier. Curiously there

were no guards anywhere, not one. It was as if they had all

disappeared into thin air. I didn't know why, but frankly I

didn't care. With the way cleared, I decided that the only

sensible way into Friedlich was on the back of Lily; she

would be my deliverance. Together we would ride through

the Black Forest hidden within the shadows of the trees

until we arrived at the edge of town.

Making my way to the stables was no easy task. I

had left the cumbersome boots at the end of the driveway,

and my feet were feeling the effects of the rock-ribbed

terrain. I went to the back to get Lily's saddle and bridle.

She was glad to see me, but Atlas was obviously unhappy

about being disturbed for a second time this morning, and

he became rambunctious at my presence. He practically

screamed out as he watched me saddle Lily and walk her

outside the stable.

"Shh, Atlas! Your girl will be back soon, I

promise!"

As we stepped outside, a damp fog rolled in, and a

light rain began to fall.

"Perfect! Ok Lily, you're gonna have to help me

through the forest. You know it better than I do. No offense

girl, but I wish you weren't so white. We're gonna stick out

like a sore thumb!"

As I mounted her, trying to stay as low as I could so

as not to be seen, the rain became heavier and denser,

which meant mud in the already saturated forest. At first,

we rode very swiftly as we crossed the grassy areas, but as we entered the forest, we had to slow way down. The darkness blinded me, and all I could do was let Lily be my eyes to get through to the other side. Certain areas were more unstable than others, and the thick trees with low branches were a recipe for disaster. I wanted both of us to make it to Friedlich healthy, and in one piece, but after only a few minutes of travel the rain became so heavy that I could scarcely see my hand in front of my face. Our pace had slowed to a walk, and I could tell that this whole experience was not only frightening for me but as thunder and lightning rumbled through the sky, Lily became spooked and reared back throwing me to the ground. Trying not to lose her, I jumped up, covered from head to toe in mud, and grabbed her reins.

"It's ok girl, I've got you. We'll do this together."

Now walking, I slowly led the way, wishing that instead, I was on the truck with Carson. No sooner did the thought cross my mind, then I heard shouting from the main road east of the forest. As I took a closer look, I saw that the truck which I was supposed to be on had been stopped by none other than Halag and a band of soldiers. Now it made sense why there were no guards on the grounds. Halag had taken them all. They were making everyone exit the vehicle, and then loosed their vicious Shepherds to sniff out every recess. He had singled Carson out from among the others and began interrogating him. When Halag saw that I was not on the truck, he screamed in Carson's face.

"Where is she?"

I could tell by Carson's body language that he was playing dumb, making every attempt to convince Halag of his innocence in the matter of the missing girl and that he had no idea what he was talking about. Clearly irritated, Halag moved nose to nose with Carson and said something; something I'm sure that was vile and venomous. To my dismay, I watched as Halag pushed him to the ground and pointed a pistol only inches from his head as he continued his ranting and raving. Thankfully, even though he teetered on the edge of insanity, the situation quickly de-escalated, he holstered his weapon and hastily returned to his car. He probably knew better than to shoot Alrik's number one man. I hoped that the caravan of cars would turn back to the estate, but unfortunately they took off towards Friedlich, and everything inside of me said that they were heading for Malachi's store.

I was so thankful that I didn't get on that truck. It wouldn't have just been detrimental to me, but to Carson as well. There were ten other people on the truck, and yet they had targeted him out of all the others. Somehow Halag knew that he was trying to help me. Poor Carson. I had no doubt that they were watching his every move, and if it came down to it, they would have no problem killing him just like they did Leta's father.

I didn't exactly know what to do once I entered town. With Halag there patrolling, I would need to remain in the shadows, but I wished that I could see Carson one last time and insist that he get Adina out right away, and leave Germany.

"Good girl, Lily. Everything's ok. Let's go, girl!"

We carefully continued making our way through the forest, until finally we arrived at the edge of Friedlich. The first thing I came to was, or what I believed to be anyway, the cottage where Adina lived. How I wish I could knock on the door and go in and sit with her. I wondered if Carson had made it there yet. I looked around the now quiet town that had a stranger in their midst and was thankful that in a few short hours, everyone would be up and out and about their business. Most importantly, I would be gone. But first things first. It was my highest priority to reveal to Malachi information that would save him and his loved ones from being sucked into the ghettos and camps.

I could *feel* Halag nearby. Most likely he was parked somewhere, waiting, hiding like a snake, to catch me walking into town.

Holding Lily's reins tightly, we walked down the back alley of the stores, knowing it wasn't safe on the main street. Trying to remember exactly which store was Malachi's was difficult. I was unfamiliar with this area and had only been to his store once, and that was during the day. Looking up at the various buildings that all seemed to look the same from the back, left me confused. All of a sudden a trashcan crashed right behind us, causing me to whip around, eliciting a loud cry from Lily.

"Whoa girl, it's ok. It's just a stupid cat. I hate cats!"

Finally, after calming Lily and collecting my wits, I cautiously once again began walking slowly down the long, dark alley. Without warning, from behind me a hand came up and grabbed and covered my mouth. I started to scream and fight my way from whoever this captor was.

"Beni, Beni, it's me, Carson. I wanted to make sure you made it ok. Listen, I had to warn you ... Halag is looking for you."

"I know, I saw him stop your truck on the road. I'm so sorry!"

"It's ok. That was a smart call you made! Halag wouldn't believe you weren't there. He's smart and cunning, and scarcely wrong about much. The whole thing made him go a little AWOL. The thing is, he suspects me. I don't know why, I've been real careful, but they have eyes everywhere."

"Oh Carson, I'm so sorry!"

"No problem, kiddo. It's all gonna be fine. We just need to get you back. Another thing, Alrik knows you're gone too, and he's furious. It's a good thing you're leaving

- I've seen him this way before, and it's not good. He only sees red, is an unreasonable mess to be sure, and is very dangerous. Well, Malachi's store is right up this way - two more up. I'm gonna stay with you until you go, ok?"

"Thank you! Hey Carson, remember what I told you about the airplane? Just ... don't get on it, no matter what, ok?"

"Ok, Beni!"

"Promise me!!"

"I promise - now let's move!"

"Wait, Carson, go to Adina right now, and leave this place, please!"

"Beni, don't worry about me, everything's gonna be fine, okay?"

I handed him Lily's reins while I went and knocked on the back door of Malachi's store. After a few knocks, he opened the door holding a candle.

"Yes, who is it?"

"It's me, Malachi!"

"Adina? What are you doing here?"

"No Malachi, it's Beni!"

"What? Why are you still here? Why haven't you returned to your own time?"

"Because I don't have the Tempus Vector, remember? I left it here!"

"No my dear, it's not here!"

My heart sank within me. What was he talking about? I left it here.

"Malachi, remember, I left it here, in my bag under your chair!"

"Who is that with you?"

"It's Carson, my Uncle Carson. He's been helping me."

"Adina's Carson?"

"Yes, hello sir."

"Both of you, come inside. It's not safe."

After tying up Lily, we walked into Malachi's kitchen, dripping water and tracking mud all over his floor.

"Benidette, I thought you would have been gone days ago!"

"What do you mean, Malachi. How could I?"

Malachi sighed deeply. The distressed expression on his face mimicked my troubled spirit.

"When I sent the wooden shoebox holding the pink shoes, I devised a compartment below that held the Tempus Vector. Between the note and the heaviness of the box, I hoped that you would discover the secret compartment containing the frame and your ring."

He moved very close to me with a frantic expression of scrutiny.

"Beni, where is that box now?"

"Oh my gosh, are you are kidding me?"

I held my head in my hands and cried.

"Beni, tell me where?"

I sat there, almost lifeless, hoping this was just a bad dream, and I would surely wake up any moment.

"It's at the Richter estate, up in my room. But I can't go back! I just can't!"

"You must, my dear. You have no choice. All will work out as it should."

"How can you say that? You have no idea what I've gone through these past few days. I just can't go back!"

I sat sobbing uncontrollably before Malachi and Carson, and couldn't seem to stop.

Carson placed his hand on my shoulder, trying to comfort me.

"It's far too dangerous for Beni to go back. What if I went instead?"

Before the words had even left his lips, we both shot that idea down in unison.

"Carson, thank you, but Malachi's right, it has to be me! But before I go, Malachi, you have to know why I came here in the first place; the real reason I'm here. It's because of you. There's something that I have to tell you!"

"Stop, stop! Say nothing, Benidette! You can't! If you do, you will be trapped here for the rest of your life."

"But, Malachi!"

"Go now, Benidette. Go!! God be with you!"

He opened the door wide, and looked away as if he hated good-byes as much as I did. As I walked out the door, I took one last look at my dear friend.

"May I just ask you something?"

"Of course, my dear. What is it?"

"Why was this task given to me? I've failed miserably! I've let everyone down, and wasted my time here!"

Malachi cradled my face in his hands.

"Benidette, remember one thing - being the Carrier of the Tempus Vector is many times like looking at a fine tapestry from the back. All you can see is clusters of frayed threads, it makes no sense, and appears to be a waste of time. But when you turn it over, the complete and beautiful picture is revealed before you. There will be times that you won't find any sense in the chaos, but that does not mean you've failed. On the contrary, you are really an instrument being used to make something magnificent. Have faith, my dear, you're not alone, and never will be. Remember too my Beni, if ever you feel overwhelmed, just keep moving forward, and take one step at a time!"

"Ok, thank you, Malachi, thank you!"

It was as if Malachi could see into my thoughts. A frayed mess of threads was all I could see ... I had to try to reach deep and find the faith that I needed to complete my task.

Carson walked out with me, with his arm around me.

"Beni, you could stay you know. I mean, if you don't want to go back to Alrik's, you can stay here with Adina and me."

"Oh, Carson, I can't - you know I can't. I don't belong here. I must find a way out of this, and you need to go home to Adina. You know, I have never seen anyone more in love than she was with you."

Carson's face fell, and his mood became somber.

"Beni, you are walking back into a very dangerous situation. Your only hope until you find the frame, is going along, and *getting* along with Alrik. He's your only defense against Halag. Be careful, kiddo. I'm gonna make it out of here so that I can be part of your life. I would love that, you know."

"So would I, but just remember what I said - no airplane, ok?"

"Will do. Now you go before the sun comes up!"

I gave Carson a hug, and a reluctant goodbye. Would I ever see him again?

Staying within the back shadows of town, I began my return journey. Like a bitter pill, I was struck by the lunacy of my unending plight. It reminded me of a carousel spinning round and round, but artlessly ending up in the exact same spot, never making any progress. I once again would return to the Field Marshal's estate, and I couldn't believe it. I only hoped that I would be able to climb back into my room, get the Tempus Vector, and leave without anyone being the wiser. I knew one thing for sure, they certainly would not be expecting me to return, so hopefully, it wouldn't be too hard to get back inside.

My stomach churned within me as I thought about how it would feel to go back home without accomplishing the task I was sent here for. I would never forgive myself if I failed at this labor of love that would have meant so much to Adina, and that now mattered so much to me. Malachi and Carson were no longer just photos on a wall, but people I had grown to love dearly. I was reminded once again that somehow, before I left, I had to let Malachi know that he and his family had to be ready to leave before October 5, 1941.

The sun was just beginning to rise and the rain had practically stopped, which helped us to move at a quicker pace through the woods. As we approached the edge of the trees and then up to the grass pastures, I looked to see if there was any movement at the estate, particularly at the stables. At this point, there was nothing, so I yelled out for Lily to fly!

"Come on, girl!"

As we arrived at the stables, I was relieved that no one had begun their work for the day. Without wasting another moment, I walked Lily to her stall, feeling the eyes of Atlas glaring at me for keeping her out all night. Once I took off her saddle and bridle and tucked her back in, I was shocked to see how dirty she was! Both of us were covered in mud, except for her still-white coat beneath the saddle.

Quietly, I climbed back up the lattice to my room, hoping not to be spotted. I knew, however, that Alrik was fully aware, and livid, that I had left. It didn't appear that Halag had returned at this point. He probably knew better than to come back empty-handed.

Even though it had been difficult to maneuver down the trellis in the oversized boots, I would have given anything to have them back right about now. My feet were suffering greatly as a result of the past few hours of traipsing through hazardous terrain barefoot.

My mind was exploding with a well-organized plan for what I would do next. The instant I got to the room, I'd grab the shoebox and leave before I ever needed to see Alrik again. I would run as fast as I could back into the forest, and for the final time, back to Malachi's shop. After spilling my heart to him, I would finally go home. Easy!

"You can do this, Beni!"

Halfway up, I heard someone coming. It was two of the soldiers - they were back. I clung face-first to the wooden lattice, staying very still. Hair-triggering pain shot through me as thorns from the climbing roses pierced my feet. Just the thought of seeing Carig again soon though, gave me the strength and will to remain lifelessly silent and still. I could feel blood dripping from the gashes, and only hoped and prayed that the droplets wouldn't fall on their heads.

"Please don't look up, please don't look up!"

It would have been so natural, so right for them to look up, but they didn't. It was a miracle before my very eyes that they kept on walking. Once they passed by, I continued climbing, and finally made it to the top of the balcony. My clothes and I were both soaking wet and covered in mud, but I didn't care. I'd go back home grimy from head to toe. I couldn't wait! I was only moments away from being with Carig again.

I climbed over the ledge and walked towards the door leading into my room. From what I could tell, no one was there. All I needed to do now was get to the wardrobe, grab Malachi's wooden shoe box, and run.

Even though I was ecstatic at the thought of finally leaving, I couldn't help but feel grieved thinking of leaving my Uncle Carson and Malachi. I had become quite fond of them both. I almost felt like a traitor somehow. I knew the horrific events that were coming. I would escape, but they would be left.

With all that was inside of me, I willed myself to move silently while my wounded feet left a trail of bloody footprints with every torturous step I took. At this point, I didn't care about the pain though. Nothing was worth getting caught. I was relieved as my hands grasped the knobs of the cupboard, pulling open the doors. I wasn't prepared, however, for what came next. Were my eyes playing tricks on me? I looked around to make sure that I was in the right place. Perhaps there were two trellises that led into similar looking chambers? But no, this was my room. To my dismay, I was hopelessly staring into the once full cupboard that had been stripped bare. Not only was the shoebox gone, but my suitcase, everything! They had taken everything.

"No, no, no, no! This can't be happening!" Frantically, I looked under the bed; I looked everywhere, but there was nothing left. Just then I heard steps approaching my room. Without even thinking about it, I frantically threw off the wet muddy clothes and tossed them behind the screen, and then briskly submerged myself into the cold tub of water. Even though I was already freezing, my adrenaline and sheer panic lessened the impact of the frigid bath. I knew that it was utterly ridiculous to try and hide my guilt beneath floods of bath salts and hollow bubbles, but where was I to go? I couldn't leave without the Tempus Vector. Once again, I was trapped, and I was afraid. I had no idea what Alrik would do once he discovered that I had returned.

The door burst open, and Alrik walked in, first looking at the balcony door, then he scoured the room. Instantly noticing the trail of blood, his angry scowl followed it, until he slightly lifted his head and caught my eye. It was apparent by his irritated expression that he was furious. As he strode towards me, I felt paralyzed, completely vulnerable, and fully at his mercy. With a blazing glare, he stood silently above me saying nothing, which made the whole ordeal even worse. Why wasn't he saying anything? His silence was agonizing. I would have chosen screaming, ranting, raving, anything but this. He simply knelt down, putting his hands in the icy water at my neck, and ran his fingers down my submerged naked body. While his hands touched each curve, his eyes never left mine, until he brought up a cupped handful of bath water that was more mud than water, and poured it back into the tub directly in front of my face.

"Where did you go, Benidette? I know that you took Lily to God-knows-where, out into the night. She is exhausted and filthy. How dare you! You promised me no more lies, but everything that comes out of your mouth is untrue."

He stood up and walked away from me.

"Why, Beni? What did I do wrong to make you act this way? But before you answer my question, I want to know what your real name is - and don't lie to me, or I will strangle you myself!"

"Alrik, Benidette is my real name - it is, I promise!"

"Don't you dare promise anything to me! You are not allowed to promise me anything! I have given you every opportunity to tell me who you are, and like a fool, I continue believing you."

"What makes you think I am not Benidette?"

He became angrier and angrier at me, and with every syllable, his tone became harsher.

"Because Halag researched you. 'Benidette Crawford in California.' There is no such person, damn you, there is no such person!"

I stood up and screamed something at him that I probably should have never said out loud.

"You're right, ok! There is no Benidette Crawford in California, not yet! There, I said it. I told you, not yet!"

Alrik stood stunned. We were both so shocked by my statement that neither of us realized, for a moment anyway, that I was naked and dripping wet. While he still stood there, I ran to the bed, grabbed a throw from the covers, and threw it around my shoulders.

"I want to go home. Where are my things? I want them back, right now!"

He didn't respond to anything that I had just said about California.

"Your things have been moved to the master chamber, my chamber. You and I are to be married tomorrow. I will wait no longer. I believed you to be pure, untouched by another man, but then the things you said about this Carig in your dreams led me to believe otherwise."

"Hold on, you German bastard, before you go down that road of being a victim. Exactly when did you announce to the world that we would be married on Saturday? Because I thought we had agreed that we would wait a little while, but you planned this all along and then lied to me about it. Do you know how messed up this whole thing is? I hate you!"

Alrik stood there, saying nothing in return. He obviously didn't know how to respond to me telling him that I hated him. I then boldly lunged towards him, my face in his as if I were going to kiss him, and then turned and walked over to the door.

"Well, what now? You seem to have all this planned. Let's go!"

I knew the shoe box must have been put in his room, and I was past ready to get this over with.

"Can you please take me to your room then? I get it. From this point forward, your room will be my room, ok?"

Poor Alrik, he was ready for a fight, but I wasn't going to argue this right now. The wooden shoe box and the Tempus Vector were in his room, and I needed to get to them no matter what it would take. He walked over to the door, and told me to follow him.

"I will have Hildegard prepare a hot bath for you and help clean you up."

I followed him down the long hall, passing the portraits of Atlas and Chariot that were even more grand during the day. When we arrived at his chamber he opened the door, allowing me to go in first. The room was washed in warm tones of cream and gold. A dressing table with a large mirror sat by the window adorned with lovely bottles of perfume, and an ivory vase filled with wildflowers. To the right was a wardrobe, twice the size as the other, filled with beautiful gowns of all lengths and colors. Everywhere I looked, from floor to ceiling were grand furnishings and decor. He and I had never met, but somehow he knew what I loved. The furnishings were hand carved with great skill, just like the carousel horses. They reminded me of something Carig or Killen might create.

"Wow! This room is, well, it's breathtaking, really!"

"I had each item placed in here for the sole purpose of pleasing you."

He appeared so upset as he pointed out each lavish gift that he had brought in specifically for me.

"Alrik, I never meant to hurt you, but you must know this time and place is not for me. Do you understand?"

He walked over to where I was standing and looked intently into my eyes.

"I *don't* understand. I can't help but think that I am cursed because of the sins of my father on top of my own. You are my last hope for happiness. Please stay with me. Don't ever leave me again. I ... I don't want you to leave, but I want you to stay because you want to be with me, not because I'm forcing you to."

"I know it's hard to understand, but I just can't stay here."

Just then, Hildegard entered the room carrying an ivory wedding gown made of full lace. She had a huge smile on her face as though she was so pleased to be the one holding the gown that I would wear to marry Alrik. For the first time since I was here, I had no words to describe my displeasure, but I'm pretty sure that Alrik could tell what I was thinking by the look on my face. I turned around, not facing him anymore.

"I'm done talking to you!"

Alrik gave Hildegard instructions about running my bath, and then left the room. As soon as the door shut, I ran over to the wardrobe and frantically searched for the shoebox, anything, actually, that belonged to me.

"Hildegard, where are my things? Where is the wooden shoe box that was in my room?"

She looked at me, afraid.

"They are gone, Fräulein! I was told to get rid of them. All new things were brought in for you, all new beautiful things. You should be happy!"

"I am not happy. I need that wooden shoebox. Where did you put it?"

"It has been put in the trash. It will be incinerated!"

"No, Hildegard listen to me. I don't care what you have to do, but go now and get me that box, please. Go now, and when you find it, bring it to me immediately!"

She ran out of the room, and all that I could do was sit on the floor, wrapped in the blanket, and stare up at that dress. I felt completely hopeless. Everything was falling apart right before my very eyes.

What seemed like an eternity finally ended as Hildegard returned to the room. I stood up to meet her at the door, but was instantly plagued with disappointment when I saw that her hands were empty.

"I am sorry, Fräulein, the trash has been incinerated - early this morning. But I make you nice bath. Everything will be good!"

I couldn't believe it! I feared it was a possibility the moment I walked away from the frame, leaving it in Malachi's store. I had sealed my fate. It felt as though I was once again being swept off of Devil's Knuckles, but this time it destroyed me. I was lost forever. I had nothing left, nothing left to lose. I would never see Carig again, and I would be forced to marry a stranger. Not only did I accomplish nothing, but I ruined my life, *and* Carig's life. I was a complete and utter failure who would forever be known as the one who lost the Tempus Vector on her maiden journey. Malachi was wrong - I had ruined everything.

For the rest of the day, I stayed confined to the walls of my new room, grieving over my newly revealed destiny, and trying to move forward just like Malachi told me to do. Informed that I had become the lady of the house, Hildegard entered the room and began the process of preparing me for dinner.

Sitting in front of the mirror, watching Hildegard brush through my tangled mane, I glared with rage at my reflection, and was tempted to throw one of the costly perfume bottles at my image, never wanting to look at myself ever again. I was discouraged and ashamed of myself.

As the time was drawing nearer for the dinner bell to sound, she pulled my hair back tightly off of my face. The black bruises that remained on my neck seemed to stand out on my overly pale skin even more than I had noticed before, matching the circles under my eyes. It would have been best if Halag would have just finished the job. At least I wouldn't be stuck here for the rest of my life. It wasn't simply my own unfavorable circumstances that were eating away at me, but Carig - what would this do to him? I couldn't even stand the thought of him being alone and doubting my love for him. Without warning, the reality of it all hit me. This couldn't be about me anymore! Wallowing in a pool of self pity wouldn't help anyone. I needed to take my eyes off of myself and create beauty from the ashes.

Although completely devastated, there was nothing that I could do to go back at this point. I would have to use my historical knowledge and wisdom to help as many people as I could. By whatever means necessary, I would have to make Alrik my ally, which I felt positive I could do. But first things first. I would convince Alrik to send Carson back to the United States immediately, so that he and Adina would be safe and able to live out their lives together. Secondly, I would do everything within my power to get Malachi and his family out of Germany. Maybe Carson could help me. I was determined that something good was going to come out of this.

"Fraulein! Fraulein, your gown!"

"Oh, sorry Hildegard."

As I stepped into the exquisite lavender gown,

Hildegard buttoned up the back and then dabbed on

cologne from the royal blue and gold decanter. I wasn't

hungry, and I didn't want to go to dinner, but if I had

discovered one thing, it was that most of my time seemed

to be spent doing things that I really didn't want to do.

Perhaps it was the lavender dress, but I looked gaunt as I

once again glared at my reflection. All of the physical and

emotional trauma of the past week had taken its toll on me,

and it certainly didn't help that I couldn't swallow real

food. On top of everything, I was wasting away and I

looked horrible. What I wouldn't give for my jeans, my

oversized sweatshirt, and a bowl of Mari's cullen skink. I

became choked up just thinking about it; her soup always

made everything better. But that time was gone forever.

As I entered the dining room, Alrik was there to

meet me.

"You look lovely, Benidette!"

"Thank you!"

"You remember Dr. Carson. He will be joining us for dinner tonight. He was kind enough to come back from Friedlich so that he could be present for our wedding tomorrow. He has agreed to stand with me."

My poor attitude, I could tell, was felt by both gentlemen.

"Really! Stand with you. How very kind of him. It's nice to see you again, Dr. Carson."

Carson kissed my hand, looked at not only the bruises on my neck, but he couldn't help noticing my overall paleness and the brooding sorrow in my eyes.

All through dinner, Alrik and Carson spoke about the greenhouse and the most recent accomplishments of the experiments, while I sat there alone. I could hear them talking to one another, but my mind was elsewhere. I was losing myself. I hardly knew who I was anymore.

"Benidette, my dear, are you alright?"

"Fine, thank you!"

Carson was very concerned, yet he couldn't let on as if he cared.

"Excuse me. I'll let you two talk. I'm going up to my room."

"I'll walk you up!"

"No, I'll be fine. Dr. Carson, I guess I will see you tomorrow at the wedding."

Carson looked completely confused. He had no idea that the Tempus Vector had been destroyed, that I would be staying, and most importantly, that I would be marrying Alrik.

I went upstairs and wanted to cry, just cry and never stop, but I was numb and no tears came. I felt as though Carig had died, and I died with him. As if I were not me anymore, and the man I gave my heart to would not even be born for another fifty years. I was about to give myself to someone who was not Carig, and it was eating me up inside.

I could tell Carson wanted to help in the worst way. Why else would he come back so quickly when he could have stayed with Adina? He must have received word that the wedding was still on. But nonetheless, there was nothing he could do either. He would stand with Alrik and watch me as I walked down the aisle.

A few minutes later, Alrik walked into the room. I stood up and just stared at the man who was soon to be my husband, who had made every attempt to make me his, including the final measure of moving me into his room. What was the point in fighting him off anymore? I was done! I would just get this over with once and for all.

He brushed up behind me, and began taking the pins out of my hair, allowing my curls to fall freely onto my shoulders. I closed my eyes trying to imagine that he was Carig. Brushing my hair aside, he kissed the back of my neck, my back … and I smiled as I saw only Carig's face. I could feel him unbuttoning my dress, slowly kissing every inch of where a button had once been. Like a statue, I stood unmoved as he reached within my dress and caressed my body, savoring each touch, stroking my flesh, pulling my body into his. With every touch, my tears finally came. I was grieved in my very soul, and my emotions were finally unleashed. I turned around, allowing my lavender dress to fall to the floor. I was finally giving Alrik what he wanted, just standing there naked before him. His excitement was uncontrolled while kissing and caressing my body. Then moving slowly, he stood close before me, and gently holding my chin, kissed me lightly. My lack of expression and unreturned affections made him stop and back away from me. He looked deeply into my eyes, and instead of seeing love gazing back at him, he was met by grief-filled emptiness. He picked up my dress, easing my arms back in, and then walked out of the room. This should have been a total relief to me, but instead I felt more confused than ever. I felt paralyzed by my grief, and was unsure of what I should do next.

There was only one thing that made sense to me and motivated me to move forward, and that was Malachi. I had to get the message to him - the message I was sent here to give him. Now there was nothing to hold me back. I was no longer limited by the constraints of the Tempus Vector. Because Carson would be at the wedding, I would send a message to Malachi through him. No matter what ended up happening with me, Malachi would know what was coming. This journey would not have been in vain. I sat down at the desk in the corner of the room and wrote down what would be my first and last task given to me by the

Tempus Vector.

My Dearest Malachi,

I am grieved to tell you that I have failed. In

every way that someone could fail. I know you

had faith in me, but it was unwarranted. I'm

not sure what will happen to me, but I do know

what's coming for you. Please heed my words,

and prepare. On the morning of October 5,

1941, your store will be overrun, and you,

Estee, and your closest friends will be taken to

camps set up to imprison and destroy Jews. I

am not sure what happens to you there, but I

do know that you will never be heard from

again. As far as I know, you are all killed in

this camp. Please Malachi, you need to get out

of Friedlich and move to safety. Make sure

everything valuable in your store is hidden, or

it too will be found. This is all I know, and why

I was sent here in the first place. The home and

the Germany that you have known will soon be

gone forever. I love you, Malachi!

Beni

P.S. Please remind Carson about the plane.

He'll know what you're talking about.

I folded up the letter, and would put it in the sleeve
of my wedding gown. At my first opportunity, I would give
it to Carson.

Chapter 13

FRAULEIN RICHTER

"Wallowing in a pool of self pity wouldn't help anyone. I needed to take my eyes off of myself and create beauty from the ashes."
~Benidette Hammell~

The morning was bustling with the noise of chairs and tables being set up, along with trucks pulling in filled with the finest foods and spirits of Germany. I had fallen asleep on top of the covers while crying my heart out, and someone, probably Hildegard, came and tucked me in. Although this was Alrik's chamber, he must have stayed the night in one of the other rooms, leaving me alone. I'm pretty sure that he had no idea exactly what to do with me, except be patient for the time being. I felt like rolling over and going back to sleep as I thought about what this day would bring.

Today, I would no longer be Benidette Crawford, but would now become Benidette Richter. Funny reality though, I hadn't even been married long enough to Carig to legally change my name to Hammel, and now I was marrying for the second time in one week. That in itself was insane, but to compound matters, Field Marshal Richter was one of the highest ranking officials in Hitler's regime, and I would now go down in history as being his wife and partner. Adina would roll over in her grave if she knew.

While I was deep in thought, Hildegard quickly entered my room to help me get ready for the big day. She along with three others came in to prepare the bride. It was certain that particular instructions were given to one individual whose sole purpose was to bathe and prepare me for the wedding night. Irma had remarkable skills that I didn't even know existed in this century. I soon found out that the art of hot wax was alive and well in 1940 Germany, and I'm pretty sure that she thoroughly enjoyed the pain she inflicted. Hildegard oversaw the other two as they worked on my hair and make-up.

"What time does this even start?"

"Two o'clock, Fräulein."

"What time is it now?"

"It's nine o'clock."

"Why so early?"

"The Field Marshal wants photo pictures taken of you. It will take much time - we must hurry. You must go out soon."

When the time came to put on the wedding gown, I recalled the night I put on Adina's gown and married Carig. That glorious evening seemed a hundred years ago, almost as if it was a dream. Right now, this was real; this was really happening.

All of my so-called maid servants in the room

gathered around and began dressing me in my lace gown. A

pearl choker that covered my entire neck was clasped on

next, most probably to hide the bruises.

"Beautiful, Fräulein. Ok, ok let's go!"

I took a deep breath, and followed them out.

"Wait, hold on! I forgot something!"

I went over to the desk and grabbed the note that I

wrote to Malachi and tucked it into my sleeve.

"Ok, I'm ready!"

Hildegard followed me, holding my veil. This dress

was far different than Adina's. It had a very full and flowy

skirt with a bodice made of elegant, but itchy, lace. It was

nothing that I would ever choose, as it was completely

extravagant like everything else in the Richter estate.

Walking down the stairs, I was met by the blue-eyed gaze

of Alrik. There he stood in his black and red uniform which

was adorned with dozens of gold decorations. There was one thing to be certain, he was extremely handsome, and the uniform only intensified his good looks.

"You look lovely, Fräulein - a vision! Before we go out for the photos, allow me."

He took my left hand, and placed the ruby ring on my finger.

"Now, you are complete!"

For some unknown reason, it was important to him that I wear this ring that was far too big and too heavy for my hand.

"Come now. I have hired a man who has harnessed an even greater technology of photographs than even your Americans have. This day will forever be remembered not only in our minds, but with many photograph cards. His skill methods are the way of the future."

"Ok, I'm ready!"

"Where is Annaliese? She will walk with you down the aisle."

He called her name, but she didn't answer.

"She's probably in her doll room. I'll get her."

I went to the stair door and gently knocked.

"Annaliese, are you in here?"

"Hello, yes, I'm here. Oh Fraulein Beni, you are so pretty! You are my new pretty mommy!"

Annaliese was doing her usual thing, dressing her doll, and in this case, in a matching dress to the one she was wearing - pale yellow lace with a blue sash.

"You look beautiful as well! Will Inga be joining us?"

Annaliese nodded her head yes. I went over and picked her up.

"Yes Annaliese, I am going to be …"

427

Before I could get the words out of my mouth, my heart nearly stopped beating as I noticed Malachi's wooden shoe box sitting on the floor, brimming with doll clothes! It had not been destroyed as I was made to believe, but instead, set aside for Annaliese to use as a miniature travel chest to store her doll clothes.

"May I see your pretty doll clothes?"

"Yes."

Picking up the box, I was relieved, as I could tell by the weight that it still housed the Tempus Vector, but exactly how to open it was a mystery. I frantically looked for some kind of lever or button, but found that both the inside and outside of the box were completely smooth.

"Benidette, Annaliese! It's time to go."

I couldn't keep from smiling. I was saved! I would be going home.

Alrik reached out his hand and helped me up. Pulling me into his arms, he lightly kissed me on the mouth.

"I love you, Beni. I have always loved you. I *will* always love you, and it is so good to finally see you smile!"

I felt both relief and conflict over my discovery which would restore my life, but destroy Alrik's. We walked outside together hand in hand. I was so happy, so thankful!

The photographer took full advantage of my wholehearted smiles, with the constant clicking of his "new", but antiquated contraptions, all the while commenting that he had never seen a happier looking couple.

"She is clearly in love with the Field Marshal! What an exquisite couple they make!"

I tried, but couldn't contain my joy, which everyone, including Alrik, believed to be a result of steadfast love for my soon-to-be husband, or for those that knew better, a resolved yielding to my ordeal. My sudden change in attitude about marrying the coveted Alrik Richter, opened the floodgates to a sea of gossipy chatter among the staff. They too were thrilled, knowing that if their master was content, they would also benefit from his happiness. But little did they suspect, my elation was not because of him. I had been reunited with my traveling companion which would see me safely home, and that had lifted the weight of the world from my shoulders!

As we continued with wedding pictures, I found myself observing the over complimentary photographer, Rollie Hermann, and his young apprentice, Uri. Rollie was an older gentleman, trying to coordinate three cameras that were dangling around his neck. One was an old Regent that looked like it belonged in the accordion family. The other was a silver and black camera, probably representing the "new" technology that Alrik was talking about. And the third one looked like a small box, but was a movie camera. This poor man was bogged down by three cameras while yelling out instructions to Uri of how to pose us. It was actually rather amusing to watch Rollie fumble around with all the doodads and doohickeys that seemed more like showy devices than essential tools of his trade. I could tell that he was nervous as there was a chill in the air, but he was sweating profusely. More than likely being chosen to do wedding photographs for Field Marshal Richter was unnerving, to say the least. He was probably afraid of failing in some way and then being sentenced to a gruesome fate.

Starting in the front of the house, Rollie snapped picture after picture of the two of us while Uri continued to move and adjust our every pose. Poor Rollie was a sweaty mess, but continued in his efforts to get the perfect pictures, giving us instructions for every move. Once we had made our way through the various backdrops of the Alrik Estate, Lily and Atlas were brought out for the final shots. After my extensive photo shoot with Lily, I was hoisted side saddle onto Atlas' bare back, squeezing in next to Alrik, where more photos were taken of us together. Alrik held me tightly and continued kissing my hand and my cheek.

Once we were done, I looked at Alrik knowing that this would be the last time I would ever see him, and I surprisingly felt guilty abandoning one so in love. As with Malachi and Carson, I also felt very strongly that I owed him a warning. I turned my body, so to face him completely.

"Alrik, there's something that I need to tell you. I would be lying if I told you that I didn't love you. I do, and I always will."

I touched the side of his face and for the first time kissed him, really kissed him because I wanted to, and he knew that it was real. At the same time, he could see the bitter finality in my eyes as my lips brushed past his. As we talked, the photographer continued snapping and winding his camera, obviously pleased with our impromptu poses and conversation.

"Beni, whatever it is you have to tell me, please don't let it be goodbye."

It was as if down deep inside he was sure that this would really never happen.

"Alrik, just listen carefully, and don't ask me how I know this. You need to take Annaliese and leave this place and never return."

"What? What are you talking about, Beni?"

"Just listen. I care ... very deeply for you and Annaliese, and I want you both to be safe and happy. I know you have a contingency plan in place in case you have to leave, and I'm just telling you that you need to do it now, before it's too late. Alrik, oh God, how do I tell you this? Germany will lose this war, but before they do they will be responsible for the deaths of millions of innocent people. Your country will be red with blood, and those such as yourself who worked so closely with Hitler will either take their own lives like cowards, or stand trial before the world, be convicted, and put to death. I know that you're a good man, and the things coming are not things you would ever be alright with. Promise me that you won't stay. If you do, you and Annaliese will be ruined forever."

He grabbed hold of my hands and told me that wherever he goes, I would be going as well.

"No Alrik, I'm not going anywhere with you. I can't stay any longer, and I need for you to understand."

"But I don't understand - none of this makes sense. How could you know such things? You are marrying me today!"

With each question he asked, he became decidedly more upset, and held my wrists even tighter. But then he stopped, stared at me, and without looking away he loosened his grip, and ran his hand up my lace sleeve.

"What's this, Fräulein?"

He felt the note that I had tucked into my sleeve to give to Carson.

"It's nothing, Alrik!"

Before I could stop him, he pulled out the note.

"Alrik, no, give it back. It has nothing to do with you. Give it back!"

Not saying a word and ignoring me as if I wasn't even there, he tucked the note in his pocket, delivered me to the front of the house, and then motioned for his guard to come and help me down.

"Watch her closely, and when the ceremony begins, walk her out. Don't take your eyes off of her for a second."

I yelled out his name, and he turned and looked at me.

"Choose what's right, Alrik. You know what's right!"

With a guard on each arm, I felt as I did the first day I arrived here. As we entered the house and they began walking me back to the library, I spoke up and asked if I could stay in the room under the stairs - Annaliese's doll room.

"There's a lock on the door, you can put me in there until the wedding begins."

One soldier held my arm while the other opened the door where I entered gratefully with no struggle. Joyfully, I watched as they closed the door and locked me in, then settling down onto the pillow, I was finally alone with the wooden box.

Thinking of the scene that just took place, I couldn't believe that Alrik had taken the note from my sleeve! How would I ever warn Malachi now? Weighing my best interest of leaving, alongside the life and future of Malachi was killing me. It seemed that no matter how hard I tried, I couldn't get that message to him. Perhaps it wasn't meant to be, but why else was I here? Once again, I felt like a dark blanket of failure had fallen upon me, and I was overwhelmed with grief over Malachi's and Carson's fate. How could I ever live with myself after this?

First things first though. I picked up the wooden shoe box and tried to open the secret panel to remove the Tempus Vector. I soon found that this small chest was locked down tighter than Fort Knox! I couldn't find even one clue of how to open it. Becoming more and more frustrated, I shook it as hard as I could, and then threw it against the wall, hoping to set off whatever latch was holding it shut. I realized Malachi's purpose for making this puzzle so difficult, but even after hurling it against the wall, I was still perplexed as it remained perfectly intact. After a few more minutes of no success, I heard voices coming from down the hallway. Mainly, above the others, I heard the voice of Halag asking where I was and demanding to see me at once. The sound of his voice made me panic, and again, I frantically began shaking and hitting the box, but still I couldn't figure out how to open it. No matter what, I had to leave this room before Halag came because in my heart I believed that his goal was not to retrieve and bring me to the ceremony, but to kill me before I could marry Alrik. He had already proven his hatred towards me, and had no fear of consequences, having free reign to get away with murder.

I had to run now, into the tunnel that would ultimately lead to Annaliese's garden. Hearing his steps moving closer, I stood up and made my way over to the rack of shoes. Oh how I wished that I wasn't wearing this unmanageable dress that was making it so difficult to move around. I pushed on the wooden clogs, and the door opened.

The tunnel stairs were steep; they went straight up, and curved around into a dark void. I had no idea what I would run into going through it, but I had no choice. I grabbed the box and climbed up the stairs. I could tell at once that this way of escape was made for a child, not an adult. Quickly pulling myself and the skirt of the dress into the small cubby in the wall and closing the panel, I heard the unlocking of the door and even more men approaching.

It was filled with darkness like I had never seen. I remained quietly sitting on one of the stairs trying not to make a sound as they came into the room. I had no idea if they were aware of this escape within the walls, but just in case they were, I knew that I needed to keep moving forward. I had no intention of waiting around for Halag to crash through the door and find me. Either way, I knew that he'd be right behind me and wouldn't stop until he found me.

The stairs turned into a tunnel, a very small tunnel. There wasn't room for me to hold onto the box, so instead I had to place it in front of me and push it forward as I pulled myself through. Inch by inch, I started my narrow journey down the dark passage.

All of a sudden I heard Halag scream out, "Where is she? You idiots, you've lost her!"

I could hear frantic scurries of the desperate guards who had misplaced me. They foolishly searched under pillows and behind racks, turning the place upside down while pleading their case. Frantically, they tried to explain that they had left me in this room and locked the door, and that I had mysteriously disappeared into thin air. I knew that it would only be a matter of time until Halag figured out where I was. I had to start moving and get to the other side of wherever this would lead. If only I could see, I could try to release the Tempus Vector from the box and disappear here and now, but with total darkness and cramped space, I could do nothing but inch forward. Even worse, my efforts to move along quietly were utterly impossible. The wooden box made too much noise as I pushed it across the tunnel floor, making short stretches of scuffs that could be heard through the walls. Upon hearing a light knock on the wall beside me, my heart practically stopped beating. His constant tapping reminded me of a war cry for blood, followed by eerie rantings from the man who already tried to kill me once, and for whatever reason, still wanted me dead.

"I hear you, Fräulein. I know what you are - just a dirty conniving rat dragging yourself through the darkness. If I had my way, you see, I would destroy you here and now."

I could hear him cock his pistol and skim the barrel across the wall where I lay, threatening to shoot me through the wood and stucco.

"If I kill you now no one would ever know, until your corpse rotted in the wall. You stupid American, coming in here and pretending to be Caprice. You are nothing like her. She was an angel ... she was mine until Alrik stole her from me, and then he let her die. I would have never allowed her to endure the torture his father put her through. It was my pleasure to kill him, just as it will be my pleasure to kill you."

Each syllable that left his mouth was spiked with poison, and twisted with cords of insanity. If the devil himself spoke out audibly, he would sound just like Halag. Even though he continued with his vile rant with me, I proceeded moving forward until I reached a place where I could no longer hear him. Was he still there talking to me, or was he waiting for me at wherever this place would end? In a complete panic, I began moving faster and faster. I didn't care how loud I was. Terror and claustrophobia set in. It didn't help that spiders and their webs were covering me. I had to get out.

The further I went, the smaller and narrower the tunnel became. There was no way someone such as Halag or Alrik could have maneuvered through, so I knew no one was behind me, but what would be waiting for me on the other side, I had no idea. Before I knew what was happening, the tunnel curved into a downward slide leading toward the ground, and I could see light. There was a small metal gate that led out of this maze. As I looked through the slats, I saw a beautiful garden just as Alrik had promised Annaliese. I cautiously looked on each side of the array of plants and flowers, and discovered that it was enclosed in a glass building, a greenhouse. In every corner of this small glass nursery, there were colorful florals of every kind. If I had more time, I would have stopped to appreciate the beauty, but I knew that this was my only opportunity to run. Pushing the gate open, I was relieved that I saw no sign of Halag - he must not have known where the exit to the tunnel was located. But one thing I was sure of, he was searching for it and for me right now, and I had to move quickly.

Pulling myself from the tunnel out onto the ground, I stood up and frantically swept webs and spiders off of my dress and out of my hair. I knelt down at the box, and once again tried to open it. I was desperate to get the Tempus Vector before it was too late! In front of me was a small planting station equipped with various garden tools. Using the handle of one of the tools, I hit wildly at all sides of the box, still making no progress. I had a feeling that the simplicity of opening the box was probably key to the puzzle. I only wished that Malachi had left me some kind of a hint in his note. Opening and closing the lid again, and then pushing and pulling on every part ... for the life of me, I still could not discover how to open it.

I suddenly had a sinking feeling in the pit of my stomach as I heard Halag's voice bellowing out orders from around the corner of the house. He was coming in my direction, and my only option was to run as he would most certainly spot me through the glass walls. From a distance, I saw him running in my direction with his pistol drawn, so I decided to go, keeping my body close to the side of the house, hoping he couldn't see me through the clusters of flowers.

Still holding the box, I ran. Within seconds, I heard him calling for me to stop. He was quickly coming towards me, and gaining ground. Trudging through the mud while wearing this blasted dress made my escape from him impossible. I could practically feel his breath on my neck, and then all at once, he was there, grabbing my arm and slamming me against the rough wall. So to finish what he had started, he held me against the house and began strangling me once again. The pain from his strong grip squeezing my already bruised neck, and the sensation of the pearls digging into my flesh, was unbearable! Pushing him away with one hand didn't even phase him. I needed a weapon. Using the wooden box as my only means of survival, I hit the side of his head as hard as I could, causing a huge gash down his face that instantly started bleeding profusely. My defenses against him not only stopped his assault on me, but the impact of the box hitting his skull created the perfect jolt to open the secret compartment within the box! I watched as the Tempus Vector along with my wedding ring, flew through the air, both landing in the mud. I ran over and grabbed the frame, along with a handful of mud where my ring lay. I could hear distant voices of Alrik and Carson behind me, but they weren't calling my name. They were desperately calling Halag's name, telling him "No!" and "Stop!" Without warning, I heard one loud blast explode behind me, followed by another.

Instantly, Halag was gone. I could no longer hear Alrik or Carson, but I was somewhere else. I was lying on our beach inside of a burrow like the one Adina and I used to dig on the Fourth of July. Fireworks kept bursting in the sky, making a huge explosion. Except for the fireworks, it was very dark. Within the black of night, I saw a shadow coming towards me. At first, I could barely make out a silhouette, but then the hazy profile became a face. It was Adina walking towards me. I sat up to greet her, and felt complete joy at her presence. She laid down in the burrow right next to mine, and we watched the fireworks together. She held my hand tightly, and then I sat up and started to

447

cry, unable to speak a word. I tried to talk but nothing came out. Shame and self-loathing consumed me! Ashamed of my failure. I had let everyone down, and because of my failure, because of me, Malachi, Carson, and Estee will all die. I had been defeated and couldn't even look at her, for fear that I would see disappointment in her eyes. All I could do was cry. The more I cried, the tighter she squeezed my hand.

"Beni, I'm here! You did well, everything will be alright. Just because your eyes are closed doesn't mean you can't see. Have faith. Remember what I always told you, faith is believing that which you can't see."

After those few words, she was gone, pain overwhelmed me, and I was beat down by a frigid breeze beating against me. And then I felt nothing.

Chapter 14

THE GUARDIAN CHRONICLE

"Well, first let me ask you a question, if you saw someone shot and killed before your very eyes, would you spend the rest of your life searching for them?" ~**Annaliese Richter**~

What shoulda' been just a few minutes without Beni, had now become nearly seven of the longest an' most excruciatin' days of my life. In sortin' through Gran's chronicle and notes about his vast experiences with Adina, it appeared that he never encountered anythin' even close to this hell of a nightmare - not that he mentioned anyway. He never seemed to be distressed about her. Maybe he just hid it well, but I never once remember him pacin' the floors worryin' whether or not she'd be returnin'. Instead, he'd be all up in his chair, sippin' tea, and readin' one of his favorites. The thing is this, he was Adina's guardian and helper, but not "bone of her bone, and flesh of her flesh." With that bond, I'm certain it woulda been an entirely different inward suffering to be sure. If it woulda been my grandmother walkin' out that door, he may not have been so calm.

Malachi's strong feelin's that the Carrier of the Tempus Vector stays unmarried ... well, became staggeringly transparent. To be honest, it was the only thing I could see clearly at this moment. His words of wisdom were not only for the good of the Carrier but also for the sake of the poor lad left behind.

Be that as it may, my feelin's about Beni hadn't changed, they'd never change. I just dunno if my heart can endure a lifetime of this. I thought I was strong, but when it comes to Beni, I'm often a bit weak in the knees. Until now, I defended this callin', while Beni saw it for what it was and what it would be. She was right. I was ready to put that frame away forever. Perhaps I would whittle a dog bone out of it, and throw it to the wolves. I hoped that, just as it had chosen Beni, it would surely choose another if she

450

walked away. Could the lass even walk away if she wanted to? I didn't know.

I felt so desperate inside the more I thought about it. Sittin' here alone, I kept seein' her face, rememberin' my body next to hers, and I knew one thing for sure, no matter what, I would stay true to her, always and forever, she above anything else had become my calling, and I would do anything for her. I just had to get her back! But what else could I do? Was there something I'd missed? Had I let her down in some way?

All of these questions inside my head were makin' me crazy. Just a few nights ago, I was at my wits' end thinkin' that she was in trouble and needed me, but I had no way of gettin' to her. Like a fool I walked out onto the balcony thinkin' it would somehow take me to her, but I just found myself standin' there staring out at the water like I do so often. But this time it was a lil different. The waters, like my spirit within me, were troubled. Roarin' like they too were fightin' a battle, risin' up not knowin' if they'd be able to keep movin' forward onto the shore. I could hear them moanin' as they were bein' held back by the strong layer of ice on top of the water. At that moment I realized that there would come a time when the power beneath the icy caps would break through and they'd keep movin', just as God had intended. They were only held back for a time. I too had to be ok and let my faith grow bigger than what I could see right now.

Day after day, I looked for comfort, for some kind of peace. Normally, it could be found in the tower, but now, just like my heart, I watched the great sea struggle to pound through the paralyzing chill. Without Beni I was cold and empty, I coveted the warmth of her body. I paid no attention to the icy wind at the top of the lighthouse; anywhere was better than the solitude of that third story room. The thought of spendin' even one more second watchin' that balcony door, was like bein' in chains. I had stayed there every moment except for my few escapes to the lighthouse, and the half-day trip into Portland to visit Annaliese Richter.

After discoverin' the 1940 wedding photo of Beni in Alrik Richter's biography, I was devastated to say the least. The hauntin' photo left me no choice, I had to find out what had become of Beni, or should I say, what was *currently* happenin' with Beni. I was hopin' that if I kept diggin' deeper maybe I'd find the answer to that question, and whether or not she was comin' back. I was half afraid to dig too deep, fearful of what I might find. Had she fallen in love so quickly with another man, in such a short amount of time? It just didn't make sense to me that she would do somethin' like that. She had never been one to give her heart away so easily. But then I remembered Adina's warning to her, of how easy it was to lose yourself in the midst of another world, compounded by another time. Had she forgotten who she was? Who I was? The way she was lookin' at Alrik, didn't seemed forced, and I had seen that look before, thinkin' it was only meant for me. I couldn't let myself dwell any longer on that picture, I had to know more. After unearthin' the information that Alrik had lived here in Maine until his death in 1999, survived only by his daughter Annaliese Richter who was now the sole proprietor of Richter Farms in Portland, for my own sanity, I had to go and see her.

I called ahead, introducin' myself, and hopin' that she would wanna speak to me. At first she said no, and nearly hung up the phone, that is until she heard Beni's name. Still a bit reluctant to say yes, probably not knowin' if she could really trust me or not, she finally agreed. After a bit, she even seemed somewhat excited to meet me.

The ongoing distractions of Beni's absence, mixed with meetin' the daughter of the man who is, or was, tryin' to steal my wife stirred such a disturbin' conflict within me that I hardly remembered my drive into Portland.

Just as Annaliese had instructed, the right-hand fork in the road dead-ended into an iron gate marked with a profound "R." Initially, when I saw that letter blarin' out at me, I was firin' hot! This inexcusable offense against me and the woman I love certainly deserved at least a duel against this man; a man known to all as a charmin' womanizer whose good looks and great wealth tempted the hearts of many. I wasn't even allowed to kick his German ass, cause the bastard was already dead. I felt as though I was hoverin' in The Twilight Zone, pissed as a red ant that the man was dead. Who could blame him for fallin' for Beni? Surely she swept him off of his feet without even tryin'. Just the thought of it all made me feel at sea inside. If I were to be honest, it all came down to losin' the only girl I've ever loved, and I hated the feelin'!

The one-lane winding road that led up to the Richter Estate, was surrounded by hundreds of acres of blueberry plants covered in a sea of snow, all of them lyin' dormant through the winter months. To the side of the main house

was a vast conservatory, larger than I'd ever seen before,

which must have been another fifty acres or so. It was the

perfect set-up I suppose, for year-round bounty. Maine was

the perfect place for such a thing - nothin' could survive the

wrath of these bloody cold elements.

A wall made of gray stones paralleled the driving

path which finally led up to the main house. As I pulled up

to the bottom step, there swayin' in perfect rhythm on the

porch swing, was Annaliese Richter, the only child of Alrik

Richter, and hopefully, the key to findin' out what had

happened to Beni. From a distance, it looked as though her

eyes were shut; I thought she was nappin'. But as I started

walkin' up to the house, she jumped up and faced me. I was

alarmed straightaway by such an unexpected reversal of

demeanor. I remember wonderin' why I didn't see any

updated photos of her, but after lookin' upon her unnervin'

ashen blue stare, I could see why. What had happened to

her? Of course, I had only seen a small picture of the lass when she was just a wee thing, standin' alone, holdin' on tightly to her doll. But now, with eyes as colorless as her alabaster crown, she somewhat resembled a kelpie. Gran warned me of these ghosts of the waters whose eyes were like white flames of fire.

I reached out my hand to introduce myself and shake hers, but she kept her hands down at her side, first lookin' at my friendly gesture, and then up at my face. As I looked down at her hands, I saw that they were curiously covered with white cotton gloves. Apparently she didn't like touchin' anyone or anythin' with her bare hands. This whole thing was gettin' way too strange for me, and I felt as though I needed to leave. Along with her ghost-like appearance and unnatural-lookin' eyes, this desolate place made me feel as if I were in the midst of somethin' evil.

Just as I was about to turn around and get the hell out, she spoke.

"You came. I wasn't sure you would show up ... Carig, right? Let's go in. As much as I love the snow, it is quite cold out here."

I followed her in, but didn't want to make myself too comfortable. I didn't have a good feeling about being here. I tried not to stare, but it was difficult. Her unsettlin' appearance wasn't just because of her face, but her presence altogether was unnervin', as if all her color had been stripped away. It occurred to me, after lookin' only a few minutes into the eyes of her soul, that it, along with her heart, spilled over with a clouded darkness. The only thing for sure that had any color at all.

I tried to talk about somethin', anythin' to break down the barrier of silence. I began talkin' about her home. It was quaint and homey with wood floorin' and tones of pale yellow. What I noticed most was standin' in the far corner of the room. A grand white wooden carousel horse with a pole that held it from floor to the ceilin' captured my attention. Even though the paint was chipped and aged, I couldn't help but focus solely on the fine craftsmanship of this great beast. I was so captivated by the magnificent antique horse, that I ran my fingers over the lines on the face, and then knocked on the wood. It was completely solid; I had never seen anythin' that compared to it.

"You like it?"

"Aye! In all my years, I've never seen anythin' quite like it!"

"His name is Chariot. He was my mother's horse, well a replica of my mother's horse. I don't remember very much about her. Before I was born, my father had a grand carousel made for the two of us. This was the only piece that was salvaged; the rest was destroyed in the war."

I could tell that even now, talkin' about the war that took place so many years ago pained her deeply.

"However, we're not here to talk about me or my mother, but the lovely Miss Beni, right?"

She stood there, seemin' a bit nervous, and then came over to where I was standin', also skimmin' her hand over the wooden sculpture and touched my hand. I could even feel the iciness through the gloves. It gave me the willies, and I quickly pulled my hand from hers and walked away. She stayed there, still facin' the corner where the horse stood.

"Now, let's see…. Miss Beni's horse was named Lily. My father gave it to her soon after she arrived. Lily was white, just like Chariot."

Annaliese continued pausin'; she seemed to get lost in her own thoughts.

"When we left Germany, most everything we owned, including our horses, had to stay behind. Somehow my father knew that we would be leaving. He had this one carousel horse crated up and shipped weeks before we left though."

Her story about Alrik givin' Beni her own horse stung my heart a bit, and she could tell that I was bothered, but seemed to find a bit of pleasure in my distress.

"Come sit down, Carig. Let's talk!"

She showed me over to a small love seat that was sittin' right in front of a rustic stone fireplace. Normal people might have had a roarin' blaze goin', but hers was just embers. I asked her if she'd like me to make a warm fire within the pit, but she shook her head, and told me there was no wood, even though a full basket of timber sat on the hearth covered in cobwebs.

Sittin' on the table was a pot of hot tea and blueberry scones. She poured me a cup, and served up a pastry, but since I wasn't wantin' to die today, I didn't touch any of it. I felt guilty for judgin' Annaliese by her looks. She was tryin' real hard, but I didn't trust the peculiar lass. There was somethin', no, a lot of somethin's, not quite right with her.

"So, Miss Richter ..."

"Please, call me Annaliese."

"Annaliese, may I please ask ye how ye knew Beni?"

"Well love, honestly, I haven't seen Miss Beni since I was a child."

"Wait, she didn't marry your father?"

"No, she most certainly did not. It wasn't meant to be, but I will never forget her and the first day that I saw her. I was playing with my dolls in my room under the stairs. I heard her voice in our entryway - she was arguing with my Uncle Halag, and he was yelling back at her. I cracked open my door just enough to see what was going on. Halag, along with his guards, were holding on to her.

She was distraught to say the least, and insisted that they let her go. Over and over again, she fought to get out of their grips."

Another very strange thing I noticed as she continued talking, was her tone and expression when she spoke about her Uncle Halag. I had never heard the name before, didn't even know *who* he was, but she knew him well, and wore a sinister grin every time she said his name.

"Halag hated her with a deep-seated hatred. He still does! I mean he never stopped loathing even the air she breathed. My father on the other hand, who was a bit of a fool, loved her the moment he laid eyes on her. I looked at my father at the top of the stairs when he first saw her standing in front of him, and I will never forget the expression on his face, and the way he was looking at her. He was enamored and instantly in love. That evening when he was tucking me into bed, he told me that she had come to be my new mommy, and he was so happy because we wouldn't be alone anymore. She was nice to me, and I wanted her to stay, but it wasn't to be. For many years after we moved to America, my father kept photos of her all around our house. He was certain that he would find her … but one day, without any explanation, he just took them all down, like he had given up hope. He seemed to finally realize that she was gone and never coming back. Have you ever been around someone who had lost their purpose for living? It's a terrible thing to watch, and there's no cure for it."

"Do you still have those photos?"

"I do, would you like to see them?"

"Aye, I would love to!"

Annaliese walked over to a wooden bench, liftin' the lid and pullin' out a cardboard box, and then handed it to me. It was filled with at least a hundred photos of Beni posed with Alrik. Some were just too difficult to look at, as he held her with great passion and longin'. When they touched one another it looked as if it was with real intimacy. As far as I could tell, Beni was just as fully engaged and filled with desire as he was.

It seemed that Annaliese could tell how disturbed I was.

"Love, where are you from originally with that adorable accent of yours?"

"I came over here from Scotland when I was a lad. My grandparents brought me over after my parents died, and they raised me."

"Really, your grandparents lived here? What were their names, if you don't mind me asking?"

"Not at all, Killen and Mari Hammell."

She sat there looking a bit shocked.

"Adina's Killen and Mari?"

"Ye, but how'd you know them and Adina?"

"Well, the first time we met Adina, it was...oh my, 1948, at the Catwalk Ball. My father and I, after leaving Germany, had originally moved to New York. Honestly, I believe that he thought he might find Beni there, but he never did. Six years later, he insisted on moving to Maine. It was always his intention to be a farmer, and he thought this beautiful state of Maine was the place to do it. Funny that he would choose this climate over somewhere more adapted to farming, like California, but he insisted on living here. He was immediately taken with Adina. Now that I think about it, when he first saw Adina, he thought she was Beni. They certainly did resemble one another. My father and Adina remained friends for many years, but something happened. I'm not sure what. Something that caused him to never speak of Beni again, and for that matter, never another mention of Adina either. The friendship we all had with Adina ended. One morning I woke up to the sound of

466

my father throwing all of the framed pictures of he and Beni in the trashcan. He was angry, making sure that the glass broke as he threw them away. Later, I sifted through the broken frames and glass, and pulled out the photos, putting them in this box. He and I never spoke of her again, and after that, it seemed that my father's hope and joy had disappeared forever. He was never the same."

Annaliese seemed to disappear into the shaded corners of the final years of her father's life.

"Beni was with us for such a short amount of time, but I can honestly say that she changed our lives forever. There was something unusual about her. She wasn't like any of the other women that my father would bring around. She was confident. Usually women would do whatever my father asked of them, but not her. She hadn't come there trying to capture his attention. She was independent and opinionated, unlike the women of Germany who were made to be subservient. So many people were intimidated by my father and his position and rank, but not her. She wasn't impressed by him at all … she wasn't well, you know, swept off of her feet by him. He was never moved by those other women. He would call them 'empty headed whores' who only wanted his money and status. I'm not saying he was right to do what he did, but he used them and then refused them. So can you only imagine Beni walking into that world? My father could think of nothing else but her. When she was in the room, his complete attention was hers and hers alone. He devoured every word that came from her mouth, and found great pleasure in how she spoke - kind of oddly. My father would always chuckle at unusual terms that she would use. She saved us, you know."

"What do you mean, she saved you?"

"Well, my father didn't tell me this until years later when I criticized him for continuing to search for her. She told him to take me and leave Germany, that it was dangerous. She told him things that no one could have known."

Annaliese slowly sorted through the pictures in the box, and once again became lost in her own thoughts.

"What sort of things did she tell your father?"

"Aside from the warning about the coming danger, she somehow knew the fate of Germany and Hitler. Hitler held so much power that the thought of him or his purpose failing, was very difficult for my father to believe. She told him that if he stayed, one day he would be tried as a war criminal."

She laughed out loud as if someone had just told a funny joke, but nothin' here was very funny.

"I know you never met my father, but he would have never hurt anyone, he didn't have the killer instinct that a German Field Marshal should have had. He was more kind and gentle, and forever grateful for the warning from Beni. His love for her never stopped. You see he was heartbroken over my mother dying, of course, but when Beni came it was like he was alive again. It was the first and last time I ever saw him happy. Well you know what I mean. When she was here he had this flame in his eyes, but when she disappeared that flame disappeared with her."

"What do ye mean disappeared? What happened to her?"

Even after all the years that had gone by, Annaliese still spoke of the experiences of Beni with skepticism. As she told about Beni and her father, she had a definite undertone of bitterness. Strangely, when she spoke of her memories of Germany and Hitler, she lifted her chin up high as if she was proud of her corrupt heritage.

"It was their wedding day, and they were having their pictures taken, these pictures."

She placed her hand over the box and closed her eyes.

"Everything seemed fine, I guess, until Beni told my father something that upset him. I'm not sure what it was. Maybe that she didn't love him, or maybe that was the moment she warned him of what was coming. But whatever it was, he became furious, and then put her under heavy guard from that moment on. I watched as she walked into the house in her wedding gown, surrounded by guards as if she were a criminal. And then I wondered why my father rode away on Atlas, leaving a cloud of dust that rose with fury. I can't help but think the problem from the very beginning, was that Beni was never free at our house. For some reason, he was always so afraid that she would leave, or maybe it was just because she was an American and he didn't trust her. I guess he was right in a way, because within a week's time, she had come and gone. He wanted her and her heart, but I don't believe it was ever his. He was a fool! Although I was a child, I always felt that her heart was never his for the taking, and because he forced her to stay, he never gave her the chance to really prove that she loved him. Instead of setting her free, he kept her in chains, unwilling to take the chance that she would never return. But in the end, he lost everything, and spent his life searching for a ghost.

"Their wedding was doomed from the very beginning - rather than an atmosphere of joy, there was only conflict. Honestly, conflict seemed to always be the cornerstone of my life. The closer that moment came for her to walk down the aisle, the tighter he held on to her."

She shook her head in disappointment, and exhaled deeply.

"Nothing about this day was joyful, and what should have been the happiest time of their lives, ended in tragedy. I never wanted to tell my father, but really all she wanted to do was leave."

"You were but a child, how could you know that?"

"Well, you're right, I was a child, but I knew something that the rest of them didn't. When they brought her back into the house, she begged them to lock her in the room under the stairs; the room where I spent most of my time. You have to understand, our estate was immense with dozens of places where she could have asked to go. Places with doorways and windows where she could have possibly found an easy escape. But she chose my doll room knowing that they would lock her in from the outside, and there were no windows and no doors. Carig, my love, there was only one reason that she would request to be held in that particular place."

I was completely confounded by Annaliese's reasoning. Her words were twisted with definite traces of mental illness loomin' about.

"What do ye mean? Why would that mean she was tryin' to leave? It doesn't make any sense. Sounds like just the opposite!"

"I've gone over this a thousand times in my mind, and until this very moment I have never told another person what I'm about to tell you. The day before the wedding, Beni came in my doll room, and sat and played with me. She was one of the few who ever did. I was very excited at the prospect of her being my new mother. Anyway, I showed her something that I had never shown anyone before. It was a secret passage that led from my doll room to the outside of the house. My father had it built for me, knowing that war was coming, and it was his way of keeping me safe. Carig, don't you see? She requested that room so that she could escape, and not have to marry my father."

At her words, I felt such relief in my heart, and my spirit within me was renewed. Beni didn't want to stay there, she was tryin' to escape and come back to me.

"So did she escape?"

Annaliese put her head down, looking bothered by her remembrances.

"Well, yes and no. She made it through that tiny passageway which was quite a feat because it was so small, made for a child. But when she finally got through and tried to run away, she was shot and killed. My uncle shot her in the back as she was running, and then another man, a friend of my father's, shot Halag. In my entire life, I've never known a darker day. I never saw her again after that. She died immediately. I don't even remember them calling a doctor or carrying her away for that matter; she was just gone. The entire scenario was done and over almost as quickly as it had begun… she had been killed and swallowed up into the earth…. like she never really existed. She was just gone. My father was inconsolable. He was devastated, and then he disappeared for weeks after. When he finally came home, early one morning he and I quietly walked away from our grand estate in Germany and never looked back."

Upon hearing her say that Beni had been shot and killed, I became paralyzed with grief and fear. I couldn't move. I couldn't breathe.

"Wait, are you sure she died?"

"Are you ok, love? You look so pale. I can tell that her life is very personal to you … you never told me on the phone how you knew Beni."

"Na, I didn't. Let's just say, I loved her like your father did. Thank you for lettin' me come and talk with ye."

When I stood up to leave, she walked right into my space and grabbed hold of my wrists like she had no intention of lettin' me go. Her voice swiftly changed, becomin' muffled-soundin', and she looked at me in the strangest way, almost as if she had become a different person.

"Are you sure you're ok to drive? You didn't think you would find her here, now did you?"

Her question was silver-tongued, filled with rhetorical tones of sarcasm. She absolutely knew more than what she was tellin' me.

"I'm not sure what I was lookin' for to be honest …. thank you for your time, I really do appreciate it! You helped more than you'll ever know."

"Carig, one more thing. Perhaps you can solve this mystery that's been plaguing me for years now."

"What is it?"

"Well, first let me ask you a question, if you saw someone shot and killed before your very eyes, would you spend the rest of your life searching for them? To this day, I can't quite fathom why my father believed that she was still alive. And for the life of me, I honestly never knew for sure if she really was indeed alive, or if he was just out of his mind with grief. Every time I asked him about it, he would simply say that she endured the fate of Enoch. I've wracked my brain, and I have no idea who Enoch was, or how my father knew him, or even of what fate he was speaking. But the thing is this, after the tragic events of that day occurred, I ran over to where he was kneeled down in the mud. There was Halag lying face down in front of him, but Beni wasn't there. She was gone, almost as quickly as she had fallen. Here and now, I still play it over and over again in my mind. More so since my father died. I even dream about it. I see my father sitting there covered in mud, and I hear him calling her name and begging her not to leave him - but she was gone.

"Aww, I'm sorry dear. Just the rantings of an old woman! If you ever discover more to the story, I would really like to know what it is. My father was never at peace, and it seems he's passed that legacy down to me. So I guess for both of our sakes, please remember me if you find out anything about Beni."

All I could do was nod, but then walked away from her, chokin' back a sea of tears that was risin' up in my throat. I couldn't help but to turn around and look back at her one last time. She looked at me satisfied. It somehow seemed that she felt pleasure in my sufferin'. She had planted seeds of discord within my mind. All of it disturbed me greatly.

After our goodbyes, I got in my car and headed back to Bar Rousse.

The trip home was difficult, trying to see through the tears that filled my eyes. Was she really dead? I just couldn't bring myself to believe it. Was I gonna be like Alrik waitin' and searchin' my whole life for Beni? The thing was, if that's what it took, I would search and wait for the rest of my life. After all, *home* didn't mean anything without her. She is and had always been my home. Within a week of marriage, I was filled with the ache of a widower and was alone.

Everyone I ever loved in the world was gone. I was far too distressed to drive any longer, and decided to pull over and get out of the car that was all but closin' in on me. I just started walkin' through the mist of fallin' snow. Lookin' up to the sky, I watched the sun break through the clouds for but a moment, makin' the entire countryside glisten like diamonds. With that instantaneous light, my hope was immediately renewed as somethin' that Annaliese said was ringin' through my mind. I hurried and got back into my car, and drove' like a maniac until I reached the first hotel in my path. With brakes screeching, almost forgettin' to turn off my motor, I ran into the lobby of the Portland Moose Inn. The poor mom and pop standin' at the front desk dressed in matchin' green shirts with the names "Sharol" and "George" embroidered on them, must have thought me a loon the way I ran in so frantically. After catchin' my breath, I blurted out somethin' that I am sure neither of them expected to hear.

"Do ye have a Bible?"

"I beg your pardon?"

"A Bible, does this hotel have Bibles?"

"Sure as heck do. Got a Gideon in every room, right next to the bed in the side drawer. Are ya just here for the night, son?"

I put my head down on the counter, tryin' to get myself together.

"You alright, son? You must be desperate runnin' in here asking for a Bible."

"I'm sorry, I just need to see one for a minute, please. I'm on my way back to Bar Rousse, so I won't be needin' a room."

"Sharol, go get the boy a Bible!"

Sharol left and went into the closet and brought a thick leather-bound book with gold letterin'. I started turnin' the pages, goin' back and forth, skimmin' from front to back.

"You know what, keep it Red, and next time you're in this neck of the woods, come by and stay a night."

"Thank you, I will!"

I took the holy book out to my car, and closed my eyes still hearin' Annaliese say the name Enoch. If I was rememberin' right, Enoch was a name in the Bible. His name, his story had some kind of similarity to Beni, at least in Alrik's mind. As I began searchin', I was shocked at what I found. This one crumb of scripture must have become the only way that Alrik could make any sense out of what had happened. There it was, plain as day; Hebrews 11:5. "By faith Enoch was taken up so that he should not see death, and he was not found because God had taken him. Now before he was taken he was commended as having pleased God."

I don't know how long I sat there, but after reading those words of old, I knew Beni was alive. More than likely, after she was shot she vanished right before his eyes. Holdin' on to this scripture, and applying it to Beni's mysterious exodus motivated Alrik to never give up searching for her. This is what Annaliese was talking about when she mentioned her father's explanation "she suffered the fate of Enoch." But that alone was not the only thing she mentioned that assured me of both Beni's survival and her desire to leave there and come home. First of all, she said that Beni was trying to leave, but being held against

her will. That means she was tryin' to come back to me, not

tryin' to stay with Alrik. No matter what the pictures

looked like, she wasn't in love with him; her heart was still

mine, it was all a facade of survival. Secondly, she said

that Beni was shot and killed, but after, it seemed that she

just evaporated - evaporated into thin air. I wasn't

absolutely sure, but maybe Beni vanished because the

Tempus Vector brought her back right after she was shot.

Maybe, just maybe, she didn't die, but only disappeared,

and is comin' back!

Chapter 15

THE MARK

"Our journeys are commonly marked in one of two ways:
Either by the light gold dusting from angels' wings,
or the dark-blistering brand of the devil's tail on our backs."
~Malachi Coffee~

For the first time in days I felt hopeful, but my

hope was soon clouded by the reality that if and when she

comes back, she would be comin' back hurt; more than

likely, very badly hurt. Within the instructions for the

guardian of the Carrier, one in particular stood out in my

mind that my Gran had made very clear. That was that no

matter what kind of injuries Adina came back with, he was

never allowed to take her to a hospital for attention, no

matter what. Thankfully, along with those unreasonable

instructions, he left a name and phone number of a highly

qualified doctor who would be discrete, and available if I

needed him. I hoped that I'd never be faced with havin' to

reach out to this man, but there was no choice. This journey had proven to be so difficult for both Beni and myself - like

bein' baptized by fire. With a renewed sense of hope and

urgency, I got back in the car and headed home. In my

heart I felt like she would come home and everythin' would

be ok. At this point, I was goin' to assume that she was

alive.

I came home half expectin' that she might be there,

but to my disappointment once again, she must have still

been battlin' to get back. I wondered at this very moment

what she was goin' through. To best be prepared for

whatever came, I called the number that Gran had left for

me. Just like him, he had left extensive notes in his journal

on exactly what to say, and what not to say. "Hello, I'm

callin' regardin' repairs on my lighthouse at Adina York's

Estate." And then after that, leave a call back number. I did

just as his instructions said, and within five minutes or so I

received a call back from a man who sounded like he had

just run a mile, bein' out of breath an' all.

"Hello, I am calling regarding repairs on your lighthouse. To whom am I speaking?"

"This is Carig Hammell. Killen was my grandfather, and now I am the keeper of the lighthouse."

"Is this an emergency, or can I come over in the morning?"

"Well sir, it could very well be an emergency."

After a moment of silence, he told me that he was on his way.

"Thank you!"

After hanging up the phone, I felt that he and I had been talking in code. It was a bit on the odd side - this situation was anything but normal and needed to be handled in a most delicate way. I'm sure he could get in a lot of trouble for not reportin' somethin' such as a gunshot wound, and I for one was thankful that he was comin'.

487

About twenty minutes later, I could see headlights approachin' the house, and figured it must be the doctor or whoever this mysterious person was. Makin' my way downstairs, I walked out to his truck to meet him. To my surprise the truck really seemed to be a servicer of lighthouses. *Dean's Lighthouse Repair* stood out as big as day, which made me even more curious about his real occupation, and who he really was. When he stepped out of the truck I couldn't help but notice that he looked more like an old sea captain than a doctor, but there was something very familiar about him. Maybe I was recallin' a time when I was a lad, when maybe he came to see Gran. Naw, that wasn't it. Where did I know him from? As I was starin' right at him, trying to examine his face without him thinkin' I was a loon, he clearly became just a wee bit annoyed. His dark complexion was covered with a scruffy beard, and he had short salt and pepper speckled hair. His unkempt bristle and scruff were somehow throwin' me off.

What I recognized was the face beneath it - the wide smile and reassurin' eyes.

"Son, have I got something in my teeth? Why are you lookin' at me like that? Is there somthin' you'd like to ask me?"

"I'm so sorry, Doc. I'm not meanin' to be rude. It's just... where do I know you from?"

He even had a distinct limp. At first I thought that he might have a peg leg to go along with his sea rover look, but in fact he had two legs intact, one with a bit of a stagger. But to help him along, he used a rather dapper lookin' staff.

He looked up at the tower and smiled.

"Ahh, she's a beauty! So, let's go inside and take a look."

We walked into the lighthouse, and he sat down in my Gran's red velvet chair, makin' himself comfortable. It was quite obvious that he had been here before, but *here* was not where I remembered seein' those kindly eyes.

"So, tell me what's goin' on."

I think he could tell that I was apprehensive as to how to respond.

"Why don't I tell you a little bit about myself first. People call me Chief, but my name is Dr. Dean, Ray Dean, and I knew and helped your grandfather with Adina for many years. He told me before he passed that there would come a day that you would be calling me. I'm retired Navy, ya know, served for forty years patchin' up ensigns to admirals. When I retired, I came to Bar Rousse and started workin' on lighthouses, even whipped this one into shape. Son, since I worked with your grandfather for years, you don't need to be nervous about me. I know everything there is to know. Your grandfather trusted me, and I hope you will too. So enough about me, tell me what's goin' on."

490

"Well sir, Beni's not back yet. As a matter of fact she should have been back days ago, and I … I'm not just her guardian, I'm her husband and I ..."

Dr. Dean could tell that this was wearin' on me in a great way, so he stood up, put his hand on my shoulder, and spoke to me with a great confidence as to what the outcome of this would be.

"Everything's gonna be ok! I can tell you're having a hard time son, but we need to be ready when she does return. And Carig, she will return!"

I was so thankful that he was here. It made me feel better to have a voice of reason standing by me, ready to help.

"Tell me everything you know, so that we can be as prepared as possible."

"Well, all I really know, or what I'm thinkin', is that she will return with a gunshot wound to her back.

Honestly, I don't even know if she'll be alive. There may be more, but I'm not sure. I think though, if I have my days straight anyway, and if time is flowin' the way I think it is, it could be tomorrow or maybe the day after. I'm not positive really."

He could tell that I was very upset, and was probably thinkin' that my grandfather seemed to handle these things far better than what he was seein' from me.

"Carig, are you ok? Son, you're gonna have to toughen up. Your job will never be an easy one, but she won't be able to do this without you, and without your strength."

"With all due respect, sir, my grandfather cared greatly for Adina, but he wasn't married to her. Beni is my wife, so that makes this a bit harder for me to take."

"I see. Well you're right about that … they weren't married, but he would have given his life for her. You may

492

not have been party to it, but he spent many an hour worrying about Adina. You know, you can't let this, whatever's happened here, stop her from going again. You understand that, right?"

I could feel the anger buildin' up within me. He had a lot of nerve sayin' anything to me about her goin' again.

"At this point here, sir, if she does come back, this is over. I will never allow her to go through anything like this again. Do ye hear me?"

"Loud and clear, son!"

I could tell he quickly decided that this was neither the time nor the place to have this discussion with me, so he started in with the process of what he knew best.

"Ok, so help me unload these supplies from my truck, and let's take them up to the third story room. Since we don't know what kind of shape she will be in, we need to be set up there, and prepare for the worst."

The first thing we carried up was a large rubber tarp folded up, which we laid down as a base. Followin' that, we carried up what looked like a gurney, but was actually a foldin' surgical table, then fifteen plastic totes of supplies, several tanks of oxygen, and a large ice chest. Pullin' a large foldin' table from the closet, he constructed a work surface in the corner of the room so efficiently that it was obvious he had done this before. However, it seemed like he was bringin' an awful lot of stuff in. As I watched him set up a makeshift emergency room, I was sure that he knew what he was doin'. Before I knew it, right across from my sittin' area, I was now lookin' at a complete surgical unit. If my Gran trusted him, so did I.

When we had finished the preparations, he gave me a hug and once again told me that everythin' was going to be alright.

"When she arrives, no matter what time it is, call me just like you did today, and say that the tower light's

494

gone out. I won't be calling you back though; I'll just be comin' right over, ok?"

I told him that I would get in touch with him as soon as she came back, and then thanked him for everythin'. The expectation that Beni would return with a gunshot wound made me feel so very strange. Was it happenin' right now? My heart broke as I thought about her havin' to go through this alone, and all I could do was, once again, watch the door and wait for her to return.

After another night of sleepin' upright in my Gran's plaid covered chair, I was awakened by the sound of snow hittin' the balcony door. Greeted once again by frigid temperatures and more snow on the way, I grabbed a thermos of coffee and made my way out to the lighthouse. I couldn't even imagine goin' through this and not having the thunderin' company of the sea, which was the only thing that eased my pain. Standin' on the catwalk and watchin' the icy waters strugglin' to make a wave, I heard somethin' out of the ordinary comin' from the house. Runnin' to the other side of the tower, I made out a bangin' noise comin' from the third story. It was the balcony door opened wide and caught in the clutches of the wind, slammin' over and over again into the wall … oh my God, she's back!

I couldn't get to the house fast enough. While on my way, I rang the doctor and left him the message that the tower light had gone out and to please come quickly. My heart was leapin' for joy that Beni was back, but I'd be lyin' if I didn't admit that I was also nervous and afraid of what I might find. As I ran up the stairs, I began callin' out her name.

"Beni, I'm comin!"

Desperately enterin' the room, I spotted her first thing, lyin' face down on the floor, already covered with a blanket of snow! The wind was poundin' the door back and forth against her body, and it looked as though she had barely made it over the threshold when she collapsed. The dauntingly familiar wedding dress from those damn photos was now sodden with miry filth and veins of scarlet.

In that moment it was as if my world ceased to exist, and it was all I could do to move towards her at a lumberin' pace. Finally, my hands that had ached to touch my bride once again, reached down and gathered her fragile body into my arms, and cradled her to my chest. "Please, Lord, let her be alive--don't take her from me!" As I gently turned my love's beautiful face towards mine, I couldn't tell. The bone-weary evidence of her broken state spoke volumes, revealing my deepest fear, that all life had been drained from her.

THE END

COMING SOON – SJ3 THE BLOOD CASTE

Made in the USA
San Bernardino, CA
20 November 2017